A DEADLY DRIVE-BY

HAUNTING AVERY WINTERS
BOOK V

DIONNE LISTER

Imprint: Dionne Lister

Sydney, Australia

Contact: dionnelisterauthor@gmail.com

ISBN 978-1-922407-40-5

Paperback edition

Cover art by Robert Baird

Editing by Hot Tree Editing

Proofreading L. Brodey

CHAPTER 1

I cringed. Was it just me, or did everyone turn into an uglier version of themselves when they were sitting at the hairdresser? I was never sure if it was the black cape cutting off my neck or the lighting, but I was positive I hadn't looked this unattractive in my bathroom mirror this morning. So ugly. If only I could shut my eyes for the whole haircut and not look weird. At least no one was here to see me other than the hairdresser… oh, and the ghost who was hanging around. Simone, the hairdresser, not the ghost, had opened A Snip in Time super early for me because I had an interview at 8:00 a.m.

"My darling's doing a lovely job with your haircut," the curly purple-haired old lady said from next to my chair as Simone did her thing. I ignored the ghost, even though I agreed with her. It would be hard to get this haircut wrong, though, since it was a simple inch-off trim.

"Do you have any kids, Avery?" Simone pinched my blonde hair between her fingers and snipped.

"No way. I'm too young. Also, I don't have a partner, and I'm in no way, shape, or form ready to be a single parent. Or any parent... really." I shuddered. I was only just getting out of the hole my life had become and finding my independence. Having a baby would be the biggest mistake ever. Being responsible for shaping another human, let alone keeping them alive, sounded like a task I wasn't up for, and I wasn't sure I ever would be.

Simone smiled. Sadness floated across the old lady's face. "My poor sweetie. She has a gorgeous young'un. But she never sees him."

My forehead furrowed. That was sad. I didn't really want to get into a deep and meaningful, but I should ask. Maybe she wanted to talk about it, and she did ask me first. "What about you? Do you have any kids?" She'd been in the village only a few months longer than me. I'd never seen her with any children. Not that I'd been following her everywhere, and people didn't tend to drag their kids to work.

Simone looked down for a moment, then resumed cutting. "Ah... Um..." She took a deep breath. "Yes. He lives with my mum."

"Do you see him much?" I didn't want to pry, but then again, maybe she needed to talk about it.

Her voice softened. "No. I chat to him on the phone every day, but...." She sighed, a long, painful exhale that made the ghost's shoulders sag.

"How old is he?" I watched her in the mirror, but she avoided my gaze, concentrating on my hair, which was probably a good thing if I didn't want a wonky haircut.

"Five. He's so smart and determined. He could walk at nine months and count to ten at three. He started school this year and loves it." Her smile contained a hint of sadness and a lot of pride. "One day, he'll come live with me. The time just isn't right... yet."

The ghost's lips pinched together, and anger hardened her face. If only I could talk to her about it without looking like a crazy person, but then again, did I need to get involved in every problem I came across? I liked Simone, but I didn't know her that well. Surely she had friends who helped her when she needed it? "If you ever need help or to talk, let me know. I'm up for a coffee whenever." I smiled. Okay, so I couldn't help offering. If she felt anything like I did at times, the world could be a scary and depressing place. No decent person deserved to go through that with little or no support.

Her smile was happier this time. "Thank you, Avery. You're fairly new to the village, too, aren't you?"

"Yep. It's not easy settling into a new country, but I've met a few really lovely people, and my job's awesome. I'm enjoying living here. Zero regrets." I grinned because I meant it. Other than the Stick sisters and seeing ghosts, oh, and being almost murdered a couple of times, moving here was really the best thing I'd ever done.

"I might just take you up on that offer of coffee. I've met some great people, too, but I could always use another friend." She grinned at me in the mirror.

The ghost jerked her head and looked out the window, as if something had startled her. Her jaw dropped open, then she covered it with her hand and fixed a panicked gaze on Simone. Surely being friends with me wasn't cause for that much trepidation.

A loud thwack and the crash of smashing glass came from the shopfront window. Instead of protecting myself, my instinct was to turn and stare. A few small slivers of window peppered me, and a brick landed amongst the shards on the floor.

I jumped up and ran to the front door with Simone. Seemed as if she was like me—running towards the danger rather than away. One day I'd change, but not today. I wanted to see who'd thrown it.

A black Mercedes sedan idled out the front of the shop. The

man in the passenger seat stared out his window at Simone. His balaclava covered most of his face, but his ice-blue eyes stood out, and a russet beard poked out around the mouth hole. His voice revealed an English accent. "I told you I'd find you, Mandy. Your mum's next, and then the boy is mine." Mandy? He must have the wrong woman. I parted my lips to say something, but he lifted his hand and pointed a gun out the window. Without saying anything else, he pulled the trigger.

Two shots cracked before I had time to react.

Simone fell. The car tyres screeched, and the vehicle took off.

I leaped out of the doorway and committed the number plate to memory. I ran back and grabbed my phone from my bag before returning to Simone, who lay on the ground bleeding. I called 999. "Ambulance, police, or fire?" the woman asked.

My heart raced and tears threatened, making it difficult to keep my voice steady. "Ambulance and police. A woman's been shot." I relayed the address and told her the number plate and make of car, just in case I forgot later. When I was done. I put my phone on the ground and cradled Simone in my arms. Blood soaked her shirt around her stomach.

Her face was pale, and she stared up at me with terror pulsing from her eyes. "Don't leave me."

"I won't." I lifted her shirt. It was hard to see the stomach wound under all that blood, but I had a general idea. How she could survive this, I didn't know, but I was going to do my best to keep her alive until the paramedics arrived.

I replaced her shirt and put pressure on the wound, the blood sticky under my palm. I looked into her eyes. "It's going to be okay, Simone." I was about to say, I promise, but the words wouldn't come. It was one thing to comfort her, but it felt wrong to lie. I blinked back tears and pretended everything was fine. "Can I call your mum? She'll want to come see you in the hospital."

She opened her mouth and tried to take a breath to talk, but all that came out was a gurgle.

"Stay with me, Simone. Please." I pressed more firmly on the slick mess of her stomach. I knew it wouldn't do any good, but it didn't matter. Maybe a miracle would happen?

"That scumbag. My poor darling." The old lady knelt next to us, her hand stroking Simone's hair. Simone's eyes widened as if she could feel it. Her eyes fluttered closed. I swallowed. Oh, God, no. She was dying.

"No. Simone. Simone!" Damn it!

Her head slumped to the side, her body limp, her heaviness sinking through me.

Simone's ghost appeared, standing next to us. Her eyes wide, she noticed the old woman. "Gran?"

The old lady stood and threw her arms around her. "Oh, I still can't feel you." Her gran frowned. A flash of brightness came from inside the hair salon. The old ghost grinned. "It's time for us to go together."

Tears fell onto Simone's cheeks. "But Adrian. I can't leave him."

"It's too late now. We have to go, sweetness."

"But—"

"We must hurry."

Simone stared down at me. "You can see me even though I'm dead?" She was quick to catch on.

"Yes."

"Please do me a favour. Save my son. That was my ex, Rusty."

"Is Mandy your real name?"

"Yes." She and her grandmother started drifting backwards towards the light.

"Where does she live?" A rush of noise swarmed the salon, like the sound of crashing waves and cicadas.

Mandy said something, but I couldn't hear. She was close to the light. I had to squint against the brightness. Her voice was an echo. "Whatever you do, don't tell the police. Mr Puddles. Get Mr Puddles. Evidence."

Huh?

Before I could ask her anything else—and I had questions upon questions—she and her gran melded with the light. Another flare, and it all disappeared.

I sucked in a shaky breath. What in Hades had just happened? I slumped against the doorframe and stared mutely at the few people who had gathered on the footpath to stare. I wanted to shout at them and ask why they weren't helping, but maybe they could see there was nothing to help.

Simone… or Mandy, rather, was dead. And there wasn't anything I could do about it.

CHAPTER 2

I sat in the salon chair I'd been in before, Sergeant Bellamy sitting in another wheelie chair opposite me, and tried not to replay the morning over and over in my head. Although that was hard, considering Bellamy wanted me to describe the whole thing in great detail. The salon owner, Verity, watched us from the basins on the other side of the room. She raised her hand to her chest, then dropped it. Every now and then, she shook her head slowly, her eyes glistening. Someone really needed to check on her, see if she was in shock.

Bellamy had out his pad and pen. "So, it was a black Mercedes sedan with the number plate *h k* one eight *l m r*."

"Yes." We'd been here for twenty minutes already, going over everything that had happened. I stared down at my palm, making a fist and opening and closing my hand slowly a few times. Cracks formed in the dried blood and my composure. Tears threatened. I looked up at Bellamy. "That's all I've got. Can I go home and have a shower?"

He glanced at my arm and hand. At least I'd been wearing

the black cape, and it seemed to have spared my clothes… mostly. "Of course. But I have one final question."

I sighed and nodded.

"You said she said it was her ex, but we had one shooting with the same description about twenty minutes earlier. Are you sure she wasn't just delirious? You said the shooter was wearing a balaclava."

"I also told you that he said he was going to kill her mother and take her son... Adrian I think his name might be." She'd said she couldn't leave Adrian, and I had to assume that was her son. She hadn't mentioned any boyfriend or husband. I left out the bit about Mr Puddles because she'd specifically said not to tell the police. I had no idea what the evidence in Mr Puddles could be and who it implicated in what, so until I figured that out, I'd keep it to myself. Maybe that was wrong, but how could I ignore a dead woman's wish? Maybe there was someone in the police she didn't trust? Or maybe whatever was in the evidence implicated herself or someone she loved in something?

"But you said he called her Mandy?"

"Yes. She admitted to me afterwards that that was her real name, and that her ex was called Rusty." I resisted the urge to scream just a little bit. We'd been over this, and I really, really wanted to get the blood washed off, and a calming cup of tea would be nice too.

"I'm not convinced, I'm afraid, but we'll check it out this afternoon." He looked over at Verity. "Your employee, Simone, did she ever tell you she had another name? Is Mandy her middle name?"

Verity blinked and shook her head. "No. All her paperwork checked out. Her tax details are all under that name, her licence, etcetera. And Amy is her middle name."

Bellamy jotted something down. "Have you ever met her son or mother?"

"No. She only spoke of them a couple of times. I got the impression she didn't want to say much. It probably upset her because she missed him." She shrugged. Her attention wasn't long on Bellamy before her gaze drifted to the russet smears on the floor near the door. At least they'd taken the body away.

"Did she have a boyfriend or a partner?" Bellamy was asking all the usual questions. At least I was here to hear the answers.

Verity shook her head. "No. She was single."

"Okay, thank you." He looked at me. "Right, well, I'll look into this, but I think it might be a case of mistaken identity. From what my officers on scene have told me, both women look similar. Obviously, we won't rule out there is an intentional connection, but I had a case five years ago where a killer murdered three men. He wanted to throw investigators off, send us on a wild goose chase. It almost worked. Because we had a mountain of evidence to sift through and so many people to interview, it gave him time to get away, but we caught up with him five months later."

My forehead furrowed. If only Mandy hadn't gone to the light so quickly. I didn't have any other information. How was I meant to find her mum and son and help them with no other details? The task seemed impossible. "Was the other person this morning killed?"

"Yes."

"Who was it?" If I knew their name, maybe it would help me figure out who Rusty was, and if there was any connection. Rusty sounded more like a nickname than a real one. Maybe neither murder was a mistake.

"I don't have her name at this stage."

"Can you please let me know when you do?"

"It'll be in the news soon enough, so sure. You'll get about a one-hour head start." He made a good point.

"Oh, right. I wasn't thinking."

"That's understandable, Miss Winters. You've just had an incredibly stressful morning." He was the master of understatement.

"Mmm, you could say that. Anyway, if I can help catch that scumbag, I'd feel a lot better. M—Simone was such a nice woman. She didn't deserve that." She was only about my age. Young for a mother of a five-year-old, maybe, and she had her whole life in front of her.

I went to Verity. "Are you okay? Do you want me to come back and help you clean up when everyone's gone?"

Bellamy cleared his throat. "Sorry, but you can't touch anything at least until tomorrow. Our evidence team has a lot to go over."

Verity shut her eyes for a moment, then opened them. "It's okay. Thanks, Avery. Maybe I can come see you tomorrow and fix that haircut?"

"Oh, that's right. She was only half done." My eyes burned. I shut them and took a breath, then looked at Verity. "Um, okay. What time?"

"Will eight in the morning work?"

"Yep. Sounds good. Thank you. Are you sure?"

She shrugged. "Life goes on, even when we're not ready." A tear slid down her cheek. "She was a great employee, and she was sweet, you know. She didn't deserve that. I just don't understand how...."

"I know." What else could I say? My phone rang. "Sorry, I have to take it. It's work."

"See, life goes on." She gave me a "what can you do" look.

"If you need anything, let me know." As she gave a nod, I pressed Answer and lifted the phone to my ear. I turned and walked out. "Hello, Vinegar. Thanks for covering that story for me." I'd hated to bug him, but seeing as how it was money in his pocket, I didn't think he'd mind too much.

"Hey, Lightning. It's the least I could do. Are you okay?"

"Um, kind of? I'm usually at the murder scene *after* everything's happened, not during. If the guy had wanted to, he could've killed me too." I swallowed, and my stomach dropped at that realisation. Bloody hell. If it was random, I'd been spared, and if it wasn't random, I'd also lucked out. What if he'd thought not to leave witnesses?

"Are you still there?"

"Yeah. Look, I'm going home for a shower. I'll be in the office later. Can you let MacPherson know I'll be about an hour? I don't have the energy to call him right now."

"Okay. If you need anything else, let me or Carina know. Okay?"

"Thanks. I appreciate it. See you later."

"Bye."

I couldn't believe I'd been so worried my work colleagues wouldn't be helpful or kind when I'd first arrived. Okay, I could believe it a little bit. My ex was an abysmal example of how a workmate should behave. There was no point being naïve, but I wasn't going to let him ruin all my current and future relationships with journalists. Not everyone was out to get others. Yes, we might all want the scoop, but Carina and Finnegan had been nothing but awesome friends once I'd gotten to know them.

As I walked home, some people stared. Maybe I should've washed the blood off in one of the hairdressing basins. Argh. My *favourite* person was walking towards me, looking at her phone. She smirked and raised her head, scenting blood… literally. She stopped in front of me. I didn't owe her anything, so I went to step around her, but she purposely moved to block me. Unless I wanted to push her out of the way, it looked like I was going to be stuck listening to her insult me. I stopped. Five, four, three, two, one.

She sneered and looked down at my bloody arm. Her voice

was pitched at a louder-than-normal volume perfect for drawing attention. "So, you finally killed someone. I knew it was only a matter of time. I bet you killed some of those other bodies you found too. You're evil. You bought death to Manesbury."

I ignored the sting of her words—*you bought death to Manesbury*. It wasn't my fault, was it? I shook off the thought because I didn't have time for her crap today. I'd just seen someone get murdered. I might have been a reporter and used to my share of dead bodies.... Oh, yeah, I didn't find them because I was a reporter. Fate seemed to step in and put them in my way, kind of like speed bumps so that my life couldn't run smoothly.

"It's *brought*, not bought." I rolled my eyes, hoping she'd get that I thought she was stupid. I wouldn't normally hassle someone for not knowing the correct word, but she was awful and deserved any insult I could get away with. "And, yes, of course I did, Joystick. I was hoping no one would notice if I left my scythe at home. But really, I don't need that. I can just touch someone, and they, you know...." I contorted my face into that of someone dying horribly, and my tongue lolled out. I reached towards her with my bloody hand. She gasped and jumped out of reach. "What, you don't want me to touch you? Are you afraid I want you dead?"

I smiled serenely and reached out to her again. Obviously, she didn't want someone else's blood on her, and she cared little that I wanted to wash it off. What I really wished I could do was go home and cry right now, not fence in the street with an insensitive idiot. If I was lucky, I was scaring her enough that she'd give me a wide berth for a few days.

She scurried sideways like a crab, finally eager to get away from me. It was about time. "You're crazy. Don't you ever touch me."

I pouted. "You're no fun." Maybe I should go back to calling her Joyless rather than Joystick. I grinned, making it as feral as possible. It had the desired effect. She turned and speed walked towards the café. Good riddance. Now I just had to run into Mrs Crabby when I got home, and my morning would be complete.

When I got home, I managed to sneak in without a Mrs Crabby sighting. Phew! I stepped inside my flat and locked the door.

"What happened to you?"

I jumped and turned, hand at my heart. "Everly. Dammit! You scared the ever-loving—"

She laughed. "Sorry, but you should see your face." Her expression turned serious. "Is that paint or…?"

"Or." I sighed and told her what had happened.

"Oh, honey, I'm so sorry. I'd give you a hug, but…."

That was the problem with having ghosts as friends—you couldn't give each other physical comfort, which was depressing. But I guessed having someone to talk to about it was better than not having them. "It's not like she was my best friend or anything, but she was nice. We'd agreed to hang out one day." I wasn't going to go over being there to see someone shot and almost being shot myself. They were horrors I didn't want to rehash over and over. "Anyway, how are you?"

She smiled and twirled a lock of her dark, permed hair around one finger. "I have a date."

"A date?! I didn't know ghosts dated." I knew they couldn't touch each other, so what was the point?

"Yeah, we do. It's not the same, of course, but we can still flirt." She waggled her brows.

"What's his name?"

"Oliver. He was born thirty years before me but died at the same age. Cool, huh."

"Um… I guess." I didn't think dying young was cool, but it was kind of like time travel, meeting someone your age who was born thirty years earlier. "So, what does ghost dating entail?" It wasn't like they could go out for dinner. The more I thought about it, the more I realised how much being a ghost would suck. The problem was, was what happened after the light better or worse than living as a ghost? Was it more like being alive, or did you lose all sense of self? That was a waste of time wondering about. I'd never know until it was too late.

"We talk and flirt. Sometimes, our energy connects. It feels kind of tingly all over."

"Oh, okay. I don't want any more details." Just in case it got raunchier, I did not need to know.

She laughed. "You asked. Anyway, are you okay?"

"Yeah. Hearing about your dating life cheered me up a bit. I'm going to scrub myself clean and get to work. That should distract me for a while. This afternoon, I've got an interview with someone who wants promotion for their cooking school."

She gave me a mock-fascinated look. "Ooh, riveting stuff."

"I'm sure it will be. My interviews always are." I smiled. "Have fun on your date."

"I will. I'll tell you all about it later." She waved and disappeared, and I had a shower. As the sluice of red water escaped down the drain, I tried my best to stop reliving the moment Simone… or Mandy, or whoever, slipped away. Unfortunately, showers couldn't wash away the nightmare stains tainting my thoughts.

I drove Daisy to work because my interview was about a ten-minute walk from the office. Okay, that's a lie. I drove to work to make sure I avoided Joyless. Trying to laugh off or ignore her idiocy and insults became harder by the day. She was toxic and filled me with anger. One of these days, I was going to push her out of the way or punch her in the face and go to gaol. It's not that I minded going to gaol that much, but she'd think that was awesome, and I didn't want to give her the pleasure. Grrr. I wasn't usually a violent person, but she brought out the worst in me.

Hmm, how much damage could I do to her by tripping? I needed to practice being clumsy and accidentally causing pain.

Her delightful sister ignored me when I came in, as usual, but when I entered the office, both Carina and Finnegan were there. They jumped up and came over. Carina hugged me. "Oh, love, are you okay?"

Finnegan stood back and looked me over. I wasn't getting a hug, but the sympathy in his eyes was enough. "I heard you were lucky you weren't shot."

I took a deep, shuddering breath. "Yep. I mean, they weren't after me, but I'm a witness. I'm surprised they didn't decide to off me as well."

"Do you t'ink d'ey'll come back?"

Finnegan gave her a "what the hell" look before turning back to me. "I'm sure they're long gone. The police are after them now. They'll have to lie low. It would be crazy of them to come back looking for you. Don't worry, Lightning. They don't know who you are either."

"Yeah, but d'ey—" Finnegan cut her off with a narrowed-eyed, pinched-mouthed stare. "Oh, okay. I'm sure you'll be fine."

I smiled. "Thanks. I'm sure they're long gone too." Was I? I was a loose end. And I was going to look into whether he really was her ex and if her son needed saving. Surely if her son went missing, Mandy's mother would report it to the police. Was I really needed? *You made a promise, Avery*. Yeah, yeah, conscience. Thanks for the reminder. Once I found out who her mother was, I could at least ask Bellamy to check and see if a child had been reported missing. But then again, Rusty—if that was his name—

said he was going to kill her, too, so maybe I should be listening for a murder report.

I had a plan. But it was predicated on me finding the mother of a woman who I potentially didn't have a last name for, assuming the name she'd given Verity was fake. Well, I'd soon find out since I'd decided I was going to drop in to see Bellamy tomorrow. In the meantime, I had work to do.

I put my stuff on my desk and pulled out my laptop before sitting. Finnegan stood in front of my table. "Oh, by the way, I think some warning would've been nice."

My face was all innocence. "Warning?"

He raised both brows, clearly disbelieving my act. "That woman this morning was a nutter. That cutlery collection she wanted me to report on was stolen. She steals cutlery from every restaurant she goes to. She had over a thousand knives, forks, dessert spoons, soup spoons." He shook his head. "Oh, and she wore a tiara the whole time, over her knotted hair that I don't think she's washed since 1986."

Carina and I laughed. I cocked my head to one side. "Welcome to my world. While you're out there reporting on the serious stuff, I'm in the trenches pandering to the crazies that make Manesbury and surrounding locales tick."

Carina patted my shoulder. "It's not all bad. You do report on murders… frequently."

I sighed. "Yes. I guess I do, and I kind of wish I didn't."

"You're getting quite a reputation." She chuckled.

I frowned and folded my arms. "Yeah, well, Joyless accosted me this morning and accused me of murdering people. Seriously? I've got better things to do. Besides, if I was going to kill anyone, it would be her."

Carina snorted, but Finnegan's eyes widened, and he said, "If anything happens to her, we did not have this conversation." His expression sobered. "I can't believe she did that, though. I mean,

I kind of can because I've seen her be snarky to Meg a couple of times, but she's always so nice to me."

Carina rolled her eyes. "Yeah, I bet. When she's wi'd you, butter wouldn't melt. She has d'e hots for ya, Finny." The day I walked into the café to find her whispering something to him and her tongue practically in his ear came back to me. I shuddered.

He blushed. Fancy that. I didn't take him for the blushing kind. Maybe he liked her. If he did, I didn't want to hear about it. Besides, gossiping about one of his friends was stupid of me. It would be me who looked bitter.

"Anyway, I've got work to do. I think I'll write a brief article on what happened this morning, then check out the Manesbury Facebook group for more leads before I go to my next interview." The best thing to do when you were stressed was keep busy. At least that's what I'd always found.

"Well, lovie, if you need anyt'ing, just let me know." Carina smiled and returned to her desk, as did Finnegan.

When I finished my article—I mentioned nothing about her possible name change or what the murderer said—I logged into Facebook and checked out the Everything Manesbury page. The first post was about a lost dog. It had gone missing last night. Those always made me sad. I put a sad-face emoji on the post and commented that I hoped they found it and I'd keep an eye out. I was such a sucker for animals. If I could have a pet here, I would, but there was a no-pets clause in the lease, and I wasn't ready to move.

As I scrolled to the next post, I gasped. My heart rate spiked, and my cheeks heated with anger and embarrassment. "That dirty little b—"

"Avery, what's wrong?" Carina asked from across the office. My gasp must've been louder than I thought, and my almost-swearing. Finnegan must've been in the zone because he didn't look up.

"Go to the Everything Manesbury page on Facebook." How dare she! There was a picture of me walking towards her, my bloody hand and arm clear as a neon sign. So, she'd taken my picture this morning. The post said "Anyone else think it's strange that Avery Winters is always there when someone gets murdered?" If I had the money, I'd sue her. I took a screenshot, then sent a message to the page admin to have it taken down, or I'd get the police involved. Not that they could do much, but the page admin probably didn't know that. Besides, people who managed these things usually didn't want drama.

Carina swore. "She's got a hide!" She stood and pushed her chair back. "I'm going to have words."

I sighed. "Don't bother. You don't need a target on your back too."

Finnegan finally looked up. "What's going on?"

"Your girlfriend just slandered Avery. She accused her of being a murderer."

"She did what? Where? Also, she's not, and never will be, my girlfriend."

A whirlpool of rage stormed inside me. "Facebook. The Everything Manesbury page. I've messaged them to take it down."

He went online and looked it up. "Wow, you weren't wrong. She really does have it in for you."

Carina rolled her eyes. "Ya t'ink?"

I chuckled. How could I not? She was the best person to have in your corner. "Don't ever change, Carina."

"I wasn't planning on it." She winked.

Finnegan looked at me. "You should message the page admin."

Carina and I looked at each other and laughed.

"What?" Finnegan's gorgeous face screwed up in confusion.

"Typical man. You never listen." Carina rolled her eyes. "Avery just did d'at."

"Oh, okay. Also, I was working. Pardon me for concentrating on work." He folded his arms and raised a brow.

"Pfft. You like a chat d'e same as d'e rest of us, Finny. Don't BS me, son." She grinned.

"Me, BS? Never!" His dimples flashed with his smile. Damn him for being so attractive. I wasn't swooning. Not at all.

I refreshed the page. Relief smoothed over my anger. "It's gone. Thank God for that."

"Sandra manages d'at page. She's okay, and she's not particularly friendly wit' Joyless." Carina nodded. "I do like your name for her. I t'ink d'at's what I'll call her from now on."

My eyes widened. "To her face?"

She chuckled. "No, lovie. As you said, I don't want a target on my back, but we can laugh about it *behind* her back."

I smiled. "Yes, we can, and we will."

Finnegan shook his head. "You two are trouble."

I cocked my head to the side. "We're as much trouble as a wasp nest. We're fine if you leave us alone, but poke us with a stick, and you'll cop it."

Carina laughed. "I love d'at analogy. It fits."

Finnegan looked at me. "Did you do something to upset her?"

Disappointment bled through me. His comment had thrown me into the past. It was something Brad would've said. Every negative thing that happened was my fault, according to him. He'd known her longer than me, though. Bad luck if he was blind to her questionable personality. It did make me sad that he didn't trust me or know me enough to give me the benefit of the doubt. "I don't think so. I think it's the mere fact that I exist and turned up here. She takes it personally, like I picked here just to upset her."

Carina frowned. "She doesn't like Avery because she hates competition." She stared at Finnegan. "Anyone who takes the spotlight away from her is fair game, according to her. She's chased you for ages. She sees Avery as a t'reat for your attention."

His forehead wrinkled. "No. That's ridiculous. I don't like her that way… never have. And I'm not about to date Avery either. She's wasting her energy competing against Avery. *If* that's what she's doing. Isn't that what women always say if another woman doesn't like them?"

Carina's gaze burned into Finnegan for a moment. Then she shook her head. "Oblivious. Typical man." She looked at me. "I've got your back. Okay."

I smiled. "Thanks. You're the best." I wanted to add that she and Meg were the most amazing friends I'd ever had or could hope to have, but getting mushy wasn't my style. Her kind words soothed the sting of Finnegan's rejection… not that I wanted to date him, but my ego didn't know that. "Right, back to work for me." I put my things into my bag. I'd look at the Everything Manesbury page again later for interview ideas, but it was time to go to my next interview. I stood. "See you guys later."

"Later, Lightning. Try not to sting anyone." He chuckled.

"I'll do my best, but I can't guarantee anything." If I saw Joyless in the street, I was going to say something. It might start an argument, but if I didn't, she'd think she could say what she wanted and stomp all over me. Everything had consequences. I wanted her to know that. Also, if she knew I'd make a scene later, it might make her think twice next time.

Carina stood and wiggled her bottom towards me. "Wasps forever, Avery."

I laughed and wiggled my bottom too. "Wasps forever! Later." Hopefully that wouldn't become our new way of greeting each other. I snorted as I walked out.

On the way to my car, I got a couple of dirty looks. Bloody

Joyless. *Deep breaths, Avery. Deep breaths.* It didn't matter what strangers thought of me. If I repeated that enough, I might get to the point that I didn't care, but right now, I cared. I was finally fitting in somewhere, and now this. I got into my car while blinking back tears.

Why did I have to see ghosts? If it wasn't for that, this wouldn't be happening. Sure, Joyless would still dislike me, but she wouldn't have anything to accuse me of. If only I could tell people, I could see spirits. But that would just make everything worse because no one would believe me, and I'd look like the lunatic that Joyless wanted me to. I sighed.

Pull up those big-girl pants, Avery. You survived lightning and two murder attempts. Stupid Joyless and her hateful antics aren't going to break you.

I sniffed, rolled my shoulders back, and started the car. She wasn't going to win. I wouldn't let her.

The drive to Xanthia Mariopoulos's place only took a few minutes. She lived in a semi-detached cottage on the main road just out of town. A few homes hugged both sides of the road on this stretch. Her short driveway had space for two cars side by side. I parked next to an old red Beetle that had seen better days. A couple of the panels were dented, and rust bubbled up on the boot and one of the wheel guards. How did that even pass its MOT? Maybe it hadn't.

The cottage looked to be in okay condition, but an assortment of potted plants littered the front porch. Some of the pots were cracked or chipped, and many of the plants were dead, brown strings of desiccated plant matter draped over the edge of the ceramic or plastic containers. They reminded me of a person reaching out for someone to save them, but it was too late. I was here because she wanted some advertising for her cooking school. She obviously didn't grow her own herbs or vegetables. At least I hoped she didn't. Maybe it was a new way of cooking that was kinder to the plants. Don't pick them when they're alive. Let them die first, then harvest. I snorted.

At least her bell worked. I heard a thud and swearing. After another few seconds, the door opened. A tall, large woman opened the door. She must've been about six foot tall. Brown hair peeked out of a blue hairnet, the kind workers of food prep wore. She smiled for a second. She dropped it like a hot potato. "You're Avery?"

"Yes." Where was she going with this?

"I don't want to do the interview anymore. I've heard a few *things* about you, and I'd prefer if you didn't come into my house." She made the sign of the cross.

I tried not to let my irritation show. "So, you saw that Facebook post this morning in the Everything Manesbury group?"

She lifted her chin and assumed a haughty expression. "Yes, I did." She glanced at my arms, probably looking for blood.

"You know it's not true. I don't kill people." If I did, Joyless would've been long dead.

Her narrowed eyes screamed *murderer!* I held in a sigh. I was getting excellent practice at that.

"I'll believe a Manesburian over a stranger any day." She threw a final disgusted look at me and slammed the door.

I stood and blinked. Wow, that was.... I shook my head. I'd say it was unbelievable, but people were idiots, so I could totally believe it. As I walked back to my car, I typed the altercation into my phone notes. If this affected my job, I would have grounds to sue that piece-of-poo woman. Not that I had the money, but gathering evidence wouldn't hurt.

I slid into my car, called Julian, and explained the situation. Double covering my butt. "Winters, that's despicable. And you got them to take it down?"

"Yes, but the damage has been done, it seems. I don't think it's up anywhere else, but I suppose I should check."

"I'll get IT onto it and legal. I'll see if we can send Miss Stick a lovely letter."

I swallowed my emotion—his unwavering support was unexpected. Not that I thought he'd be on Joyless's side, but I figured he'd tell me to brush it off and keep going. Him taking it seriously was everything. "Thank you, Julian. I appreciate your support."

"You're one of our best journalists." He chuckled. "And I know we only have three permanents in this office, but I'm speaking more widely. You give all the other journalists in our organisation a run for their money. I won't be sending anyone else out to cover that story either. That lady can lie in the bed she made." He cleared his throat. "Right, I have a meeting to get to. If she gives you any more problems, let me know." Gratitude filled my chest.

"I will, and thanks again. Bye."

He hung up. Warmth at the support outweighed how angry I was at Joyless and that idiot Xanthia. I'd just have to forgive the woman for being stupid. It wasn't her fault she had a defective nice-person radar. Her bad luck.

I had some time to kill, and I needed to eat, so I went to Meg's pub rather than back to the office. I could figure out who to interview next while I was there.

It was a little early for lunch, but the place was still half full. I went straight to the bar. The new guy, Mike, was there. "Hey, Avery. How are you today?" His smile was genuine.

"It's been a hell of a day." I'd let him take that as he wanted. I didn't really want to get into everything with him. Besides, he probably didn't have half an hour to chat.

His face turned serious. "I heard what happened this morning. Are you really okay?"

Thank goodness the sweet people outweighed the idiots

around here. "Mostly." I forced a smile. "Nothing a Riesling won't fix."

He grinned. "Coming right up. House okay?"

"Definitely."

He poured my drink and handed it over. "There you go. That'll be a fiver."

I handed the money over. "Thanks. Is Meg around?"

"Yep. Grab a table, and I'm sure she'll be out any minute."

I gathered my drink and sat at a two-seater table next to a window. I didn't really need to talk to Meg, but I did want to say hello. This was leading into their busy time, so I hadn't planned on hanging out with her.

I set up my laptop and got into Facebook. I checked that page, and the post was still gone. Good. I tried to look up Joy's page, but it didn't exist. Ha, she'd blocked me. I rolled my eyes. Sneaky cockroach. I'd just ask Carina to monitor it for me. Or I could start a new account and look from there, but honestly, I couldn't be bothered. I had work to do. After missing out on that story this morning, I needed to organise something else.

"Hello, Avery."

I jerked my head up. Standing across from me in front of the table was Meg's great-grandmother, Mary. I pulled my phone out of my bag and put it to my ear—thank heavens I wasn't born in the 1970s when mobiles didn't exist. "Hello." I smiled. "How are you?"

She chuckled. "I'm good, thank you. What are you up to?"

"I'm just looking for my next story." Again, I didn't want to go into my morning, so I didn't explain why I needed one ASAP.

"I've got one for you."

"Oh, do tell."

Her gaze flicked around the pub, then back to me. "A new singer is starting here tonight, Reece. He gave a performance for an hour last night as a trial, and the kids loved him." By kids, I assumed she meant Meg and Bailey. "He's from Exeter, and he's a lovely boy. Maybe you could cover that for the pub? Give us a bit of a lift." They didn't really need a lift—lunch and dinner were normally full—but I was always up for promoting the Frog and Trumpet.

"That's a great idea! Thanks for the heads-up. What time does he start?"

"Six. The sign's out in the hall."

That explained why I didn't realise, because I'd parked out the back and come in that way. "I'll be here at six on the dot." I smiled.

"Excellent." She turned her head. "Meg's headed this way. I'll let you say hello. Bye, Avery."

"Bye." I pretended to press the End Call button on my phone and put it in my bag. "Hey, Meg." She stared at me, her face serious. She was probably trying to gauge how I was feeling. I smiled. "I'm fine. Well, as fine as I can be." Now was okay, but tonight would probably suck. I doubted I was going to get much sleep with the goriness of this morning playing through my brain.

She jerked the chair out from the table and dropped into it. "I only have a minute, but sheesh. Dad told me what happened. He saw the tail end of it on his way here. He said there was a lot of blood. Carina also messaged me about Joyless. I'm so sorry."

I swallowed my anger. "Don't worry. She's a troll. One day, Karma will come and bite her on her scrawny behind. Until then, I'll bide my time. Besides, what's happening to me is nothing compared to poor Simone." Or Mandy. A heavy stone sat in my stomach. "She was only our age. So young. She's left her son behind."

Her eyes widened. "I didn't know she had any kids."

"Yeah. He's started school this year, apparently. Anyway, I'll deal with my stuff. I'm still here, and that's what I'm going to focus on." And finding out who the killer was.

She gave me a shrewd look, as if she could read my mind. "Are you going to see if you can track down the killer?"

A smile hijacked my lips. "You know me so well." I'd only known her for a few months, yet she knew me better than anyone back home, except maybe my sister. Maybe it was because she'd taken the time to really look because she cared.

"Do you need any help?" She stared at me like an eager puppy. She was so adorable. How could I say no? Unfortunately, I might have to.

"I'll let you know. I'm meeting with Bellamy tomorrow, although he doesn't know it yet." I smiled. "I'll call you as soon as I'm done." Hopefully he'd give me something. He hadn't known much this morning, but he also hadn't offered anything but to let me know about the other woman's name. Come to think of it, he hadn't called me. He was probably flat out, given what had happened.

She cocked her head to the side. "Um, Avery, turn your head."

"What?"

She made a spin-around motion with her pointer finger. I turned one way, then the other. "Um, is it my imagination, or is your ponytail longer on one side than the other?"

"It's not your imagination. This morning happened in the middle of my haircut. Verity's going to come to mine in the morning and fix it."

Her face fell. "Oh, yeah. Sorry."

I shrugged one shoulder. "It is what it is. At least I'm still alive." I would've said more, but the urge to cry snuck up on me. I took a deep breath and pushed it back down.

Meg leaned across the table and grabbed my hand. "Thank goodness for that. You've had so many close calls lately that I'm beginning to think you're cursed." She released my hand. "Speaking of being cursed, I have to get back to work." Meg chuckled and stood. "If you need anything or want company tonight, let me know."

"Oh, I'm coming here for dinner. I need another story, and I heard you have a new performance person."

She laughed. "Performance person. You're hilarious. Yes, we do, and he's all kinds of hot."

"Ooh, bonus."

"Total bonus. Okay, so I'll see you later, then."

I grinned. "You sure will."

When Carina and Finnegan found out I was going to the pub for dinner, they decided to tag along. We'd snagged a four-seater table near the stage, which had a perfect view of the soulful, and yes hot, singer. He had an acoustic guitar and played a mixture of fast and slow songs from a few current famous artists, like Taylor Swift, Ed Sheeran, and Jessie J. We'd been here for twenty minutes, our food having just landed on the table. I'd also warned Finnegan off using tonight for an article.

"It's fine, Lightning. I have more important articles to write. I'll let you deal with the inconsequential stuff." He smirked, then sipped his beer.

I smiled sweetly. "Your generosity knows no bounds. Neither do your compliments."

Carina watched us both and grinned. "Who needs an entertainer when I have you two to watch."

Finnegan and I both turned unimpressed gazes on her. She just laughed.

Meg stopped at our table. "So, what do you think of Reece? He's good, hey?"

I smiled. "He's got a great sound. Love his voice. And you were right—he's hot."

"Is he single?" Carina asked.

"I haven't asked. I didn't think Chris would appreciate me flirting with another man. Maybe you ladies should." She grinned. Chris Lark was her long-distance boyfriend. She hadn't mentioned him much lately, and I wondered how much longer they'd last.

"Hmm, maybe we should." I didn't want to date, not really, but was it wrong to want a brief fling with someone I would never have to see again if I didn't want to? He lived in Exeter, according to my brief research, so it would be easy to avoid him later. Maybe seeing someone casually would be fun. And while he wasn't quite as gorgeous as Finnegan or Bailey, he was more than pleasant to look at. He had shoulder-length, thick, blond hair, slightly tanned skin, and a killer smile with dimples. Not to mention his slightly raspy, sexy voice and guitar-playing talent. Musicians had it going on. I wasn't sure why. Maybe it was because they could display emotions. It made them seem deeper than the average person. Okay, so it might not be true if the reported promiscuous lives of famous musicians were anything to go by, but a girl could hope.

Finnegan looked at me, his face carefully casual. "I thought you didn't want to date anyone after your disaster of an ex?"

"Well, Reece is from Exeter, so it's not like I'd have to see him again. A casual fling might be fun." Meg side-eyed me. Who was this new Avery talking about casual flings like an old hand? What happened to the woman who wouldn't sleep with anyone unless she really knew them? I think she died with the realisation that she didn't know Brad very well or knew how awful he was and slept with him anyway. I chuckled. There was no way the hot guy strumming his guitar could be worse than Brad, and he was probably better in bed.

"Good for you." Carina grinned. "If you don't want him, maybe I'll have a go."

Finnegan glanced at the guy before looking back at me. "He might reject you; you know." Ouch!

I laughed incredulously. Carina's eyes bugged wide, and she slapped his arm. "You did not just say d'at!"

"It's okay." Meg grinned. "He's just worried because he knows the guy will say yes, and then his chance with our girl might be lost forever."

He rolled his eyes. "Please. You know I don't date." He eyed me. "No exceptions."

I waved a hand. "It's fine. Vinegar's just being honest. The guy might reject me, but really, who cares? After everything I've been through today, a rejection is nothing."

Carina nodded. "You make a good point, lovie. But if he rejects you, he's eid'er gay, or needs glasses." She was sweet. People were attracted to what they were attracted to. If he rebuffed my advances, I wasn't going to take it personally.

Meg looked across the room and gave a nod. She looked back at us. "Sorry, guys. Gotta get back to work. I'll drop by later." She hurried off.

Finnegan swallowed a mouthful of food. "All joking aside, are you going to investigate what happened this morning?"

Carina leaned forward.

"What do you think?" Looked like I'd lost any semblance of secrecy about looking into this. Not that it mattered now that Bellamy wasn't swearing me off investigating crimes.

"Do you need any help?" His blue eyes drilled into mine. "I won't steal any stories, if that's what you're worried about."

"Um, it's not that, but, ah, aren't you worried about getting injured or killed after last time? I don't want to be responsible for getting anyone killed." That was one reason. The other one was that when ghosts told me things, sometimes it was impossible to explain away how I knew what I knew. Meg was one thing because she wasn't suspicious by nature, and she didn't really have time to follow me 24/7, but Finnegan was another. He was a journalist—it was his job to weigh up everything I said and look for holes. He also had time to become a pain in my behind. Not that I didn't appreciate the offer. It came from a good place.

Carina speared me with the look of a teacher about to give a disciplinary lecture. "You're not supposed to investigate t'ings by yourself. You should say yes. One of us should be wit' you whenever you leave the village to question anyone."

Oh, sweet baby Jesus. They weren't going to let this go. I would imagine Bellamy would repeat the same thing—after last time, he made me promise. I could pretend I promised for that one case, but I'd never hear the end of it if anything happened to me. "Look, some of what I'm researching is confidential. I don't plan on interviewing anyone dangerous just yet. Besides, what if I have to hurry somewhere and none of you are available to come?" I appreciated their concern and even agreed with them to a point, but I didn't want a babysitter for everything.

"Not good enough." Carina was like a dog with its favourite stick.

"Look, I can't promise, but I'll do my best to have one of you along whenever I'm going to interview someone I think is a suspect. But if that happens, you can't pester me for facts if I don't want to give them. You need to trust me, or we don't have a deal." That might give me some leeway with spirit-given information. I wouldn't have to explain myself every five minutes.

They narrowed their eyes and gave me sceptical looks. Finnegan was the first to crack. From his spot opposite me, he reached across the table. "You have yourself a deal."

I shook his hand and ignored the sensual feeling of his skin against mine and the zing that travelled down my arm to my belly. Before my thoughts showed on my face, I imagined a big dog poo.

His forehead wrinkled, and he snatched his hand back. "No

need to look so disgusted about touching me."

I laughed. "Oops. Sorry. I was thinking about… something else."

Carina grinned, glancing from Finnegan back to me. "It's okay, Avery. He's not used to women being turned off when he touches them." She was evil, teasing him like that, but it was still funny. "I also agree to your terms." She shook my hand too.

"Excellent. Now, are we getting dessert?"

After a small apple tart with a scoop of vanilla ice cream, we chatted until the music stopped. That was my cue. I grabbed my handbag. "Okay, I'm going to get to work."

Carina chuckled and winked. "Work. Yup, I understand. You go get that hottie."

I gave her a "seriously" look. "Ha ha. Thanks for having dinner with me. I'll see you both tomorrow."

"And don't forget." Finnegan stood. "Be careful, and make sure you take us with you or at least let us know where you're going when you're interviewing."

"I will." And I meant it. He was giving me an out with the "let us know where you're going" bit. I'd take it. Finnegan gave me a wave and sent a stony-faced glance to the singer, and Carina gave me a quick hug. They left, and I made my way to the bar where Reece was sipping a beer and eating nuts from the bowl on the counter. I smiled and pretended my heart wasn't beating a little too fast. Maybe I wasn't going to flirt. And maybe I wouldn't work up the nerve to ask him out. "Hi, I'm Avery. Did you know those nuts probably have faecal matter in them?" I slammed my hand over my mouth. Bloody hell. I opened my mouth, and that's what came out?

"Hey!" Bailey had obviously heard. He folded his arms and raised his eyebrows. "Are you dissing my nuts?"

I laughed. "I would never diss *your* nuts. It's just a well-known fact that nuts on tables at bars have gazillions of germs because people don't wash their hands after going to the toilet, then they dip them in the bowl."

Reece smiled, his dimples showing. His expression was part amused and part not sure what to make of me. I couldn't blame him. "Thanks for the warning, but I'll risk it."

"A man who lives dangerously." I'd start by asking if he minded giving me an interview, and maybe by the end of that, I'd have the courage to ask him out. "I'm Avery, and I'm a friend of Meg and Bailey's. I'm also a reporter with the local paper, the *Manesbury Daily*. I was wondering if you'd answer a few questions for the paper, so I can pimp out your act and the pub."

"I don't get enough pimping offers by beautiful women, to be honest. It would be my pleasure." Ooh, he was smooth. I almost blushed, but he was probably always flirty, being a musician and all. Not that he would have to try hard with those looks and talent. Maybe it was part of his act, a barrier of superficiality he wore when in public.

"Excellent. Thanks." I smiled and ignored the annoyed expression Bailey threw the guy's way—not that Reece had eyes in the back of his head, thank goodness. I took out my notepad and pen. "Can we sit somewhere? This'll only take ten or so minutes."

"Sure."

We returned to the table I'd sat at for dinner. I asked a few questions about how long he'd been singing—since he was a kid—who his influences were and what he enjoyed about performing. Once that was done, I recorded the details of his performances at the pub. He was going to perform two nights a week for the next six weeks. If that went well, they'd keep him on for a while. He'd been friendly, polite, well-spoken, and relaxed. He gave off an air of someone who was chill at all times. By the time we were done, I'd lost my nerve. There would be no asking him out. He was too attractive, and given he'd mentioned he'd had quite a bit of success online and with a few songs he'd written and put on streaming services, there was no way he'd want to go out with me.

I slid my notebook and pen back into my bag. "Thanks for that." At least I'd made up for the disaster of this morning's aborted interview.

"No, thank you. I haven't done many interviews. It was fun." He grinned, which did gooey things to my insides. I was pathetic. Maybe my lack of dating experience was messing with my hormones. And maybe it was because my ex was such a horrible person that even two steps up from that looked better. Not that this guy was only two steps up, but you know. Someone even a bit nicer seemed enticing. Hmm, it could also be because of the number of losers I'd had to suffer at the pub's speed-dating night. Wow, so many reasons. "Did the pub owners strongarm you into it?"

"What? No. I needed another article for today because one from this morning fell through. It was actually my idea. It'll be in tomorrow's edition."

"Oh, what happened this morning?" He leaned forward, looking for all the world as if he really wanted to know. Well, this was unusual—a guy who could've kept talking about himself but wasn't.

"Um.... Well, stuff happened this morning, and when I got to my interview, they didn't want to talk to me." Argh, now I'd done it. How to explain that away?

"And? You're not going to leave me hanging, are you?" His gaze bored into mine. An exciting kind of warmth settled in my belly. Was he flirting? He couldn't be. Why was it so hard to tell?

Throwing all good sense to the wind, I told him what happened this morning and Joyless's actions afterwards. If there was any flirting before, I surely just killed it. "So, you see that you actually helped me out."

His mouth hung open. "You were almost killed, and she had the nerve to talk smack about you. What a numpty." He looked genuinely concerned. "Are you sure you're okay? That's… a lot to have happen. I mean… I've never even seen a dead body, let alone had someone killed next to me." He shook his head.

"Well, when you put it like that… I should be upset, and I guess I am, but this isn't the first time I've been in such a stressful situation." I really, really didn't want to date him, apparently. Way to go, Avery.

His eyebrows rose to heights they might have never seen before. "What? You've seen someone killed before?"

"Not exactly. I've just been unlucky enough to come upon dead bodies more than once. Anyway, that's enough about me." I stood before he started to agree with Joyless's assessment of the situation. "Thanks again, and it was lovely to meet you."

He stood, his amber eyes still on mine. "Not so quickly. This might sound cheesy, but are you single?"

Oh my God. Oh my God. I ignored my freaked inner voice and feigned calmness. "Yes. Are you?"

"Definitely. So, now we've established that, I'd love to take you out for lunch one day. Would you be up for that?"

Ooh, lunch was risky. He was going all out. If we didn't get along, he'd be stuck with me for about an hour and a half. Coffee was the easier option. I could explain I didn't want to get serious right now, but then he might think I just wanted a booty call, which wasn't exactly right either. *Argh, brain, just calm down. Stop overthinking everything.* "Yes, thanks. Lunch would be nice. Do you want my number?"

He smiled. "That was going to be my next question." He unlocked his phone and handed it over. I punched my number into it. I caught Bailey in my periphery, frowning at us from behind the bar. That made me sad, but dating him would be way too complicated if anything went wrong, so I told myself for the hundredth time. Besides, he'd taken someone out a couple of times recently, and she was really nice. From what Meg had said, he liked her so far.

"There you go." I wanted to ask when he might call or text, but I didn't want to seem desperate.

"Right, well, thanks. I'll be in touch."

"Great." Cue awkwardness. He leaned towards me, but we weren't on hugging terms, so I raised my hand in a halfwave, turned, and walked to the rear entrance. Had I just done something stupid? Whatever. If he called me, he called.

I stopped walking before I reached my car and sucked in breath. What in Hades?

Large white writing spread across my bonnet. Was that shaving cream? *Leeve Manesbury, murderer.* At least it wasn't an evil genius. The message was upsetting enough without them not being able to spell "leave" properly. My last bit of energy syphoned from me, and it was all I could do not to sit on the ground. People sucked.

Was it Joyless, a friend of hers, or a town nutjob who'd seen her post? I took a photo and called Bellamy's mobile. Since he'd been at work this morning, it was unlikely he'd be at the station now, and he already knew about everything, so it was best to talk to him. It had been a ridiculously long day, and I didn't have it in me to explain everything all over again.

"Miss Winters, it's a bit late for this to be a social call. What's up?"

"Sorry to bother you, Sergeant, but there's been a small incident. Nothing major, but I wanted to report it nonetheless."

"Right. Trouble seems to follow you, Miss Winters." Ha, that was an understatement, and we both knew it. "What is it this time?"

"Well…."

CHAPTER 3

The next morning, Verity came over to finish cutting my hair. I sat at the kitchen table, and Everly observed and made comments. "Why don't you try something different, like your friend Carina? Blonde hair is so boring."

I almost answered her. Thankfully, Verity chose that moment to speak. "I still can't get into my shop either. I have a few home visits to keep me busy today instead, but I didn't sleep last night." Her face was drawn, and her eyes brimmed with sadness.

"I don't blame you. I didn't sleep much either." The whole day was crazy—from almost being killed, to seeing someone be murdered, to being harassed, and getting a guy's phone number. How was this my life?

"I'm so sorry, Avery." She took another section of hair and snipped.

"It's not your fault! And, as you've probably heard via the grapevine, I have a habit of finding bodies.... Although this was way worse." I figured Verity was trustworthy—I could bring this up with her because she wouldn't believe Joyless's idiotic opinion. At least I hoped she wouldn't.

Everly managed to get in a "Go pink. Pink hair rocks" before Verity answered. I flicked an annoyed glance Everly's way. At least there was no mirror reflecting it back to the hairdresser.

Verity stopped cutting and came around to my side so I could turn and look at her. "I don't for one second believe those stupid rumours. I've heard it all. When people get in my chair, they lose all sense of decorum. The things that go on in this village, well, even you'd be surprised. One thing I know is not to believe everything I hear second-hand. If you want the truth, go to the source of the rumours. Besides, I'm good at reading people, and I like you, Avery. Joy… well… let's just say, she can be difficult. I've known her for a long time, and she's never been my favourite person. There's probably more people than you think who would take her words with a grain of salt." She moved back behind me. "Now, let's get this finished."

Everly shook her head. "You're so boring. I'm outta here. See ya." She disappeared, and I smiled. Thank you, powers that be. It was too early to deal with badgering, especially since I hadn't had enough sleep. I yawned. *Argh, don't think about being tired.*

"I feel you." Verity laughed. She smoothed her hands over my hair. "Right. You're done. Come into the bathroom, and you can see it."

She followed me into the bathroom. When I reached the mirror, she held a round mirror to reflect the back. I smiled. "Thank you. That looks perfect."

"I'll just sweep up."

"No, it's fine. You've got enough to deal with today." I smiled.

"Are you sure?"

"Totally." I checked my phone. I was supposed to be at the police station in twenty minutes to see Bellamy. I'd managed to get an appointment with him when I'd called him last night about my car. Now there was just enough time to get there. I gave Verity cash and a hug, and she left.

After I called Bellamy last night, he sent a couple of police down to take photos and evidence. The pub's video camera was working, so they took that footage too. I doubted anyone was stupid enough not to disguise themselves, but you never knew. We were going to go through the footage together today.

I gathered my stuff and went downstairs. Just as I opened the building's front door, Mrs Crabby opened her front door. I sighed and stopped. No doubt, she was going to say something awful to me, but I didn't want to be rude and shut the door in her face and walk off. Okay, so I *wanted* to, but I wasn't going to. Enough people were trying to run me out of the village. I didn't need to lose my apartment and make it a reality. I turned around. "What do you want to ream me out about now?"

Her mouth already open, her eyes widened. She hurriedly regained her composure, her face shifting into an irritated mask. "I heard about yesterday morning. Did you have anything to do with it?"

I so wanted to be snarky and say yes, but I wasn't in the mood to move today. "Of course not. I'd be in gaol right now if I had. What about a little sympathy? I was standing right there when it happened." I wanted to scream, "I held the woman as she died," but I didn't. Instead, I swallowed. I was not going to cry in front of the old bat. What was wrong with people?

She sniffed. "Sympathy? There's some here that don't like you, young lady. And I tend to agree with them—you always seem to be in the wrong place at the wrong time. Are they going to find me dead soon and you standing over my body?"

If only I could get away with that.... Ahem. "Look, I don't have time. I'm going to be late for my next appointment." If my nonanswer worried her, good. I turned and hurried to the gate, slamming it closed behind me. I was sick to death of her crabby attitude. She took every opportunity to harass me. Maybe I should start looking for another place. Why wait for her to kick me out and be on the back foot? Oh, that's right—I'd signed a lease. I was stuck. And even though she had obligations, too, she could break the lease, and there'd be nothing I could do about it. I wasn't going to spend time and money fighting her. Argh.

My stomach was in knots as I walked into the laneway. I'd cleaned off the muck last night. If there was more, I didn't have time to grab a bucket and wash it. And what if whoever it was damaged my car this time, like slashed the tyres or dented it? Maybe I could ask Charles to watch over it at night. It wasn't like he had anything else to do.

There she was. My beautiful car. My feet stopped automatically. Adrenaline warmed my stomach, and tears burned my throat. Someone had toilet-papered my car. I shut my eyes and took a deep breath. *Turd.* I supposed it could be worse. Whoever did this could've smeared themselves all over my car.

I opened my eyes and went to my pride and joy. "I'm sorry, Daisy." Okay, so the car wasn't a living thing, but still, I felt bad. I looked around. No one seemed to be watching, but just in case, I rolled my shoulders back and held my head high. No one was running me out of town.

Right. I cleaned the toilet paper off the windows and windscreen and checked her over for any dents or scratches. At least the mess wasn't permanent or disgusting—the toilet paper appeared to be unused… until now.

I got in my car and drove to the police station. It didn't escape my notice as I drove through Manesbury that everyone stared at my car. A couple of them laughed. They were women about my age. Probably Joyless's friends. What had I ever done to her or anyone here? Okay, so people never needed an excuse to be horrible. I'd just have to rise above it. Karma would show up sooner or later and deal with the peanut brains, surely.

Finally, I made it to the police station. I found a spot on the street and pretended my car wasn't plastered with toilet paper as

I got out and locked her. At least no one knew me in Cramptonbury. Oh, scrap that. A young woman trotted down the footpath towards me. And by trotted, I meant like a horse. She stopped next to my car and shook her head as if shaking out her mane. Her lips vibrated as she made that noise horses do.

"Hi, Carly. How are you?" It was the young woman I'd interviewed about show jumping, not knowing she was rider and horse all in one.

"Hello, Avery." She smiled. "How are you?"

"I'm good, thanks. How have you been?"

"Really well. Since you interviewed me, I've had a couple of offers for other interviews, and I'm going to be on TV in two weeks. It's been grand. So thank you again. And I appreciate you being so nice. Not everyone gets me." Okay, so I didn't totally understand her desire to be a horse, either, but she was a lovely girl. Plus, she wasn't hurting anyone, except maybe herself. I hated to think how her hips would feel in twenty years.

"It's my pleasure. Good luck with the other interviews."

"Thanks." She smiled and waved, then trotted off down the street.

Inside the station, PC Adams buzzed me in. It was nice not to have to weasel my way in here anymore. I knocked on Bellamy's door. "Come in."

"Hi, Sergeant." I shut the door behind me.

Bellamy sat in his chair, paperwork spread out on his desk. Sergeant Fox stood next to Bellamy's chair. They greeted me simultaneously. "Hello, Miss Winters." Bellamy gestured to the seats on the other side of his desk. "Please, sit."

"So, have you got any leads on the murder?" If they found the killer super soon, I wouldn't have to do anything. Surely Mandy's mother's number was in her phone.

He shook his head. "Still chasing witnesses up, I'm afraid. We're classing it as a random crime until we can prove otherwise.

Either your friend or the other woman was likely in the wrong place at the wrong time, and frankly, it's a miracle you weren't shot." So, he hadn't found evidence to back up what I'd said she'd told me, and he was still assuming he was investigating *Simone's* murder.

"What about her phone? Did you call her mother?"

"There were only three numbers in her phone. One was Verity's, the other was for one of her friends here, and the last one we tried to call a few times, but no one answered. Now it's disconnected." His gaze travelled to the papers on his desk. I could tell avoidance when I spotted it.

"Doesn't that strike you as odd? Who has only three numbers in their phone? And one just happens to disconnect after you try and call it? Also, if Simone really is her name, and she has a child, doesn't it stand to reason, you would've found out some information on her? Where is her family—parents, siblings, her child? I'm sure you're going to tell me that you found none of that. Please don't gloss over things. I don't have time." I took a deep breath before I said something I shouldn't. Might as well get to my car issue. "Have you got any leads on who toilet-papered my car last night?"

"We have nothing on who vandalised your car. The video footage from the pub is grainy at best, and the two perpetrators had their faces covered. As for Simone's case, her having only three numbers is odd, as is the fact we can't find her family, but we'll get there. I'm afraid that's all the information I can give you at the moment." He shuffled the papers on his desk, avoiding my gaze.

I looked at Sergeant Fox and raised my brows as if to say, what's going on? He shrugged. I narrowed my eyes. I didn't buy any of this. He was thorough and likely had at least one lead by now. "So, you're cutting me out of the investigation?"

He finally met my eyes. "I would hardly say I'm cutting you

out, Miss Winters. We're analysing all the evidence and speaking to many, many witnesses. At this stage, there's nothing to tell, and you've helped all you can. Unless you can think of something you didn't tell me yesterday?"

A flicker of doubt about Mr Puddles came to me, but I ignored it. There was a reason Mandy had said not to tell the police, and I was staying mum until I figured out what it was. "No." I folded my arms and gave him my cranky face. I wanted him to know that this wasn't on and that I wasn't going to forget about it.

"Look, when we get somewhere with it, I promise you can have the scoop. Okay?"

"I won't say no to that." Could I just leave it to them, knowing her son and mum were in danger? Looked like I didn't have a choice. With no ghosts to talk to and Fox not giving me anything, I didn't know what else I could do. But I'd made a promise. Argh!

"As for your toilet-papered car, that video, as I mentioned, wasn't enough to go on. It's impossible to tell who it is, even how old they are, or whether they're a man or woman."

Frustration fermented inside me, the gasses threatening to explode and spatter my body all over the room and Bellamy. I stood before I voiced my ire. "Right, well, I have to go now and wash my car." I turned and left. Yes, it was rude, but he wasn't telling me everything, and he knew I knew. I was sick of being nice to everyone, trying to smooth things over. I'd been doing it my whole life, but not any more. I'd made a promise to Simone… Mandy. And Bellamy was making it impossible for me to help. All I could do was cross my fingers that the police would find something within the next few days that exposed the killer.

But did her family have that much time?

Probably not.

CHAPTER 4

Before returning to the office, I stopped at a do-it-yourself car wash—I wasn't driving back into Manesbury with my car the way it was. I refused to give Joyless and her cronies the opportunity to laugh. I also stopped to get a takeaway cappuccino from outside of the village. After what Joy had done, I couldn't bring myself to go inside the Heavenly Brew Café. I wasn't a coward, but I also wasn't a sucker for punishment.

Back in the office, Carina was in. We said hello, and I got straight to work, typing up the article about the pub and its new entertainment. I added a photo I'd taken of Reece mid-song, strumming his guitar, his eyes shut, mouth open, holding a note. He'd have a few more fans when this article came out. I couldn't help the sigh that escaped. He really was good-looking.

"What are you sighing about, d'en? It wouldn't be d'at hottie you interviewed last night, would it?"

I grinned. She was sharp, that one. Just when you thought she wasn't paying attention. "I'm not answering that question on the grounds that it may incriminate me."

"So, did you go home wit' him?"

I looked at her as if she'd grown a beard. "Um, no. Of course not."

"Missed opportunity, if you ask me."

"I didn't."

"Did you at least get his number?" She looked hopeful.

"No. He's got mine, though. If he calls, he calls." At least I couldn't embarrass myself by texting him too soon. It was a good thing I didn't have his number—it would be too tempting to use it.

She twirled a few strands of her blue hair around her finger. "Did you tell Finny?"

"No. Why would I?"

"Oh, no reason." She was such a mischief-maker.

"Oh, how's your mum?" Carina's mum had broken her ankle a week ago and had an operation.

"She's okay. My sister says she's being annoying again, so she's definitely on d'e mend. I'm going to go home and see her d'is weekend, give my sister a break."

"That's good." I was pleased with myself, seamlessly changing the subject.

"So, if you need to check out any suspects, you'll have to take Finny wit' you." That gleam in her eyes wasn't normal, and my ruse had failed.

"Or Meg." Not that I had anything against taking Finnegan. Carina just seemed to think sparks would fly or something. Wasn't going to happen, and I enjoyed messing with her just as much as she enjoyed messing with me. "Maybe I could take Bailey, or the musician guy?" If he called, but I wouldn't let reality stop my musings.

"Hmm, maybe. Oh, how did things go wit' Bellamy?"

"Not great. He wouldn't tell me squat. Well, he said they didn't know anything yet and that I couldn't help." I slumped against the back of my chair. And this time, I couldn't even get

Fox on board. I'd have to ask Charles about that later. He'd become such a help to me. Who would've thought a child ghost would be one of my best friends and source of information. Truth was so much stranger than fiction sometimes.

"But you don't believe him?"

"No, and I don't know why they're giving me the run-around."

"D'ey?"

Oops. I almost said too much. "Well, the police. You know." Not the two sergeants—one living and one dead.

"If d'ere's anyt'ing I can do to help, let me know." She smiled.

"Thanks. You're the best." My phone dinged with a text. Ooh, maybe Bellamy had changed his mind about sharing information. I looked at my phone. It was a number I didn't recognise. My heartbeat sped up. It was either one of Joyless's minions harassing me, or it was Reece.

Hey, Avery. Want to catch up for a quick dinner before I play at the pub tonight? I could meet you there at 5. My set starts at 6. Reece 😊.

Phew! I grinned and replied. *That would be great. See you there at 5.* I considered using an emoji because he had, but I didn't usually use them, and he might think I was copying him. Actually, no, he probably wouldn't. Why did I have to overthink everything?

"What's d'at smile? D'e one you had a second ago?"

I looked at Carina. "Do you miss anything?"

She rolled her eyes. "I'm a reporter, lovie. Remember? Now, stop trying to change d'e subject."

"Reece just texted. We're having dinner at the pub before he performs tonight."

Finnegan strode in, stopped in front of my desk, and peered down at me. "What's this about dinner at the pub? Are we going again?"

Carina chuckled. "You missed d'e first part of d'e conversation. Our Avery is going on a date tonight with the musician."

"Oh!" He smiled. "Wow, he was quick asking you out. Means he's keen. Have fun." And just like that, he dropped it and went to his desk. Carina looked a bit put out because he didn't take her bait. Proved that he really was okay with it. I shouldn't be disappointed that he didn't care, but I was. What was wrong with me? I didn't want him, so why should I want him to be sad someone else was taking me out? I was such an idiot sometimes.

"Thanks. I'm sure I will."

My phone dinged again. *Excellent. Can't wait to see you.* 😀

"Was d'at him again?"

"Yep."

"He really is keen." Carina winked.

Being keen wasn't the only prerequisite for a good date. Hopefully, he was just as pleasant as when I met him the other night and didn't have weird hang-ups I was about to find out about. "Seems to be. Anyway, I have to go out. I've got an interview."

Finnegan looked at me. "Is it related to the murder?"

"No. Bellamy wouldn't give me any info, and I have practically nothing to go on." Maybe Verity would know something, even if she didn't know she knew. I'd have to go and talk to her, but maybe I'd leave it till tomorrow, give her five minutes to absorb what had happened. Actually.... I picked up my phone and dialled Julian.

"Hello, Winters. What can I do you for?"

"I was wondering if you would let me do a small article for A Snip in Time. Verity's looking for a new hairdresser, and considering what happened, I think it would be nice if she didn't have to pay for an ad. What do you think?"

I could hear the smile in his voice. "That's a great idea. Good thinking, Winters."

"Thanks. Have a good afternoon. Bye."

"Ciao." Ooh, a goodbye. Okay, so it was in Italian, but I'd take it.

Right, so since I had a reason to go see her, that would help. I might as well go later today, after my next interview. I stood and shoved everything into my bag. "See you guys later."

They simultaneously said, "Bye." As I walked out, Carina was jinxing him for saying the same thing at the same time. I chuckled. They were like brother and sister sometimes, giving each other a hard time whenever possible. I'd really lucked out when I landed the job here. I couldn't have ended up with a nicer group of people.

Well, look at that. My car was still clean. It didn't take much to make me happy these days. My property not getting vandalised was a new high for me. I chuckled at my life. Was there a group of gods or creators up there, looking down on Earth and laughing at what they put everyone through? Honestly, life was a joke at times. If I didn't laugh, I'd cry, and there was no way I was going to cry for anything idiot Joyless did.

Today's article was about the star in a local nursing home. Mavis Bartholomew was turning a hundred and three today, and they were holding a party. From what Karen from the nursing home said, Mavis was still with it. She was there because she had osteoporosis and couldn't look after herself, but Karen had let slip that Mavis loved Maltesers, so I stopped at a supermarket on the way to the nursing home.

The place was about a fifteen-minute drive from Manesbury. The traffic sucked the whole way. Must be my week for annoyances. I finally pulled into the grounds, which were rather nice. Hedges lined the driveway, and there were islands of vibrant flowers dotting the vast lawns. A group of oldies was playing croquet in a particularly level section. I parked near a white two-storey building, then made my way to the entry. The reception desk was just inside the main doors, and there was a tall security gate between us and the rest of the nursing home. I assumed it was to keep the residents in rather than other people out.

"Can I help you?" The forty-something woman behind the reception desk had short brown hair and kind eyes. "Who are you here to see?"

"Hi. I'm Avery Winters. I'm here to cover Mavis's birthday celebrations for the *Manesbury Daily*." I held up the Maltesers. "I also come bearing a gift."

She smiled. "Oh, you will be welcome, then. I'll buzz you in and show you where the party is."

I walked into the facility, the gate locking behind me. The woman led me down a wide corridor that smelled of disinfectant and something sickly sweet. The hallway eventually doglegged to the left and kept going. We passed many doors—some closed and some open. Off-key singing that sounded like a chicken being murdered came from one of the open doors, and the receptionist called out, "Great singing, Frank," and kept walking. Frank sang louder, probably to please his audience. I wished he hadn't. "Poor Frank. He's got dementia and had one of his legs amputated. He's happy enough to watch TV, but when he's sick of it, he sings."

"If he's happy, it's not poor him, then really, is it? It's more like poor everyone else who has to listen to his singing." Hmm, was I being too harsh? Maybe I should've kept my mouth shut. Damned thoughts, escaping again.

She laughed. "Yes, poor the rest of us. You learn patience, working in a place like this, and most of the residents on this floor are too out of it to care. Some of them talk to themselves and yell out. Some are just medicated and in their own world." Wow, how depressing. This party better be the highlight of my week. I was due for some fun. "Oh, look; here we are."

Laughter bounced through a large reception room leading to

the garden. A crowd of elderly residents mixed with younger people who were likely to be Mavis's family, and there were more than a few ghosts, all of them elderly. I'd had my ghost-seeing stone put on a necklace that I wore nestled against my chest. It made my life a lot easier. There would be no more looking like an idiot in public for me… at least where seeing ghosts was concerned.

A buffet table was set up in the middle of the room, and a separate, smaller table held a three-tier cake covered in pale-pink icing with colourful flowers spilling from the top to the bottom, covering a third of the cake. It was gorgeous. Before introducing myself, I took a few candid shots around the room and a couple of the magnificent cake. I'd have to see whether the cakemaker was local and, if they were, do a story on them too.

Mavis sat in a chunky armchair holding court. I had to excuse myself and push through the throng. I wasn't the only media person here either. Two television crews had set up near the cake, lighting on stands ready to go. Two reporters with their cameramen chatted next to them.

Trying to get through the crowd was like swimming in quicksand—slow and torturous. I didn't want to push the oldies too hard. If I knocked one of them over, they could break a hip, which was pretty much a death sentence for people in this place. As I eased past one short, round, elderly woman, she jerked her head towards me and grabbed my arm, her hand much stronger than I would've imagined. "No pushing in! I was here to see the Queen first. You wait your turn."

I froze and stared at her. How was I supposed to extricate myself without hurting her? I gently put my hand on hers to remove it, but she slapped it. "Ow! That's not very nice."

"I won't let you push in. So rude!"

I lifted my hand again, but she held her other hand up, ready to dispense with another slap. Feisty old lady. "I'm sorry, but I'm here to interview the Queen for the local paper. Maybe I can help you get to see her more quickly. Why don't you let me help you get through the crowd? All the people in front of us have seen her already." My brain was so good to me sometimes.

Her face relaxed, and her eyes widened. "Ooh, would you really help me see her quicker?"

I smiled. "Of course. Come on." I arranged her gripping hand of death so that her arm was linked in mine. "And what's your name? I'm Avery."

"Mary."

"Lovely to meet you, Mary. Now, let's meet the Queen." I slid us through the clumps of people and threw in a few "excuse mes." Before long, we'd made it to the front.

Mary slid her arm out of mine and curtsied. When I didn't, she grabbed my wrist and jerked me down. Man, she was strong. She whisper hissed, "You must curtsy. Where are your manners?"

Mavis smiled. "Mary, it's okay. You don't have to curtsey. Just wish me happy birthday and move on."

She slowly straightened. "But you're the Queen. God save the Queen."

Mavis waved her hand imperiously. "There are so many people here to see me today. We need to hurry this up."

Mary gasped. "I'm so sorry. My apologies, Your Highness. Happy birthday. May you have many, many more."

Mavis smiled. "Thank you." She gave a nod. "You are dismissed." She looked at me. "Hello. And you are?"

"I'm Avery Winters, the reporter from the *Manesbury Daily*. Have you got a couple of minutes to answer some questions?"

"Of course, since we asked you here. Fire away. But please don't ask me my advice on how to live until this age. They've asked me that every year for the last three." She certainly was sharp. I hoped I was as with it as her when I hopefully made it to old age, although the way my life had been going, I'd be lucky to make it to thirty.

I laughed and took out my notepad and pen. "Okay, I'll try to ask you some original questions. What's your fondest memory from your life?"

"Ooh, that's a good question. Hmm…." She linked her wrinkled hands in her lap. "That would be my sixtieth birthday. All the family came to celebrate, and my Harrison was still alive. We partied until the next morning. It was a real shebang. The little ones slept on the floor, wherever they found a place, and the rest of us danced and danced. Those were the days." She smiled wistfully. "It's been a long time since I've been to a party like that."

"This isn't original, but I'd like to put some facts in the article. How many children do you have?"

Her smile disappeared. "Five, but only two are still alive. That's the problem with living until this age."

"Grandchildren?"

"Twelve. And before you ask, I have twenty-nine great-grandchildren and ten great-great-grandchildren. Put that in your family tree and smoke it." She laughed, as did a few of the people within hearing distance.

An elderly man yelled out, "Nice one, Mavis!"

I continued the interview, then took a couple of photos of her with some of her family and then a couple with the workers from the home. Just as we were finishing up, someone screamed, "No, Polly!"

All chatter cut off instantly. As one, everyone turned towards the ruckus. A tall, large woman with short, curly, white hair had a hand to her mouth, tell-tale pale-pink frosting and chocolate cake smeared on her face and covering her hand. A chunk—I suspected exactly the size of Polly's hand—was missing from the bottom tier of the cake. As she shoved in one handful, her other hand reached for more. A middle-aged male guest and one of the female staff moved to restrain Polly's arms. She twisted and turned, trying to shake them off, all while angling towards the cake.

I couldn't help it—I took a few photos. I wasn't sure if any would make it into the paper—I doubted those involved would consent to have their identities plastered all over the news, but this could be for my cheer-me-up files later. I chuckled.

Just when everyone smiled and started chatting again because they assumed everything was under control, an elderly man shuffled to the cake and dug his hand in. "Come on, everyone. Cake time!" He guffawed, then shoved the cake into his mouth. I shook my head. Those old-timers looked like they moved slowly, but there was some weird magic going on where they dove into the mischief before the rest of us could react.

I did the only thing I could think of—I started videoing.

They were like a hoard of newly awakened zombies. Seven more residents, a couple with walking sticks, made a beeline for the cake, and there wasn't enough staff to stop the onslaught. Looked like Mavis wasn't going to get any of her one-hundred-and-third birthday cake.

A couple of children, maybe six or seven years old, ran to the cake and got involved in the ruining. Cake flew, the zombies laughed, and everyone else stared. The six staff who were in attendance had given up, and Polly—the shenanigans instigator—was let loose to wreak more havoc.

I stopped filming and turned around to see how Mavis was taking it. The crowd had parted like Mavis was Moses, giving her an unobstructed view of the cake-tastrophe. Others stared at her too. We were all waiting for her to smite the sinners.

Her lips twitched and grew into a smile. She opened her mouth and laughed and laughed and laughed until tears coursed down her face. "I haven't been to a party like this for a long time. It's wonderful!"

And just like that, the spell was broken, and bit by bit, a different type of contagion overtook the room—happiness. I took one last photo of Mavis, her eyes glistening with joy. If only we could all be so resilient, willing to go with the flow, and immediately bounce back from life's disasters. On the scale of awful to tragic, I conceded that this was only awful, but she hadn't let it ruin what could be her last birthday ever. Mavis was awesome. I could learn a lot from her.

I smiled and whispered, "Happy birthday," turned towards the door, and left.

CHAPTER 5

As I drove back through town and passed A Snip in Time, I noticed a ghostly woman pacing back and forth out the front. I cringed. A massive red stain covered half of the front of her white blouse, and it wasn't from a disastrous confrontation with tomato sauce. She'd been shot or stabbed. I didn't get a good look at her because I'd had to look at the road, but she had the same straight, shoulder-length brown hair and slight build as Simone. But it couldn't be her—she'd gone into the light, and the clothes were very different. This woman was in business attire.

I parked near the office, then walked back through the village to Verity's. The timing of the ghost showing up wasn't a coincidence—so my gut said. Add to that all the blood, and well.... Could she be the other victim? What I wouldn't give for more clues. I crossed my fingers as I approached the ghost.

Stopping just before the hairdressing salon—I didn't want Verity wondering why I was out here—I lifted my phone to my ear and looked at the woman. On closer inspection, she might be slightly older than Mandy, maybe late twenties. I didn't recall Mandy wearing much jewellery, but this woman had three blingy rings on her fingers. If they contained real diamonds, she was loaded. Her nails were definitely salon-done and scarlet, matching the blood on her shirt perfectly. Gunshot wound to the chest, it seemed. Whoever had killed her was a good shot.

"Excuse me. I'm Avery. I was wondering what you're doing in front of this particular shop?"

She stopped pacing and stared at me as if she couldn't believe I was talking to her. "You can see me?"

"Yes." I glanced around to make sure no one was within earshot and lowered my voice. "I can see ghosts."

She hugged herself. Tears pooled in her eyes. "So, it's true. I am dead. I… I mean, I figured I was, but I'm still here. No one can see me, though, and I went home and tried to shower, but I passed through my door, and then I couldn't touch anything." She swallowed.

"You knew, but you didn't want to believe." She nodded. "I don't blame you. It's a massive shock."

"You're telling me." She peered up and down the street, as if she were looking for someone.

"So, why are you here?"

"I hung around for ages after I was killed, and I heard the police talking. One of them said that another woman was shot and killed here on the same morning I was. I wanted to talk to her, see if I could find out what happened."

Hmm, now we were getting somewhere. I bit the inside of my cheek to prevent my smile—I was about to get information about the other murder that Bellamy refused to give me. Maybe I'd get somewhere with help from this woman. Luckily, this lady hadn't gone into the light. "I might be able to help you work it out. I was there when it happened."

She gasped. "Oh my. But you weren't killed?"

"No. By the way, what's your name?" Bellamy had never gotten back to me, and I hadn't had time yet to scour the news.

"Naomi Ashford." She held out her hand to shake mine.

I glanced at her hand. "I'm sorry, but that won't work." I gave her a sad smile. I could've reached out to her, but I would've looked like a weirdo, and I'd had enough criticism for one lifetime. "There's some stuff I don't want to talk about right here. Can you come with me to my car? Maybe we can go for a drive and chat?"

"Will I be able to sit in your car and move with it?"

"Yes. I've done it with other ghosts. I'm not sure how it works, but it does. Actually, would you like some ghost company, someone who can show you the ropes, so to speak? I know some really nice ghosts." I peered around. Phew, I'd forgotten myself. Even saying that into the phone would sound loopy. I spoke more quietly. "Look, let's do this in my car. Is that okay? I've got a bad enough rep in this village without making it worse."

"Of course. I understand. Lead the way. The sooner we have a chat, the sooner, hopefully, we can work out who killed me and why." Her face hardened. "And when I find out who it is, they'd better watch out."

I grinned. That attitude, I could respect. "I'll do whatever I can to facilitate that for you."

She smiled at me. "Thank you, Avery. I can tell we're going to get along just fine."

We reached my car. Yay, it was clean! Not that the vandals would mess up my car on the main street in daylight. At least, I didn't think they would. I got in. Naomi hesitated, looking in at me from the street. I waved my hand, beckoning her. She took a deep breath—I still didn't understand why they breathed when they didn't have to—and reached out to the door handle. Instead of being able to grip it, her hand slid through. Her arm was next, and soon she sat in my front passenger seat, her eyes wide. She shuddered. "That felt… icky. It was the same when I accidentally passed through my front door."

"Sorry. I didn't think it would feel like anything." Hmm, so strange. None of the other ghosts I knew ever complained about that. Maybe it was something they got used to, so it was a non-issue. "I think it's time to call my friend Charles. He died when he was a boy, but don't let that fool you. He's been around way longer than us."

"Okay. I trust you."

"Charles. Hey, Charles, please come."

We waited for about fifteen seconds, and he appeared… on top of Naomi. She screamed, and he yelled. Charles disappeared, then reappeared in the back seat. "Holy mother of God! I'm so sorry. I didn't mean to land on you." His cheeks were aflame.

Naomi hugged herself. "That was… well… it didn't feel like much, but it was like a creepy vibration, and you crowded my vision. All I could see was your insides."

"His insides? You have insides?" My brain was about to explode. But then again, if they looked the same on the outside, it stood to reason their insides would look the same, but what was the point? It wasn't like anyone needed to see their insides—no more operations to fix broken bones or remove the appendix. They didn't even *need* their own insides.

Charles leaned forward and poked his upper body between the seats so he was half in the front of the car. He looked at Naomi. "It doesn't happen that often. But I agree; it's unpleasant." Charles turned his head and pinned his annoyed eyes on mine. "Next time, a bit of warning would be nice, Avery."

"Sorry. I didn't think I needed to. So, that brings me to why I called you. Naomi"—I gestured to the woman—"has recently been murdered, and she knows nothing about being a ghost. I was hoping you could show her around, give her some info."

He smiled. "Of course I can." He turned back to her. "Lovely to meet you, Naomi. As you've already heard, I'm Charles. At your service."

She smiled. "Thanks. That's really kind of you."

"So, now you're here, you may as well stay and listen in. We're trying to find out who killed her." I hadn't spoken to Charles in a few days. "Did you hear about the hairdresser from Verity's being murdered?"

"Of course. It's all they're talking about at the station." He lowered his head for a moment, then raised it and met my gaze. "I'm sorry I didn't check in on you. I've been helping Sergeant Fox, and I didn't realise how much time had passed."

I smiled. "Don't worry. It's only been a day." Now that I thought about it, that surprised me. Time had gone quickly for me too. I'd been flat out like a lizard drinking since it happened. I started the car. "We're going for a drive. There's a lovely park ten minutes away. I've only been once, but I could do with a walk, and it should be quiet." I started driving. "If people around here see me talking to myself… well, let's just say, I've had enough grief to last me a lifetime. And if I'm driving, I can't concentrate on what you're telling me. I might like to write some of it down."

On the way, Naomi asked Charles a few questions. She seemed like the sort of person who made friends easily. It wasn't taking her long to warm up to us. But how much did she know, if anything, about who killed her? Was it random, or did she suspect who wanted her gone? She revealed that she worked as a secretary in a solicitors' office. She lived with her boyfriend, who was a financial advisor. They both worked in Exeter. Her parents were good people, so she said, and she got along with her two brothers. "I don't know why anyone would want to kill me."

I pulled into the car park, parked, and got out of the car. I grabbed my handbag because leaving it there was just asking for trouble. Also, I wanted my notepad and pen handy, just in case Naomi told me something important. There was only one other car here, so that boded well for me to talk to my invisible friends without appearing crazy. Failing that, I had my phone handy.

Late afternoon sun slanted across the path that meandered through an open field, the occasional large tree stretching long shadows over the lush grass. Squirrels darted around near the base of a tree. I couldn't help but laugh. They were so cute. Australia had its own adorable wildlife, but not much came close to the cuteness of squirrels.

As I strolled along, I looked ahead. "I'm not ignoring you, but if anyone sees me, it'll look less weird if I'm watching where I'm going. There's a bench over there." I pointed to one that sat under a leafy canopy about a hundred feet away. "That will ensure no one overhears me. I can see people coming."

"This is nice, but something is missing." Naomi frowned.

Charles nodded sagely. "It's normal now, but when I died, I remember being depressed that colours weren't as vibrant, and you can't feel the breeze on your skin or the warmth of the sun."

"Oh." Her voice, sad and defeated, didn't invite an answer. What was there to say? None of us could fix it. I did breathe in through my nose and appreciate the fragrance of grass and fresh air. The gentle kiss of wind on my cheeks as I walked didn't go unnoticed either. It was a good reminder to live in the moment whenever I could.

When we reached the bench, I sat in the middle, and Charles sat on one side of me, Naomi on the other. I got my notepad and pen out of my bag. "So, are you sure you don't know who killed you?" Might as well get straight to it.

"No. It all happened so fast. I was waiting at the bus stop, reading on my Kindle, and there was a loud bang. It was as if someone pushed me back a step, but I didn't feel anything for a moment. The lady next to me screamed. She was staring at my shirt. I looked down, and red was just spreading and spreading." Her breaths came shallower, and she placed her hands to her chest, over the bullet entry point.

I reached out to rub her back, but my hand went through her, and a chill bit my arm. I put my hands in my lap and sighed. "I'm sorry for asking you to relive that."

She took in a juddering breath. "It's okay. You're only trying to help."

"Is it okay if we keep going through it?"

She nodded. "I want to get to the bottom of it. I'm hoping it was random, because there was no one in my life who should want me dead. If anyone of my friends or family organised it, I'll be shattered." She was in a terrible situation. As much as I wanted to solve the case—and her knowing the perpetrator would make it easier—I didn't want her to have to face something so horrible on top of being murdered. Dying was bad enough. And, yes, that was the understatement of the century.

"Did you get a look at the car or anything?"

"As I fell, I looked up. The guy who shot me was wearing a balaclava. I remember his eyes—cutting Arctic blue. I've never seen eyes that colour before. I definitely didn't know him." She shuddered. "I passed out after that, and that's all she wrote." She sighed. "I used to love watching reruns of that show—*Murder She Wrote*. My mum and I used to watch it together. Oh, God, she must be so upset. My dad and brothers too." Tears glazed her eyes and spilled over, tracking down her cheeks. Naomi looked up at me. "I haven't even been to check on them."

Charles leaned forward so he could see past me. "Don't worry. You can go later. All you have to do to go somewhere you know is to think about it—imagine how it looks and smells, even how you feel when you're there. You'll be able to get into your house, but you won't be able to visit places you haven't lived unless it's a business. People have to invite you into their homes." Which was why I'd suggested the park. The last thing I needed was another ghost who had unlimited access to my apartment.

She gave him a sad smile. "Thank you, Charles. That's very helpful." She sniffed and wiped her nose.

"And you definitely had no enemies?" It was mean of me, but I had to keep this on track.

"Definitely not. There was one woman at work who didn't like me much, but we weren't enemies." She sniffled. "My boyfriend and I were in love. I was so lucky–he's kind and super generous." She held up her hand. "He gave me two of these diamond rings. My parents gave me the other for my twenty-first birthday. Anyway, Kyle and I were getting along really well—we live…" She shut her eyes and took a deep breath before opening them again. "We *lived* together. We've been going out for three years and were talking about getting married. I have a good relationship with my parents and brothers, get along with everyone at work—except that one woman I mentioned–and I have a great, supportive group of friends." She stared into the distance for a bit. "You could say I had the perfect life."

I wrote all that down. Hmm, an apparent dead end… at least for now. Maybe that woman from work was an issue, but just because you didn't get along with someone at work, would you arrange to have them killed? "Did that woman from work ever threaten you?"

"No. She was just snarky sometimes."

"What was her name and the name of where you worked?" I'd best do my due diligence.

"The woman's name is Mallory Burnie, and she's another secretary at Smythe and Sons Solicitors."

"Great, thanks. I'll try and talk to her, although I'm not a police officer, so I can't force her to chat." I was going to have to figure out how to get access to her workplace. Would they be fine with me asking about Naomi for an article? The only way to find out was to try. "Okay, well, it sounds like you did have the perfect life, except for one annoying person. The only other thing I can ask is, did you know any hairdressers called Simone or Mandy?" I described what she looked like. Come to think of it, I should look up her social media and grab a pic. I scrolled Instagram under her name. Nothing. I tried Twitter, Facebook, and TikTok. Nada. I tried the surname Verity had told me with Mandy. Still nothing. Okay, so that was weird.

Charles was staring at me. "What is it?"

"She has no social media. When Simone died, she told me her real name was Mandy and that the guy who shot her was her ex. He called her Mandy before he shot her too. He said he was going to take her son, so I'm assuming he's her abusive ex and, considering she had no socials, she was in hiding."

Charles cocked his head to one side. "Yeah, but Bellamy's saying it could be a case of mistaken identity. They can't find any hard evidence yet. They're hoping to find the car soon."

"What does Fox think?" I asked.

He shrugged. "He's reserving judgement, but at this stage, he said Bellamy has nothing else to go on."

I huffed out a frustrated breath and looked at Naomi. "So, it appears as though you might be a red herring to mess with the police investigation, just in the wrong place at the wrong time. I saw the murderer, and it's definitely the same person—ice-blue eyes and a balaclava. He called her by name, and he said he was going to kill her mother and son. He was a hundred per cent after her, and we're assuming you have no connection to Mandy, so I can't see why the same person would kill both of you. Do you remember him saying anything to you?" Maybe I was wrong, but I had to make assumptions.

"No." Well, that confirmed it for me. He went to Mandy's work to kill her, and she wouldn't have been at a bus stop because she lived in the village and walked to work. He'd known where she was. A tiny piece of me said that maybe he had a reason for killing Naomi, too, other than trying to confuse the police, but since I couldn't find the connection yet, and he'd said nothing to Naomi, I was going with the easy answer for now. "What a stupid reason to die." She shook her head. Eventually, she sat up straighter and met my gaze with a determined one. "At least it wasn't someone I loved or cared about who did this to me. That's something, I suppose. But now what? I want to find the rotter who did this to me and Mandy. Where is she, by the way? I'd like to meet her, you know, since we've both been through the same thing."

Argh, how did I break this to her? She might worry, but I had to tell the truth. This was too important. "I'm sorry, but she went into the light straight away. Her grandmother was there to take her. She's not here any more."

The wheels turned in her head, lines appearing on her forehead. She eventually turned to Charles. "Why am I still here, then?" Her eyes bugged wide, and she slapped her hands on her stomach. "I'm not going to hell, am I? Oh, God, I should've gone to church. But I don't even believe in God. This is my punishment. It has to be."

Pain flickered in Charles's eyes. If staying behind was a punishment, he was being punished too. But for what? He was just a kid when he died. I hoped to Hades this didn't send him spiralling into guilt and self-loathing again. He opened his mouth to answer, but I jumped in. "You're not being punished. Charles died when he was a child. He didn't do anything to deserve it. You might still be here so you can help me figure out who killed you and Mandy." Stuff it—I wasn't calling her Simone at all any more. She hadn't lied to me, and that guy in the car was her ex. As if he'd make such a mistake. He'd been close enough to stare at her face, and the hate shining from his eyes wasn't made up. He was an angry, evil person taking revenge. "Once this is done, you might go into the light, or you might stay here." I wasn't going to give her the third option. She didn't seem like someone who should go to hell, and I didn't want her upset for nothing.

"Are you sure?"

"Avery's right. You're just like me. We have unfinished business. I think I was left behind to help. I wasn't ready to go before, and I'm still not ready."

She didn't look a hundred per cent convinced, but the fear in her eyes abated. "Okay, then."

"I guess it's time to go. Are you sure you don't remember anything else? Was the car the killer in familiar?"

"No. I honestly can't think of anything else. I mean, I work in a law firm, but we deal with corporate law, and I'm just the secretary. No clients would want to kill me. I think you're right, and I'm a red herring. I hope the police don't take too long to figure it out." She bunched her hands into fists. "I want you to find whoever killed me. I want justice." She growled. "I'm so angry, I could spit. What the hell?" She spat. "I can do whatever I want. I'm dead. What's the point of holding back now?" Her shoulders slumped. My heart went out to her. She was torn between grief and anger.

"I promise I'll do what I can to figure this out, Naomi." If only I could reach out and squeeze her hand.

"Me too." Charles smiled reassuringly.

"Thank you both." She stood and looked down at Charles. "So, all I have to do is think of my parents and where they live, and I'll go there?"

He smiled. "Yep."

"Right. Here goes nothing." She shut her eyes and disappeared.

I turned to Charles. It was time to tell him about my car being vandalised and implement my plan. "I have a favour to ask."

"Go ahead. I'm listening."

CHAPTER 6

"Mmm, this steak is great. Thank you for buying dinner, but you didn't have to. It'll be my shout next time." I'd never bought a steak at the pub before because I was a tight arse, but Reece had insisted after telling me how delicious they were.

Reece grinned. "Ah, so you're keen for a next time?"

My cheeks burned. Oh, bummer. I put my foot in it. "Um, yes, but only if you're keen too. I'm not a stalker or anything." *Seriously, Avery.* The best way to make someone think you were something was to say you weren't. I was such a verbal klutz.

He laughed. "I didn't think you were. Although now you mention it, you're the one who came here the other night to see me."

"Well, yeah. It's hard to stalk someone if you don't follow them everywhere." I gave him a so-there look. Luckily, he laughed and didn't run for the toilets.

"You're funny. I like funny." He smiled and stared into my eyes.

I couldn't help but smile back. "Lucky me, then." The warm

and fuzzy feeling in my stomach wasn't as devastating as what I had around Finnegan, or even Bailey, which was a good thing. I didn't want to get serious. It was a sensible halfway point to being attracted enough to spend time with him but not so bad that I'd be devastated when we went our separate ways.

"Are you going to stay for my set?"

"I enjoyed it last time, so yeah… unless you'd rather I didn't." Again, I didn't want him to think I was a stalker.

"I would, actually…. But only if you really did enjoy it last time, and you're not just saying it. I don't want to torture you."

"I definitely enjoyed it." I smiled. He was such a modest guy. Not at all what I thought he'd be. Seemed as if he left the confidence all for the stage.

He finished the last bit of food on his plate, put his knife and fork on the plate, then drained his beer. "Off I go. Wish me luck." He stood.

"Good luck; although, you don't need it." As he walked towards the stage, I peered around the room and caught Meg's gaze. She grinned and waggled her eyebrows. At least she accepted that I wasn't going to date her brother. Hopefully she saw the sense in that.

"Avery, come quickly!"

I jerked my head around. Charles stood nearby, beckoning me to the car park. Bollocks. Someone must be vandalising my car. I jumped up and ran out the back.

I'd parked Daisy as close to the exit as possible, and it wasn't quite dark yet. These people were either brave or stupid… or maybe a bit of both. Two guys dressed in black, their faces covered by scarves, stood in front of my car. One held a can of something he was shaking, and the other held a roll of toilet paper. I was going to sneak up on them and tackle one, but he saw me out of the corner of his eye. Damn it!

He shoved his mate, and they ran. I wasn't wearing running

shoes, so there was no point chasing them. They were gone. At least I'd saved my car and myself from washing it again.

"Avery, what's going on?"

I turned. Meg had just come out of the back door and approached me. "I had a funny feeling and thought I'd better check my car. Turns out, I was right. Two guys were about to put more crap all over her." I frowned. From now on, I was wearing sneakers, and tonight I was sleeping on top of my covers with my clothes on, just in case.

"Did you get a look at them?"

"Yes, but they were covered pretty much head to toe. They had scarves wrapped around their heads, mouths, and noses. They were both white, and I could see a bit of brown hair on one, but that's it. They looked like skinny teenage boys, but they were taller than me by at least a few inches. I suppose I should call Bellamy and notify him. Not that there's anything he can do."

Meg gave me a sad look. "I'm sorry, Aves. Bloody Joyless. I'd love to wax off her eyebrows and shave her head."

A smile broke free. "I'd pay to see that."

"Maybe we can do a special feature at the pub one night?" She grinned. "I have to go back inside now. Are you okay?"

"Yeah, I'm fine." I flicked a glance at Charles, then looked back at Meg. "I was lucky this time, but I don't know if I should risk going back inside and leaving her."

"I wouldn't worry. They've just had a close call. They'd be morons to come back tonight. Besides, our star performer will wonder what happened to you."

I sighed. "Fine."

I crossed my fingers that they wouldn't be back and let her lead me inside.

CHAPTER 7

That night, I tossed and turned, nightmares pushing me this way and that. When Charles woke me around five thirty in the morning, I was exhausted but glad to get out of my slumbering hell. I sat up, swung my legs over the edge of the bed, and set my feet on the floor. Wide-eyed and heart racing, I didn't know if I was fully awake, but hopefully, I'd wake up before I got downstairs.

"They're about to vandalise your car. Hurry!" Charles hopped from foot to foot and threw a worried glance in the direction of the laneway—not that he could see it from my bedroom. He looked at me and pulled an ew face. "Is that dribble?" I wiped my hand down one side of my face. He shook his head. "The other side."

I wiped the drool off. "What, you never dribbled in your sleep?" I shook my head. "Hang on. That's not important." I stood and took a moment for my blood to reach my brain. "Okay. Let's go." I'd done as I'd planned and slept fully dressed, shoes and everything. I grabbed my phone off the bedside table and put it to film. I was getting it all this time. I'd slept with my keys in my pocket. Uncomfortable, yes, but I didn't want to add drama to my morning and lock myself out if I was too intent on catching scumbags and I forgot to take my keys. Plus, it saved time.

I ran down the stairs as quietly as I could and opened and shut the main door with stealth—if I woke Mrs Crabby at this hour, I'd never hear the end of it. My feet nary made a sound as I hurried to the laneway in the near dark. The light was on in Josie's living room. The cheery yellow glow beckoned me in for a cup of tea. Unfortunately, I had other things to attend to, not to mention, who shows up unannounced at five thirty in the morning? And what if I did that and found she'd died? Yeah, I'd be run out of town.

I held my phone out in front of me to capture everything. My car came into view. It looked like the two skinny guys from last night. One was spraying shaving cream over Daisy. The other one smeared it with his hand and threw toilet paper over her.

Fury clawed its way up from deep in the pit of my stomach. How dare they?! I hadn't done anything to anyone. I had enough to worry about without stressing about being bullied. This wasn't high school, and I hadn't moved all the way across the world to suffer again. Add to that, Mandy's son needed me to find him and make sure he was safe, for goodness' sake, and my time and energy were being taken up with this stupidity?

I crouched low and snuck closer to my car. I was only a few feet from them, but they couldn't see me as I was hiding behind the car parked in the premium spot—Vinegar's. It was actually working in my favour that Daisy was in the second spot.

I held my breath and carefully placed my phone on Vinegar's windscreen, so it kept filming.

I snuck around to the edge of the gap between cars. Here went nothing.

Jumping up—I fancied myself to be a bit like Mel Gibson in

Braveheart, sans the blue face paint—I screamed a battle cry of incoherent noise before launching myself at the nearest vandal. I'd played rugby league for a couple of years at school, and I knew how to tackle.

My arms wrapped around his thighs, and my shoulder hit his hips. We went down. Hard. Me on top of him. I'd knocked the wind out of him, so it didn't take much effort for me to rip the balaclava off his face.

He couldn't have been older than eighteen. He looked familiar. I'd seen him around the village, but I'd never met him. Then it hit me. "Joyless's brother? What's your name?"

He stared up at me, fear in his eyes. Maybe he thought I was going to kill him? If he believed half of what his sister said... well, he deserved it. "I-I'm n-not telling you."

If only I had my phone on me. I didn't want it to break when I tackled him, but now I needed it for a photo, and it was unlikely to be filming this low down. Damn. I guess I'd just have to make sure he was facing it when we stood up. And I had to get some DNA. I ripped out a few strands of his hair.

He slammed his hand on his scalp and rubbed it. "Ow! Get off me, you crazy cow. Get off!" He wriggled around and tried to push me off, but I probably weighed more than him, so he was having a difficult time of it.

"Maybe you shouldn't vandalise people's cars, and then they wouldn't have to tackle you. And your hair is for the police. It's evidence." I put it in my jeans pocket and considered scratching him to get some skin. "All the crap your sister said about me isn't true. You think I want to find dead people? News flash—I don't. What I actually do is help find out who killed them, so I'm helping." I leaned down so our noses were almost touching and ground the words through my teeth. "Leave. Me. Alone. And just so you know, I have surveillance on my car now." He wriggled some more. Were those tears in his eyes? For Hade's sake. "You're such a baby." I slid off him and stood. "Off you go. Better get back to your sister so she can change your nappy. Tell her to do her own dirty work." Not that I wanted anyone to do dirty work against me, but it would feel really good to get her arrested.

The kid leaped to his feet and, without another glance at me, ran down the hill. *Bye, bye, idiot.* I grabbed my phone and pressed Stop on the recording. Hopefully it had at least recorded our voices.

A shiver vibrated down my spine, and I shuddered. It was as if I was being watched. I peered around, but no one was there, and the house next to the cars was all dark. There was no face at any window. Maybe I was just paranoid because of what just happened. Nevertheless, I hurried back home. When I locked my door and settled on the couch, I let out a relieved breath. Mrs Crabby was none the wiser, and I was safe. It was time to call the police. I wouldn't ring Bellamy directly because he might be asleep, and this wasn't exactly super urgent.

The police said they'd be there in twenty minutes, so I watched out the window. If they rang my buzzer, they'd wake Mrs Crabby, and she'd get angry that police were here because of me. She'd probably expect them to arrest me for something. Thank goodness she was too old to get on Facebook; at least I assumed she wasn't on there. And if she was as friendly with everyone as she was with me, she hopefully hadn't plugged into the gossip Joyless had started. If she had, I'd likely have had a telling-off by now.

Finally, two police emerged from the alley into our little dead-end street. I hurried downstairs and outside, catching them before they entered the front gate. I smiled. "PC Adams, I didn't know they let you out on occasion." It was the constable who usually manned the reception desk at the station. She was always nice to me, which hadn't gone unnoticed.

She returned my smile. "Yep, they let me run free every now

and then." She turned to the other constable. "You remember PC Patel?" He'd attended my place before, and while he hadn't been overly friendly, he'd been professional.

I gave the slim Indian man a nod. "Hello, constable. Thank you both for coming out."

He returned my nod. "We've seen your car. Can you tell us what happened?"

I went over everything, except instead of saying a ghost woke me up, I said I'd gotten up to go for a walk. Then I showed them the video.

Patel winced when I tackled Joyless's brother, and Davis smirked. "Nice work, Winters." When it came to me pulling out his hair, the phone couldn't see us because it was tilted up a bit rather than down, but we could hear everything. I couldn't help chuckling at Joyless's brother's "Ow."

I took the hair out of my pocket and handed it to PC Adams. "Here it is."

She shook her head, still grinning, and pulled a little plastic bag out of her pocket. She slid the hair inside. "You're hilarious."

The video finished with a brief view of the guy's face, then his back as he ran for his life, and of course, me gathering my phone and turning the video off. "So, is that Joyless's brother?"

Patel scrunched his face. "Joyless?"

"Ah, sorry, Joy Stick." I snorted. Such a stupid name.

His face registered understanding. "I don't know. I'm not too familiar with everyone in Manesbury." He turned to Adams. "What about you?"

"Nah, I don't know him. I grew up in Exeter, and to be honest, I don't come this way all that often. If you could send that video through to my mobile, we'll check it out when we go back to the station. So, you think his surname is Stick?"

"Yes. I think so. I'll show the video around."

"Hey, Lightning. What's going on?"

I turned. Vinegar, hot as you please in short running shorts and a muscle shirt, approached us. I was not staring at his toned arms and strong legs. Not. At. All. And neither was PC Adams. I cleared my throat and dragged my gaze to his face, but that was somehow worse. Why was he so beautiful? "My car was shaving creamed and toilet-papered again, but I caught who did it." I brought the video up again, put it to the spot that showed the guy's face, and paused it. "Do you know who this is?"

"That's Gavin Stick." His eyes widened. "He's been messing with your car? I didn't think he had it in him."

I rolled my eyes. "Don't sound so impressed. Anyway, he was crying at some stage after I tackled him. I think he thought I was going to kill him… you know, seeing as how my scary reputation precedes me."

He chuckled. "You tackled him? Nice work."

PC Patel looked at Vinegar. "So, you can confirm this is Gavin Stick?"

"Yes, sir."

"Does she have any other brothers?" I asked. It would be good to figure out who the other guy was.

"No, just the one, but he's pretty thick with a guy called Owen Mead. They went through school together, and Owen's always had a crush on Joy, Gavin's sister. I'd check him out first."

"Thank you. And your name is?" Patel held his pen at the ready.

"I'm Avery's work colleague, Finnegan Walsh."

Patel wrote it down. "And your phone number, just in case we need to ask you anything else." Finnegan gave it to him. "Okay, thanks. You're free to go."

Vinegar looked at me. "Are you all right? Do you want me to stay?" Why was he being so nice? Oh, that's right, we were friends. Just friends.

"No, it's okay. But thanks. Have a good run." I gave him a wave, and he jogged off towards the path that led to the fields.

PC Adams gave me her mobile number, and I sent her the video. "Thanks, Winters. We'll look into this today and get back to you when we have something. I'm afraid, though, that there hasn't been permanent damage to your car, and this is just a misdemeanour, so we're unlikely to arrest anyone. It will be more of a warning, unless they've got priors."

My shoulders slumped. "But what's going to stop them from doing it again and again?"

"We'll let them know that we'll bring up more serious charges next time, like stalking and harassment, destruction of property. At this stage, though, it's more like two teens pulling pranks, and we'd be wasting everyone's time trying to get them to court."

I got it. I did. They had so much serious crime to combat that this was petty in comparison. But I just wanted it to stop. I was getting tired. "Okay, I understand. Thanks for coming out."

They said goodbye and took off, and I returned to my flat to get a bucket and sponge. Washing my car was becoming a terribly familiar pastime.

CHAPTER 8

After washing Daisy, I hopped in her and drove to a farm about ten minutes away. I was doing an article on a local cheese manufacturer. Thankfully, they weren't hostile, and I wrapped the interview up within an hour. I'd decided to go with video as well because cows and cheesemaking were interesting. This piece might do well out of the area, too, since foodies were always looking for new places to try homemade produce. Being in nature had imbued me with a sense of peace I sorely needed.

It was short-lived.

I parked my car on the main street so that everyone could see her in case Joyless's idiot brother returned. It was a couple of minutes' walk to the office from there, but on the way, who should I run into but the harpy herself coming out of the *Manesbury Daily* building.

Her eyes widened when she saw me, and her nostrils flared. If only her molten-hot anger would burn her eyebrows off. That would be something to see. Shame spontaneous combustion wasn't all that spontaneous. I would bet Daisy on the fact that she was here to complain to her sister about me getting their brother in trouble. Instead of buying into her death stare, I pretended I didn't notice, smiled, and walked straight past. My heart was racing, but she didn't know that.

She grabbed my arm and spun me around. I yanked my arm out of her grip and stared at her. "You didn't just do that. Touch me again, and I'll have you charged with assault." I was done glossing over things. Stuff it. She'd poked the dragon one too many times.

She glared at me. "The police came to talk to my brother and give him a warning. It's all your fault! Also, you hurt him. He skinned his elbow when you jumped him."

I gave her a "you've got to be kidding" look. "If he hadn't been vandalising my car on your say-so, none of that would've happened. You have got to be joking, blaming me. How many working brain cells do you have, anyway? I'm thinking it's about ten." Her mouth opened and closed like a stranded fish. "Stop harassing me and stop getting other people to. Next time, I'll press charges, and because you're ruining my reputation, I'll sue you as well. I have an uncle in London, and he's a solicitor who specialises in court proceedings. He's always said if I need anything, to just ask." *Liar, liar, pants on fire.* If only I had an uncle like that, but sometimes you had to stoop to their level to win.

Her nostrils flared again. She narrowed her eyes, and her mouth pinched. There was so much she wanted to say, and I smiled, knowing she wasn't going to say much at all. Finally, she found something that was only mildly horrible. "You just watch yourself, Avery Winters. One day the truth will come out about why you were at all those murders, and I'll be the one laughing as they cart you off to gaol." Before I could respond, she turned and strode off, her blonde hair streaming out behind her. The effect was ruined when her heel caught between two cobblestones, and she flew forward. Her legs strained to lunge in front of her fast enough. Would she, or wouldn't she? Ah, possum poo. She didn't fall, but I laughed anyway because it was pretty funny. She stiffened her shoulders, then kept going. Good riddance.

I turned and pushed the *Manesbury Daily* door open. When I hurried past the reception area, I made sure not to look. Talking to three Sticks in one day was just way too much toxicity.

When I reached my office, Carina and Finnegan were there. They stared at me as I put my stuff on my desk and sat. They were likely waiting to get the rundown on this morning. No doubt Finnegan had told Carina all about whatever he knew. I could have a little fun and make them wait. I set up my laptop. They stared. I got out my phone and opened a word game. Who would break first?

I made about three five-letter words before Carina burst. She leaned forward in her chair and slammed her hands on the table. "Damn you, Avery! I can't wait any more. Tell us what happened d'is morning."

I put my phone down and grinned. Even with the day I'd had so far, she could still cheer me up. My friends were ace. I went over everything that happened, then pulled up a chair near their desks and showed them the video. "After all that, Joyless had the nerve to tell me off for getting her brother in trouble."

Carina's mouth made a big *O*. "Oh no, she didn't!"

"I'm afraid she did. But I basically told her where she could shove her attitude."

Finnegan's forehead furrowed. "This is really getting out of hand. Do you want me to say something to her?"

Talk about lucky to land these friends. Back in Australia, if something like this had happened, my last ex, Brad, would've asked what I did to aggravate the person in the first place. He never had my back. In fact, he was often the one stabbing it. "No, it's okay. I appreciate you offering, but I don't want this to escalate. Before you know it, the whole village will be taking sides. I didn't come here to cause trouble. All I wanted was to get a job and, if I was lucky, make a few friends. Most of it's gone well, except Joyless and her war. I just wish she'd leave me alone. I don't even care if she hates me, as long as she doesn't sic people onto me." I sighed, fatigue spreading down my arms and back.

"Well, if you change your mind, let me know."

"Yeah, lovie. We've got your back." Carina patted my knee.

"Thanks, guys. I really don't deserve you both." I gave them a sad smile.

"Poppycock!" Carina waggled her finger at me. "We'll have none of that talk here, young lady. We're lucky to have you here. You've helped so many people since you arrived, and you've made d'is office even more fun." She grinned and turned to Finnegan. "Isn't d'at right, Finny?"

He smiled. "Actually, it is. Don't sell yourself short, Lightning."

"Thanks. Anyway, I suppose I should get back to work." Thankfully, they didn't argue, and the office hummed with the muted clatter of fingers pressing computer keys. Even though I could count on my friends, I was sick of talking about everything, and my article wasn't going to write itself. There was also the niggle in my gut. Mandy's son was out there somewhere, and he needed my help.

After a couple of hours, I was happy with everything and emailed it to Julian. Time to source some other newsworthy material. I reluctantly went to the Everything Manesbury page.

"Avery." Charles appeared in front of my desk.

I sucked in a breath and leapt back in my chair. Carina and Finnegan jerked their heads around to look at me. "Avery, what is it?" Carina's voice held concern.

I took a deep breath. "Nothing. Sorry. I just remembered that I have an appointment in ten minutes. Yikes." I jumped up and packed everything in my bag. "See you guys later." They said bye as I hurried out the door.

Charles followed me to my car, which was, thankfully, still clean. I jumped in, put my phone in its holder, and started the car. I didn't turn to look at him in the passenger seat because that would've looked weird. "You can't just pop in out of nowhere. You scared me half to death. How many times do I have to tell you?" Getting angry at someone didn't have the same impact when you weren't looking at them, so I shot him a quick glare.

He didn't even have the decency to look contrite. He laughed. "You should've seen your face. Are you sure you didn't wet yourself?" He had his hand on his stomach and bent forward, guffawing.

I shook my head. "It's not funny. Horrible child." Somewhere in the back of my brain, I knew it was kind of funny, but getting called out by my peers wasn't. And the near heart attack was neither pleasant nor, I'd imagine, good for me. If it wasn't for my quick thinking, I might've had to spill my secret, and Finnegan would never speak to me again. After that thing with the woman who stole from his sister, abused their trust, and conned them by saying she could see ghosts and speak to their dead grandmother, there was no way Finnegan wouldn't hate me.

His laughter subsided. "Sorry, but it was hilarious. Anyway… I came to give you some news from the station."

That got my attention. "Simone's case?" He nodded. "Why isn't Bellamy calling me?"

"I don't know. He hasn't discussed that with anyone. Sergeant Fox agreed that I should let you know. I told him that you'd spoken to her ghost and that she'd told you about her son."

"At least someone over there is on my side. So, what is it?" I literally crossed my fingers on both hands. *Please be some news that would blow this thing wide open.* I hated to admit it, but so far, I had nothing to go on. Mandy had no social media presence, and I didn't have access to her phone or any of her old friends, ones who would've known about her son.

"They didn't have any luck with any of the numbers from her phone, so they ran her fingerprints. Turns out her name is Mandy Hadler, and she was arrested at seventeen for drug possession but got off with community service since it was her first offence. There's a record of her having a baby, Adrian, but there's no father named on the birth certificate. They've tried finding her mother, but it's as if she's disappeared into thin air. They called the few numbers that were in her phone, but they got nowhere. Oh, and Mandy's place was ransacked the morning of her murder, but they didn't find anything that pointed to why."

Argh, so annoying. Bellamy knew I was right now, but did he call and let me know? No. Also, why was he cutting me out of the loop? Lucky for me, I still had Charles and Fox. And what was her ex looking for? Did he feel he was owed money from her? Or maybe he was looking for the evidence she told me about, or the whereabouts of her son. "Okay, that's a lot of great information. Thank you. Can you get the mother's name for me?"

His fingers silently tapped the door. "I'll try. You could probably look it up, too, though, now I told you her last name."

"I guess I could. But I'll call Bellamy first. Give him a chance to tell me what's going on. If he won't budge, I'll do my own research." I dialled his mobile number and put him on speaker.

"Miss Winters, I'm in the middle of something, so if you could make it snappy."

Wow, what a great greeting. He clearly didn't want to talk to me. "Are you going to update me on what you've found out about Mandy?" I purposely used her real name as a reminder that I'd known before him.

"Yes, well, you were right. That is her real name, but we don't have anything else to report right now. We can't find her mother or her son. I'll let you know if that changes. Was there anything else?"

"So, you really have nothing else to tell me? I want to help. People tend to talk to non-uniforms more easily. I can help."

"Well, I can report that the car the killer used was stolen early that morning. Other than that, I'm sorry, Miss Winters, but like I said, we're working on it, and there's nothing else to report. I promise I'll call you if anything changes." *Ha, like you called me this time.* If only I'd had the guts to say that. "I have to go now. Bye."

"Right. No, wait! I have one question."

"Make it quick."

"Have you been to her mother's last known address?"

"We had the local police check, and they said she hasn't been seen at that address for a while. So we have nothing to go on, just like I told you. Look, we're working on it; I promise. Now, I really have to go. Goodbye, Miss Winters."

"Bye, Sergeant." Grrr. So frustrating. If I wanted to find out anything else, I'd have to do it myself. I turned to Charles. "I probably won't get any further than Bellamy did, but if I found her last known address, I could go there and see if any ghosts are around who know something. By the sounds of it, Bellamy really hasn't got much other info, and what he does know, he's not sharing." It was disappointing that he didn't come clean on the mother's name or Mandy's surname. Mind made up, I looked over my shoulder to check for traffic, indicated, and pulled out.

"Where are we going?"

"Home. I have research to do, and then I might be going on a little trip." For all I knew, her mother lived ten minutes from here, but I very much doubted it if she was trying to escape her ex, and Bellamy had to call the local police to check rather than send his own officers. Chances were, her mother lived on the other side of England, and I was in for a hell of a drive.

He stared at me. "Can I come?"

"Yeah, why not. I could use the company." He was also good for bouncing ideas off, and he could pop away at any time and let Fox know what we discovered.

"Shouldn't you tell Meg or someone before you go?" His worried expression hit home. If I hadn't learned anything about being careful lately, I was a bigger idiot than I gave myself credit for. It wasn't like I could ask Carina or Finnegan to go on a long trip, but I would tell Meg what I was up to.

"Once I know where I'm going, I'll shoot Meg a message. But I'm not going to stir up trouble. This is just for some information, and I'll be careful who I talk to. I might only speak to ghosts anyway. We'll be there and gone quickly. It'll be easy peasy."

CHAPTER 9

After some online investigation, I discovered Mandy's mother's first name was Jan. I texted Meg about where I was going, and we were off. Turned out that Jan Hadler's last known address was in Canterbury, which was over a four-hour drive east and slightly north. I stopped three-quarters of the way for a snack and toilet break. It was going to be a looooong day. But it would be worth it if it led to me finding Mandy's mother and warning her. Maybe she already knew? Mandy's murder had been all over the news, albeit using her alias, Simone. Funny that they hadn't corrected that. Maybe the police didn't want her killer to know they knew who she really was. If only Bellamy would talk to me.

"This is like a fun holiday." Charles grinned at me from the front passenger seat.

"Really? When I was a kid, long drives were torture. We were always asking, 'Are we there yet? How much longer?' Drove my parents crazy." I smirked. They'd deserved the annoyance. If I'd known then what I knew now, I would've been much more difficult as a kid. Most things I'd done growing up, I'd done to get their approval, which was, I'd learned, impossible. That didn't stop me from contorting myself to try and make it happen. Letting go of that desire and accepting it was an impossible task had been like having a massive truck lifted off my shoulders.

"I've never been on holiday." His smile fell, and he turned to stare out of his window.

"Oh, I'm sorry. If I were your mum and you were alive, I'd take you on holidays all the time." Every time we spoke about his crappy childhood, my heart hurt. It might have been many years ago, but it still affected him.

"Thanks, Avery. If only we could choose when to be born and who to."

"Tell me about it."

We drove in silence for the last half hour, well, except for Google Maps directing me where to go. Jan's apartment was a couple of blocks from the train station. I pulled up a few spots down from where it was because the car spaces were full. It was a busyish street lined with two-and-three storey terraces and unit buildings.

"What's the plan?" Charles asked.

I turned and looked out of the rear window. Foreboding slithered down my back, and I shivered. Was it the guilt of coming here and not bringing another human, or did I have some kind of PTSD about investigating things since so many of my previous ones had been close calls? I knew I should listen to my gut, and it was telling me to be careful. "It pains me to say this, but I'm not going to door knock or buzz any of her neighbours. The police have already established that she isn't there. I'm really hoping there's a ghost or two who might know something."

"I'll come with you."

"Thanks." I got out and took my bag with me so I didn't look weird loitering out the front of the building. I put my phone to my ear as I stood there and lowered my voice. "Hello. Are there any ghosts about who will talk to me about Jan Hadler? Hello?"

A middle-aged man ghost with a potbelly slid through the front door of the building and came over. He stopped in front of me and stared into my eyes. "You can see me?"

I smiled. "Yes. I'm pretending to be on the phone so I don't look like a nutcase."

He chuckled. "Fair enough. So, what's your name?"

"I'm Avery Winters. I'm a journalist, and I'm looking into the disappearance of Jan Hadler. Do you know anything about what happened?"

"She's been here for… well… I don't know how long, but the other day—or was it the other week?" He put a hand on his mouth as he thought about it. Argh, ghosts and their non-sensing of time. "Anyway, it was fairly recently, she upped and left in the morning. Chucked a couple of suitcases, a box, and a few toys into her car, and she and the little boy left in a hurry."

"What kind of car was it?" I looked at Charles. "Can you make sure you remember all this?" Holding my phone meant I didn't have enough hands to write in a notebook as well.

"Yeah, sure."

The new ghost tapped his lips with his forefinger as he thought. "A white Honda Accord estate. Not new or anything. Maybe eight or nine years old."

"Okay, thanks. And have you seen anyone coming around looking for her since she disappeared?"

"The police. That's it. Well, that's all I seen, anyway."

"Okay, thanks. Um, you wouldn't happen to be able to get into her apartment, would you?" I needed to know if the child had Mr Puddles. Whether Mr Puddles was a soft toy or something else, I had no idea. Whatever he was, that's where the evidence was.

"No. I lived on the floor above hers." He looked across the

road and down the street a bit before turning his gaze back to me.

"Do you know anything about a Mr Puddles, what kind of a toy it was?"

"Can't say I do."

A slim, old lady dressed in a knee-length grey skirt and white shirt, her short, wavy hair styled immaculately, approached from down the street. She stopped when she reached us. I looked at the ghost I'd been talking to and said goodbye. He gave a nod—thankfully, he understood, and I "hung up" my phone. I smiled at the woman. "Hello."

"Hello. May I ask what you're doing out here?"

"Of course. I'm Avery Winters, a journalist with the *Manesbury Daily*. I'm just following up on a story I'm covering." I pulled out my lanyard ID.

She squinted as she studied it. "Okay. I'm Beverly Davies, and I live here. What story are you doing?"

"One about a woman who was murdered recently. Her mother lived here, apparently, but she recently left. I was hoping to talk to her, but someone else who lives here told me a few minutes ago that she left the other day." Maybe Beverly could help.

Charles nudged me with his elbow, only instead of it hurting, it was cold and made me shudder. "You said you weren't going to talk to any living people."

I ignored him. He was right, but this opportunity was too good to pass up.

"Oh, I heard about that. I didn't know her well, but her grandson was the cutest. Jan mainly kept to herself, but if I saw them out and about, I always said hello." She sighed. "I miss those days when my children were little. I had three, and only one saw fit to give me grandchildren, and even they're teenagers now. Not so cute when they're older." She shook her head, disappointment clear on her face.

"Did you ever hear them mention a Mr Puddles?"

Charles was glaring at me. I kept ignoring him.

She smiled. "Oh, yes. He had this adorable soft toy duck. Although he hasn't been taking it out as much lately. Probably growing too old for it. Such a shame they have to grow up. The little ones are so easy to please, and they're honest. Not like teenagers and adults. I don't speak to one of my sons any more. I needed help once, and he refused. Imagine that, refusing your own mother. I was in labour with him for twenty hours, and that's the thanks I get."

"That's such a shame. I'm sorry." Wow, she held a grudge against her own son. Maybe he was horrible, or maybe he couldn't afford to help her. Whatever the problem, I didn't want to hear any more of it. "Did you see them leaving the other day by any chance?"

"No, I'm afraid not. First I heard of it was when the police came and spoke to my other neighbour."

"They didn't speak to you?"

"No. Only that one neighbour. She told them that she hadn't seen them for a couple of days. The two of them broke the door down and looked around in there for an hour, made such a mess—that bit I did see—and then they left. The landlord's fixed the door now, and they're having her furniture taken away to the Red Cross charity shop. Apparently after she left, she emailed them and said she couldn't come back."

"Did the police know this?"

"I don't know. I ran into the landlord when he came down. He didn't mention speaking to the police, and I haven't seen them here since they spoke to my neighbour."

"What was her name?"

"Felicity Jones. But don't tell her I told you. She's a horrible gossip, but she also likes her privacy. Won't talk about herself, just others. She probably won't want to talk to a reporter either." Well, there goes my theory about people wanting to speak to reporters more than police. Although it had been true up until now.

Charles was peering down the street. He narrowed his eyes and shuffled from foot to foot. "We should get going, Avery. I have a funny feeling."

I would have ignored him again, but I couldn't ignore that I had the jitters when we first got here, and it felt like we were being watched, although that could just be me being paranoid. "Well, thank you so much for all that information. You've been a real help. I hope you have a lovely afternoon."

"Thank you. Now it's time to watch *Pointless*. I hate to miss it. Toodles."

She turned and made her way to the front door, and I hurried back to the car. Charles was sitting in his seat by the time I got in and locked my door. "What's wrong?"

"I felt like we were being watched, and just down the stre—" His eyes widened, and he stared at the police car that pulled out of a spot across the road and down a bit. It drove past us. There was only one policeman, and he didn't give us a second look as he passed.

"It's only a police car. They're probably staking out the place to see if her ex comes by."

"But how would they know he wanted the child."

"I told Bellamy what Mandy's ex said. She'd changed her name and left her child with her mother. She was basically in hiding. Bellamy must have passed that info on to the local police." Maybe it had been more dangerous than I'd thought to come here. What if her ex happened to come by when I was out the front? I shuddered. "Maybe it was a good thing the policeman was there. We might have lucked out." I wasn't about to admit it was a stupid thing I'd done, coming here. I'd gotten some good info after all. Unfortunately, I had no idea where Jan and the boy had gone. I wrote everything down in my notebook before I forgot. "If only I could look in her apartment. Hmm…." I needed to know whether they had Mr Puddles. Hopefully Mandy's mum knew how important that duck was. "If they're giving everything to a charity shop, we'll lose our chance to go through it. I think I'm going to have to check out who owns the unit and speak to them."

"Can you do it by phone?" Charles's leg bounced up and down. He was likely still a bit put out by the chances I took.

"Yes, Charles. I can do that."

"Can we go home now?"

"Yep. Let's go." Even though I'd apparently dodged a bullet, maybe even literally, the uneasy feeling between my shoulder blades stayed with me for the entire drive home. And I had no idea why.

CHAPTER 10

When I got home that night, I texted Meg to say I was okay, and then I found out who the landlord was. Turned out, he owned the whole building. Lucky rich guy. He also happened to own an accounting firm in Maidstone, Kent. I wasn't up for another three-hour-plus drive. Luckily there was a phone number for his firm. I'd only do the drive if he wouldn't talk to me.

The next morning, I had a coffee at home—because I was never going to voluntarily be in Joyless's vicinity while she was on the warpath—then checked in on Verity on my way to work. She was still a bit shell-shocked, but she was doing okay. After that, I went to an interview I'd organised the night before the shooting. Donald Ewing was a seventy-two-year-old busker who was hoping a write-up in the local paper would help him draw more of an audience. He lived in Cramptonbury, so at least it wasn't a long drive.

Just as I pulled up outside his white, pebble-dashed bungalow, my phone rang. I didn't know whether to be happy or worried. "Hello, Sergeant Bellamy. Have you got some news?"

"No, but Sergeant Riley from Canterbury police had some for me. A certain journalist we both know was snooping around there yesterday afternoon, despite me trying to keep her away from this case."

I pressed my lips together and tried to school my voice so it was less angry. "I knew it!" Oops, it didn't work. The annoyance was loud and clear. "I thought we had an agreement. Why are you shutting me out?"

"Miss Winters, I'll only pass on information when I think it's safe to do so. Sergeant Riley so helpfully pointed out that the killer is still out there, and he's seen you. If he thinks you're trying to find him, you're likely to get the same treatment Miss Hadler did. We're doing all we can to find her mother and son."

"They're obviously in hiding. Do you know why?" No more beating around the bush. I again had nothing to lose with this man. I wanted him to admit I was right and her ex was after her, that it wasn't some mistake or attempt to throw them off the right path.

He sighed loudly. "We suspect her killer might be her ex… after what you told us… but we have no idea who he is. According to a friend of hers she knew before she came here, she had a few exes, and when we asked about a Rusty, she clammed shut. We're trying to narrow it down. Why he wants to hurt her mother and child is also a mystery. He obviously has a vendetta against her. We also don't know how it all ties to the other murder, so we might be barking up the wrong tree. According to witnesses, the same Mercedes was used, and the killer wore a balaclava. Other than that, we have little to go on. She had a drug charge against her, as you know, so it could also be related to that."

"The other murder was probably a red herring." Which reminded me—I hadn't heard back from Naomi, which meant she'd found her family.

"If there's one thing I've learned in all my years as a police officer, it's that people rarely murder for no reason. Just because we haven't found a link, doesn't mean there isn't one. Now, that's all I'm saying about the case, except stay out of it. I don't want to be waving your coffin off at the airport. Do you understand me?"

"Yes, Sergeant, I understand, but it's not as cut and dried as that. I promised Mandy as she *lay dying in my arms*"—it wouldn't hurt to pour some guilt on him—"that I would help find her ex and make sure her son was safe. And that's what I'm going to do. I'll make sure I'm careful."

"If you go against my advice, you're putting yourself in incredible danger. Someone won't always be there to save you, Miss Winters. I've seen enough dead bodies to last a lifetime, and I'd hate to see one more, especially someone I respect and consider a valued acquaintance." Ooh, now he was trying to push the guilt back on me. Nice try, but it wasn't going to work.

"I understand, Sergeant, but we all have to do what we think is right. If I discover anything I feel is useful, I'll let you know. Anyway, I have an interview to conduct, so I have to go. Bye."

"Goodbye, Miss Winters." The disappointment in his voice was palpable. It reached through the phone and punched me right in the heart. Still, I had the help he didn't—the ghosts. And if the police could solve this one all on their own in time, why had the universe seen fit to put me at the scene at that particular moment? Something bigger than Bellamy and me was asking for my help, and I wasn't going to refuse.

I grabbed my bag and headed to the front door. Donald Ewing answered within a minute of me banging the frog knocker. "Oh, Miss Winters." He frowned, and I detected a whole lot of disappointment in his voice.

Nevertheless, I smiled. "Yes. Hello, Mr Ewing. I thought you knew it was me coming."

"I did. I even requested it be you. I just lost track of time this morning. That's all." He shuffled backwards. "Please, come in." He held a cane in one hand. The hair adorning his head was white and framed a lined face. His blue eyes were kind but tired. I didn't see how this man had the energy or physicality for busking, but what did I know? Maybe someone helped him set up, and he sat and played a harmonica or something. "Go through to the kitchen at the back. I'll catch up to you."

I did as asked. His sliding back door was open, and two chairs sat at a round, glass table on the back porch. A bowl with coloured balls sat in it, and three bowling pins were on the table. There was no way he was a juggler, was there? If I'd been asked to put money on what he did as a busker, I would've lost it all.

He finally arrived, his walker clicking a slow cadence on the timber floor. "Please, sit outside."

"Okay." I sat at the table and gazed out onto the level, lush lawn. Two mature trees shaded the back of the yard. It was rather peaceful.

Instead of sitting, Mr Ewing put his cane on the back of the other chair. He picked up three of the coloured balls—a red, a green, and a blue—and painstakingly made his way to the grass. He wobbled on the one small step down, and I jumped up, ready to catch him. This was a disaster in the making. "Ah, Mr Ewing, are you sure you're okay to do this? I'd hate for anything to happen to you."

He made it to the grass, turned, and winked. He smiled. "That's not what I heard."

My eyes widened. "What?"

"Never mind. Just watch." He threw the red ball in the air, then the green, then the blue.... Then they all fell to the ground because he failed to catch them. He tried to bend down to pick them up, his body folding in excruciating increments like a rusty piece of machinery. This time, I did stand and hurried over, but not in time. He fell to his hands and knees and grunted. When he looked up at me, tears welled in his eyes.

This was so confusing and sad. "Why don't we sit up at the table, and you can tell me why I'm really here." There was no way I was here for this disaster.

He nodded slowly, and I stood behind him and grabbed under his arms. It took considerable effort, but I managed to get him upright and help him to a chair.

I sat opposite him. "Would you like me to get you a glass of water or a cup of tea?" I was pretty sure the old guy lived alone, but he obviously needed help.

"Maybe a glass of water. Help yourself to a tea if you like." He placed his arms on the table and stared forlornly at me.

"Okay. Thanks." I went in and got us each a water, then returned and put his in front of him before I sat. There wasn't going to be an interview today. This was more like community service, which was okay with me. If we couldn't show kindness to our fellow citizens, we were falling short. "Now, do you want to tell me what's going on?"

He took a sip of his water. "I heard about the hullabaloo with you and those dead bodies and that murder the other day." Ah, not again. At least he didn't seem to hate me.

"Wow, news travels far. I didn't think it would get out of Manesbury."

"My sister, Enid, lives there. She mentioned it the other morning. My great-niece is friends with someone called Joy, and she was complaining to her. She thinks you're killing people."

I rolled my eyes. "Yes, but she's wrong. She's spreading nasty rumours. Do you think I'm a murderer?"

He sighed. "No, not so much that, but I thought you might be like a bad-luck charm. But either way, it would've suited me. Although I don't want it to be painful."

I frowned. "Please don't tell me you asked me here hoping I'd kill you or you'd die." Now I'd heard everything. Maybe I could write an article about today—Journalist Named as Angel of Death Does Home Visits on Request. I tried not to chuckle. It really wasn't funny, but it kind of was.

His head dropped for a moment. He finally looked up again. "So, you're not going to kill me?"

"Oh my God, of course not! I'm a journalist. I write about murders; I don't participate in them."

"Are you sure? My arthritis is so bad, and I'm in pain. I'm tired, and I just want to slip peacefully away."

I stared at him. My heart went out to him, but I didn't feel like spending the next twenty years in prison, not to mention the killing part. "No. Definitely not."

"Please reconsider. I'll leave you my house."

"No!"

"Are you sure?" His puppy-dog eyes almost did me in, but this was one thing I could never help with.

"Positive. Have you thought about going to the Netherlands or Belgium? They have assisted death." Argh, this was getting more morbid by the minute.

"I want to die here at home."

"I can't help you, but if you need me to organise some services for you to make life easier, let me know. I'd be happy to do that."

He sighed again. "Never mind. My nephew could do that if I wanted. You've been a bit of a disappointment, to be honest, Miss Winters." Wow, harsh.

"Maybe you shouldn't listen to gossip. Do you need anything legal from me before I go?"

"No. Do you mind seeing yourself out? I need to sit here and deal with it. I really thought I'd get to go to the other side today."

I blinked, speechless for a moment. "Um, not at all." I stood, picked up my glass of water, and drained it. "I'll wash this and put it in the sink on my way through. Are you sure there's nothing I can do before I go?"

He shook his head. "Goodbye, Miss Winters."

"Goodbye, Mr Ewing. I'm sorry I couldn't be your angel of death today." What the hell was I saying? I actually wasn't sorry about that, just that he was suffering. I washed my glass on the way through, put it back in the cupboard, and let myself out. As I drove back to the office, I dreaded what else was awaiting me today. My life had turned into someone's idea of a joke, and it wasn't funny at all.

CHAPTER 11

Back in the office, Carina was gone, but Finnegan sat at his desk, typing away. When I stepped inside and turned to my work station, I stopped. My mouth dropped open. A bouquet of a dozen red roses sat on my table. A sticker closing the pale pink tissue paper surrounding them indicated it came from Petunia's Pretty Petals.

I placed my things next to them and reached for the small card. As I pulled it out of the envelope, a voice came from directly behind me. "So, who are they from? Your new rock-star boyfriend?"

I started, then turned to Finnegan, who was only inches away. "Oh my God, don't do that! You scared me half to death."

His face was all innocence. "Do what? I can't help it if I have ninja skills. I wasn't even trying to sneak up on you. So, who are they from?"

I would've said it was none of his business, but who cared? There was only one secret I wanted to keep, and it had nothing to do with dating. Okay, maybe I had two secrets—I could see ghosts, and I found Finnegan particularly delectable. I read the card out loud. "I had fun the other night. Can't wait to see you again. Reece xx." I smiled. How sweet.

"Ooh, kisses. He's serious. Next, he'll be getting down on one knee."

"Save the sarcasm. I love flowers. Just because you don't have a romantic bone in your body." I picked them up and smelled them. "Not much of a fragrance, but they're gorgeous."

"It's a bit early for flowers, isn't it? You've been out, what, once?"

"It's never too early for flowers. Besides, if every guy did things according to *Vinegar's Guide to Dating*, no one would ever date. One-night stands would become the standard. Goodbye long-term relationships and having children. Society would collapse. Do you really want that on your conscience?"

He shrugged. "There'd be far fewer broken hearts, that's for sure. Besides, the world's overpopulated anyway." His phone rang. He hurried back to his desk and answered it. "Oh, hey. Yeah, thanks for calling back." He gave me a nod as he strode out the door.

Talk about having a hang-up. That evil woman really did a number on him. Hopefully, when he met the right woman, he'd realise and take a chance.

I sat and put the flowers to the side of my desk. After setting up my laptop, I sent Reece a text. *The flowers are gorgeous. Thank you so much. And I had fun the other night too.* I typed xx, but damn it, I didn't want to put kisses. It just wasn't me. I stared at the message for a minute, then deleted them. The urge to do what he'd done was strong because I didn't want to offend him. Hopefully he wouldn't read anything into the lack of x's at the end. I hated when someone did something, and then I felt obliged to copy so I didn't make someone feel like I didn't care. Old Avery would've included the kisses, but new Avery wasn't going to. Was I over-thinking again? You betcha.

My phone quickly pinged with another message. *Can I take you to lunch tomorrow?* Yikes, tomorrow. That was too soon. Also, I rarely stopped to have a long lunch. Typically, I ate a prepacked sandwich wherever I was, and it took about five minutes.

I have too much work at the moment. What about next time you're at the pub, I buy you dinner?

OK. I'm there on Friday night. Is five thirty OK? I know it's early, but I'm on at six thirty.

Sounds good. See you then 😊.

His return message contained emoji only. 😊😘 More kisses. I wasn't sure how I felt about that. It was nice that he liked me—he was an attractive guy. However, he seemed a bit too keen. He hardly knew me.

I shook my head. What was I saying?

My previous example had been Brad, and he'd managed to get me hooked by doing not much. He gave me a few compliments early on, and he did buy me flowers, but he was always arrogant and assumed I'd just follow him around like a puppy. Which I'm ashamed to say I did. I looked up to him when I first met him. He was one of the more senior staff at the company. All the others looked up to him too. He was the "cool kid" of the office, and I was surprised and flattered that he even wanted to date me. Boy, had I been stupid. Maybe that's all it was. My aversion to Reece's affectionate overtures was because I wasn't used to it. Finnegan's teasing aside, maybe this was how decent men treated women they wanted to date.

Right, Avery. I sat up straighter. *It's time to just go with the flow and enjoy being fussed over.* It wouldn't be easy, but I'd try. Now it was time to get back to work. This morning's interview was a bust, but it gave me an idea for a boring yet helpful article on avoiding osteoporosis. There wasn't much to help arthritis as far as I could tell, but you could avoid subpar bone density if you did the right things, like have enough calcium, enough vitamin D, and do weight-bearing exercise. Apparently one in three women and one in five men over the age of fifty ended up with osteoporosis. Wow, that was more than I thought.

Finnegan returned after I'd been researching for about half an hour, but he said nothing and went straight back to work. I made a couple of phone calls to get quotes from knowledgeable sources—a doctor and a physiotherapist—then it was time to write my article. I'd almost finished when a voice came from outside the door. "Get ready, Avery. I'm coming in." I tried not to grin as Charles walked through the door. Apparently, I did a terrible job of it.

"What are you smiling about?" Finnegan asked from across the room.

"Oh, just remembering something funny Reece said the other night." He rolled his eyes and went back to his laptop. He he he. He was so easy to ruffle sometimes. I stood and grabbed my phone.

"Before you ask, Naomi's waiting outside. She's upset about something."

I just nodded and made my way out the door and down the stairs. I lifted my phone to my ear. "Why didn't she come in with you?"

"I don't know. I'm a ghost, not a mind reader."

"You're also a smart ar—"

"Avery, thanks for coming so quickly." Naomi stood on the footpath, hugging herself.

"Why didn't you come upstairs? Not that I could've talked to you up there, but you're welcome any time."

She eyed the door and shuddered. "I hate passing through things, and my popping in and out is a tad unreliable. I tried to come here and ended up in London the first time, then Exeter the second."

"I'll give you some tips later if you like."

She gave Charles a grateful smile. "Thank you. I'd really appreciate it."

As much as I was happy Charles could help her, I was impatient to find out why she was here. "So, what happened, Naomi? Charles said you were upset about something."

"Yes. Well, a couple of things. My parents are devastated. They keep crying and wandering around the house saying, 'I can't believe she's gone.'" Her eyes glistened and brimmed with tears. "How can I help them? I want them to know I'm here and I love them, that I'm okay."

Charles looked at me, and I gave him a nod. "Um, I may be able to help with that later. I'll come up with something."

Her expression lightened. "You can help me? Thank you so much!" She threw her arms around me, and they passed right through. I shivered at the chill and rubbed my arms. "Oh, sorry." She frowned, then sighed. "Being a ghost is better than disappearing forever, but it still sucks haggis."

I gave her a small smile because she was funny even when she was upset. "I understand. Hence why I'm not in a hurry to cross over. So, what was the other thing that upset you?"

"I went to see my partner, and I caught the tail end of a fight he was having with his brother. I don't know the details, but Kyle yelled, 'This is all your fault. Naomi's dead because of you.'" Her forehead wrinkled, and she shut her mouth quickly and placed her hand over it, as if she was trying not to cry.

Was it a lead, or was it the grief talking? And how could it have been his fault? "Did his brother answer?"

"No. He just stared, lowered his head, and left." She sniffled. "I can't understand it. His brother was always nice to me. Why would he do something like that?"

"What colour eyes does he have?"

She thought for a moment. "Brown."

"Well, unless he was the getaway driver, he definitely wasn't the shooter. Mandy recognised him straight away from that, so he wasn't wearing contacts. Also, could Kyle have been speaking figuratively? Does he usually drive you to work? Was your routine changed for some reason because of his brother?"

"No. I always caught the bus from that stop at that time." She shut her eyes and rubbed her forehead, then opened her eyes. "That made me an easy target. They could've been watching me for days before this."

I looked at Charles. "Can you find out if the police got security tapes from the last few days? Maybe the killer drove past there without his balaclava on?"

"Would he be dumb enough to do it from the same car, especially if someone else drove the day they killed Naomi and Mandy?" Charles made a good point.

I worried my bottom lip between my teeth. "Hmm. No. Bellamy told me they stole the getaway car early that morning, which makes sense. Still, if I could see video and check if that icy-eyes guy was driving any car past there, bingo."

Naomi gave me an "are you kidding?" look. "Avery, as much as I want to solve this and rip the innards out of the killer, do you know how many hours of tape you'd have to watch?"

I smiled. "Not many. They figured out the time you caught the bus, didn't they?"

Charles grinned, and Naomi's smile, whilst slow in forming, shone brightly once she was done. She gave me a grateful look. "You're smart. I'm glad you're on my side."

"Aw, shucks. Thanks." I turned to Charles. "I'm going to ask Bellamy outright about security tapes and if I can view them. I got a good look at that killer's eyes, after all. If he refuses, I'll have to think of a plan B."

"And what about my partner's brother? Can you look into him too? I can't believe he'd have anything to do with this, but… well… I don't want to leave any avenue unexplored. Kyle gave him money a few times when he was desperate, and I never said anything. I even lent him five hundred pounds at one point. I've only ever been kind to him. He probably didn't do it, but let's just make sure." The worry on her face said it all—she needed to know, but it might break her heart. Although what motive he could have, I wasn't sure. It didn't sound like he wanted her dead.

"Okay. If you could give me all his details—full name, address, phone number, where he works—I'll go that route. Can I also have your partner's details? I might need to sit down with them both together, so it looks less sus. I'll say I'm interviewing them for an article I'm working on that celebrates your life." I'd write that article too. Why not celebrate a kind young woman who was living her best life and contributing to society?

"Okay. So…"

I "ended the call," took out my notebook and pen, and started writing.

CHAPTER 12

After speaking to Naomi, I returned to the office, grabbed my stuff, then headed home, where I tried calling Bellamy, but he didn't answer. So frustrating. He didn't want to put me in danger, and he probably had some leads so didn't need me. Well, I had leads, too, and if he didn't want help, that was his bad luck. I'd keep going with my investigation.

Charles had come home with me, and we sat at the kitchen table. "Can you and Sergeant Fox see if he has any security tapes from near the bus stop? If he does, at least I can push him on that. I'll go down to the station if I have to."

"Yep, can do. But I don't know how lucky we'll be. They still haven't found a connection between the two murders—other than the murderer—and Bellamy's like a chook without a head because they have so many people to interview to try and find what it is, if anything."

They were police, though. They had procedures, and before they knew about Mandy, or believed me, rather, they would've gone through the motions, one of those being getting security tapes of where Naomi was killed. "They would have them, even if they've only gone through them for the day of the murder. They might not be good quality, but we have to try, don't we?"

He nodded solemnly. "We do. If it was me, I'd want someone to make it right and stop those bad people from hurting anyone else."

I folded my arms. "Exactly."

"Is that everything? I'd like to get back now."

"Yep. And if I go interview anyone, I'll let Meg know. I'll pass on the address, etc." Hopefully that would keep everyone happy when they found out later what I'd been up to. Besides, it was still my job to interview people for the paper. This was a story I wanted to write an article on. I was just doing what I got paid to do, and I doubted Kyle or his brother were dangerous.

He waved. "Bye, Avery."

"Bye."

I ate lunch and planned how I would handle the brothers. In fact, I'd told a little white lie to Naomi… or maybe only kind of. I'd considered interviewing them together, but after further contemplation, I'd changed my mind. If they were both in the same room, I might get a feel for whatever they'd been arguing about, but if I interviewed them separately, I could check their stories against each other. The younger brother, Max, lived at the parents' place in a converted garage. Naomi's partner, Kyle, was still in the flat they'd rented together. Kyle worked in finance, but Max was in and out of employment. In the last two years, he'd worked only about half that time in various odd jobs. He sounded like a bit of a loser, to be honest. That was mean of me, but when you're thirty-one and living in your parents' garage, you've either had a lot of bad luck, bad health—which didn't put you in the loser category—or you just didn't give a fig, and from what Naomi said, he was the third category.

So… who to talk to first?

I decided to talk to Kyle first because he was the obvious person I'd interview if I was doing a story on Naomi, which I was. The brother wouldn't even know I was coming, but if I did it the other way around, they'd both be suspicious from the get-go. I had a feeling it was going to be easier to convince Max that Kyle had said certain things and be able to coax information out of him that way, if there was anything to coax. I still wasn't sure this wasn't a dead end. The two women didn't know each other, so why would the same killer murder them both, especially since Mandy's murder was personal, and the killer had told her why? He didn't say anything to Naomi. And if it was Max, what was his motive? Was he in love with Naomi and thought if I can't have her, no one can? Or was he jealous of the time she spent with his brother? Goodness knew people had killed for less. But I also had the problem that Mandy had said it was Rusty who killed her. Maybe Rusty and Max had an agreement and Max had driven the car—you help me, and I'll help you, kind of thing.

I called Kyle, expecting to get his message service, but he answered on the fourth ring. "Kyle here."

"Hi, Kyle. My name's Avery Winters, and I'm sorry to bother y—"

"I'm not donating to anything at the moment, so if—" I couldn't let him hang up.

"I'm sorry about your loss."

There was a pause, then, "Oh, okay. Thanks. Are you a friend of Naomi's?"

"You could say that." Hmm, he'd given me an idea. "I sometimes caught the same bus as her in the mornings. We chatted a few times. I wasn't there the other morning when…. Anyway, I'm a journalist for the *Manesbury Daily*, and I'm doing an article on her because she was really nice, and I wanted people to know what a loss it is to our community. I also thought you and her family would appreciate it. There isn't anything else I can do for her, and I wanted to honour her. I was wondering if I could visit with you and find out more about her and your life together."

"Oh." He went quiet, and I didn't want to seem pushy, so I gave him space. I could be patient when I had to be. That's one thing this job had taught me—when to push and when to hold back. Eventually, he'd decided. "Um, okay. When do you want to meet?"

"Today or tomorrow is good for me, unless you want to wait until after the… um… funeral." That was hard, mentioning that to someone newly grieving and probably still in shock about it. "We can meet at your place or at a café. Whatever you prefer. I'm honestly so sorry to ask you, but I really want to share her story."

"No, it's all right. I'm almost numb at the moment, still processing. It's surreal. I keep thinking she'll walk through the door any moment. Maybe it's best we talk tomorrow. I don't know how I'll be… after…." He might have thought he was numb, but the pain in his voice came through the phone loud and clear. My initial gut feeling was that he had nothing to do with her murder, but I wouldn't know for sure until I'd sat down with him. Body language always gave me a clearer picture of the situation and whether the person was telling the truth.

"What time tomorrow, and where?"

"I guess my place is fine, say ten o'clock?"

"That sounds good. What's your address?" Yes, I had it, but if I didn't ask, it would be insanely suspicious. He rattled it off. "Great, thanks. I'll see you tomorrow at ten. And thanks for agreeing to speak with me. I appreciate it."

"No problem. Naomi's a… was a…" He sighed. "She was an incredible woman, and I'm glad someone else appreciates that."

He certainly wasn't talking like someone who wanted her dead. It didn't strike me as an act.

"Of course. She had many great qualities."

"She did. See you tomorrow, Avery. Bye."

"Bye."

That went better than expected. And now he thought I'd known her in real life, I could be freer with how I spoke about her. Once I'd spoken to Kyle, I could decide how I'd approach Max.

Now I'd organised all that, I'd earned some time to myself. Some hapkido practice was in order because I had a feeling I might need it sometime soon.

CHAPTER 13

The next morning, I stayed home until it was time to go and see Kyle. I'd managed to avoid Mrs Crabby the last few days, but today, I was out of luck. She caught me as I reached the bottom of the stairs. Bummer. I needed to walk more quietly, but there were a couple of stair treads that squeaked, and I'd forgotten to avoid them. She sprung out of her door in front of me like a demented jack-in-the-box. So much for arthritis slowing her down. My heart stuttered, and I halted, my hand flying to my chest. "Mrs Cr— Mrs Collins. Good morning."

She narrowed her eyes and waved a gnarled finger at me. "What have you been up to, hmm? Why were the police wandering around here yesterday? I don't want any more trouble. You've caused enough strife to last me the rest of my life."

Bellamy hadn't said anything about coming around, but they must have been following up on stupid Joy's brother messing with my car. It was nice that they were taking it seriously. "I haven't done anything. I promise. Some boys vandalised my car, and the police were just following up about it. I'm the victim in this case."

She sneered. "You, the victim? Pfft. I'll believe that when I see it. You're a troublemaker. Not one day goes by that I don't regret letting my flat to you."

Wow. Don't hold back—tell me what you really think. I shook my head. Her attitude was wearing me down. "Why do you hate me so much? I thought it might be because you hate everybody, but you seem to have a particular dislike for me. What have I done?" Good on me for being brave enough to ask. She at least owed me an explanation.

Her nostrils flared as breath puffed out of them. She lifted her chin, pinched her mouth closed, stepped back into her flat, and slammed the door. Well, that went well. Maybe I should start looking for another place to live. She was probably about to kick me out. I sighed. What a way to start the day. Oh well, no use worrying about it right now. And at least I had some savings. I was in a much better position now than when I first arrived.

The tension in my shoulders as I let myself out and walked across the street to the laneway wasn't because of Mrs Crabby. Would my car be clean or not? Surely Joyless's brother wouldn't be stupid enough to reoffend after being spoken to by the police.

I reached the laneway and smiled. Daisy was clean. Phew.

As I slid into the car, my stomach churned. Was I doing the right thing, spending time on this when I should be looking for Mandy's son? Had I lost focus on what was most important? Naomi might have entirely misunderstood the brothers' conversation, and this trip might be for nothing, but then again, the police were looking for Mandy's son, too, so at least someone was doing something. But they didn't know the significance of the soft toy. Was it evidence pointing to her ex for her murder or maybe evidence of something else he'd done? Had she recorded him threatening her? If only she hadn't been snatched away by the light so quickly.

What if Kyle or his brother did have something to do with

her murder, but I couldn't figure it out? It wasn't like I could ask too many probing questions. An idea had come to me last night, but I'd discounted it because it was cruel. It was necessary, though. I wanted the truth, but it would likely come out when I wasn't there to see it.

"Naomi, hello? Can you come to my car?" Hopefully, Charles had given her some pointers, and she'd figured out how to travel. "Naomi?"

A minute later, she popped into the front seat. She grinned. "I did it! I heard you, and it took me a bit because I ended up in my mum's car in her garage, but then I came here on the second try. I'm really getting the hang of it."

I smiled. "You are. And thanks for coming ASAP."

"That's okay. What do you need? I thought we went over everything yesterday." I guessed she figured it was yesterday because I hadn't been to Kyle's yet.

What I was asking was mean, but I had no choice if I wanted to make sure. "I hate to ask you to do this, but could you come with me to see Kyle? I would ask Charles, but he wouldn't be able to enter your home."

She worried her lip between her teeth. "I guess. But why?"

"It's more for after I leave. Unfortunately, you might hear something that confirms your suspicions, or something… worse." I stared at her, gauging her reaction.

Her eyes widened. "Oh. You mean if, if…." She shook her head. "No. There's no way Kyle had anything to do with this."

"I'm not saying he did, just to be ready for anything. I want you there for after I leave. If I ask a couple of probing questions and one of them did have something to do with it, he might get worried and call his brother. That's when you'll hear what we need." Her shoulders slumped. I was such a bad person.

She looked out the window for a moment, then slowly turned to me. "Okay."

"Thanks." There wasn't much to say after that. The drive to Kyle's took twenty minutes, and we rode in silence.

Kyle and Naomi had lived in a modern three-storey, rendered-brick apartment building on a quiet, tree-lined street. The bus stop where Naomi was murdered sat two blocks away on a busy street. I'd driven past it on the way here. It was freaky how it just looked like any other bus stop already, like a life-ending, violent, tragic event hadn't recently occurred, the people waiting for the bus reading or scrolling on their phones in oblivion. Naomi stared as we passed, her forehead bunching up.

I parked a few doors down from her building. She turned to me. "It's weird coming via car. It's like I'm still alive." Her eyes held such desperation that my nose tingled, heralding tears.

I took a deep breath—she didn't need me to pity her. My hand moved to reach out and touch her, but I stopped myself just in time. "I'm sorry I can't do anything to change that. I wish I could." Oh, how I wished. As much as I helped ghosts, I couldn't do the ultimate, the one thing they all yearned for—re-alive them and reunite them with their loved ones. "Are you going to be okay? If you really don't want to come up, I won't hold it against you."

She sat up straighter and looked me dead in the eyes. "I'm in. I want to find out what happened and get past it. I need to stop feeling sorry for myself. There's no going back. I need to move forward. Thank you for helping me, Avery. I really do appreciate it."

I gave her a gentle smile. "I know, and trust me, I feel for you in all of this. What happened to you sucks big time. You have every reason to wallow. I'm impressed with your resilience. I'm not going to give up until this is solved, and I'll be here for you afterwards."

She smiled. "Thank you. You know, I wish I'd known you in real life. We would've been great friends."

My smile widened. "If you hang around long enough, we still can be."

She grinned. "I'd like that." I'd had trouble making friends in my old life. Turns out it was easier than I thought. Just find someone you get along with and put yourself out there. Who knew? It didn't matter if half my new friends weren't on the same plane. It was kind of like being friends with someone overseas via the internet.

"Okay. Let's go." I grabbed my bag, and as I got out of the car, Naomi disappeared. I went to the security entry and buzzed. When Kyle answered the intercom, I confirmed who I was, and he let me in.

I knocked on one of two doors on the first floor. The guy who answered was around six feet tall. His shortish, sandy-brown hair curled around his ears and framed sad hazel eyes and three-day blonde growth. He didn't smile. "Hi, Avery. Please come in." Naomi stood next to him, staring at his face, longing in her eyes. I quickly took my gaze off her. If I worried about her, I'd look like a weirdo to Kyle, and I'd probably cry.

Slick, white-tiled floors ran through the immaculate living area and into the open-plan kitchen. Gold-coloured light fittings complemented large white lamps that sat on two glass side tables. A camel-coloured three-seater leather lounge faced a huge flatscreen TV. Kyle went to the four-seater round glass dining table and sat. Naomi sat in the seat to the right of him, the one I was about to pull out and sit on. I veered around it and took the seat opposite Kyle. "I hope you don't mind, but I'll be writing notes. My brain won't remember everything, and, of course, I want to get the details right."

"Not a problem. Where did you want to start?" He sat back in his chair, hands limp in his lap. He wasn't relaxed so much as drained. It looked like he was in the "let's just get this over with" mode. I couldn't blame him.

"I should warn you that I'll ask some personal-ish questions. Nothing too personal, of course, but I want to ask you what your favourite things about Naomi were." I forced myself not to look at Naomi. I loved my job, but times like this, the guilt stabbed me. I was picking at this guy's wounds—and Naomi's—that hadn't even begun to scab. It was for a good cause, but still, that was one part of my job I didn't think I'd ever be comfortable with.

He smiled sadly, but then his smile grew as he thought more about it. "She was always up for anything, and she loved having fun. She could make anything fun, too, even grocery shopping." He paused, probably remembering some outing or other. "You know how they talk about people having a positive mindset? Well, that was Naomi. If anything went wrong and I worried, she'd convince me it was going to be okay, and it always was. She's supportive of all her friends and family, and if you asked for her help, she would always give it, no matter how much she had to go out of her way. She once drove twenty-five minutes to swap cars with a friend whose car had a mouse in it. Her friend freaked out, but Naomi saved the day." Joy flooded his eyes, and he was sitting up straight.

"I remember that day. It was a cute grey mouse. My friend was practically crying in fear when I got there." She grinned.

I chuckled. "I can imagine her doing that." And I could. "She's also a bit feisty too. We had a couple of conversations about general-world stuff, and she had a real love of fairness, doing what's right." She gave me a side-eye, and I shrugged as subtly as I could.

"She did. A couple of times, she organised for our group of friends to do charity fun runs. She was into everything—clubbing, running, football, travelling. It was rare that she wanted to sit home on the weekend and relax. Nae was a bundle of energy." He sighed and slumped back again. The joy of remembering her had him collapsing into the void she'd left. Naomi flopped her arms on the table and rested her chin on them, looking up at him with tears in her eyes. Why had I thought bringing her was a good idea? It was double the grief.

I watched him carefully for the next question. "Did you know Mandy Hadler?"

He cocked his head to the side as he considered my question, his body relaxed. "No." His forehead wrinkled. "That name is familiar." His mouth made a small *o*. "Oh, wasn't she the other woman, ah, you know, shot on the same morning?" This had to be hard on him. Whether he had anything to do with Naomi's death, he seemed to genuinely love her.

"Yes. The police are still looking for a solid connection, but they can't come up with anything." At least not that they'd told me. Stupid Bellamy, cutting me out. "Anyway, moving on, I have another question." I looked at him, giving him a chance to stop talking to me. I didn't want to be accused of badgering him later.

"Go ahead."

"I take it everyone at work loved her?"

Naomi sat up again. "Of course they did. Except that woman I told you about. She was a cow. Mooey Mallory I used to call her… to her face." I pressed my lips together to hold in a laugh. She was going to get me in trouble any minute now.

Unfortunately, Kyle wasn't smiling. "Yes. It was impossible not to love her once you got to know her." His forehead furrowed. "Well, there was one woman who didn't like her because she's just a grump. Naomi used to complain about Mallory every now and then." I made another note to possibly go to her work. It was already on my list but low down. Not that having a bit of office rivalry was much of a motive, although being called Mooey Mallory might have ticked her off just a bit too much. Kyle stared past me, and I turned. A framed photo of him and Naomi about to bungee jump hung on the wall. They were hugging and grinning, sunlight warm on their cheeks.

"I remember that day well…." Naomi sighed. "I thought there'd be so many more."

Sorrow settled over me. I wished I could take their pain away, but the same old helplessness froze my tongue. There was nothing I could say to make either of them feel better. As far as Kyle was concerned, platitudes weren't going to help, and I didn't know him well enough to hug him. I scribbled something in my notebook and steeled myself for the tangent I needed to go on. "I bet your family loved her too. She spoke a couple of times about you and your brother and how you all got on well."

His gaze darted to his hands for a moment before coming back to me. He hugged himself. "My parents thought she was the bee's knees, and she was patient with my brother. He's a bit of a handful sometimes, but she was always generous with him." Hmm, what was that supposed to mean? I threw a glance at Naomi. She gave me a blank look. I'd ask her about that later.

"Generous with time or money?"

He shrugged. "Both, I guess. Don't put this in the paper, but I lent my brother money a couple of times, and she didn't complain. We were saving to buy our own flat, and what I lent him wasn't insubstantial. He was supposed to pay it back." He heavy sighed and scrubbed a hand over his face. It didn't escape my notice that he squeezed one hand into a fist. "Please don't repeat that to anyone. I'm sorry I said anything."

I put one hand up in supplication. "Forget I asked. And I didn't write it down. It's hereby stricken from my brain." Yeah, nah. I was totally remembering it. "How's your family taking it?"

"They're upset, of course. They're mourning her and worrying about me."

"I can understand that. This is off the record and is more for me because, well, what happened was more than unfair—it was tragic and horrible, and…." I swallowed. "Did the police say whether they're close to finding out who did it? Are they keeping you updated?" He frowned. "Sorry if I overstepped. I… well, I'm sad about what happened. I miss my bus buddy. I hope they find whoever did this and lock them away forever."

"Bus buddy?" Naomi looked at me as if I'd lost the plot. I ignored her.

He put one elbow on the table and half covered his face with one hand. "They have no idea. I was already at work when it happened, so I couldn't help them, even as a witness. I know they think her death might be connected to another murder that happened that morning, but they really haven't said much at all." His Adam's apple bobbed. Hmm, his body language showed discomfort, and he was basically confirming that he'd been cleared. Did he feel guilty? Was there something in what he'd fought about with his brother?

I shook my head. "That's so unlucky. Out of all the people in the world, they had to pick Naomi. It's just so unfair. Normally the police ask if the person had any enemies, anyone who'd want to hurt them, but it sounds like everyone loved her. She was lucky to have you and your brother while she was here. She always spoke fondly of you both. I know you both always had her back." Naomi looked at me as if I'd kicked a baby seal. Maybe I was laying it on a bit thick, but still. We needed results.

He covered his face with one hand before dropping it. "I was lucky to have her. I probably didn't deserve her." Hmm, what was that supposed to mean? He cleared his throat. "If that's it, I'm tired. All this talk about Nae is draining. I appreciate you doing an article on her, though." He stood and looked at the front door. I could take a hint.

Naomi stood and went to him. She tried to hug him but went straight through. He stopped and blinked, then rubbed his forehead. "I love you, Kyle."

I pushed my chair back and slid my notebook and pen into my bag. "I understand." I stood and shook his hand. "I'm really sorry about Naomi. She was one of a kind, and I know she loved you more than anything." That last bit was more for Naomi than him. Well, it could be for him if he was innocent in all this. I'd have to reserve judgement.

He gave me a helpless look but said nothing. Maybe he was trying to keep it together.

Just as I reached the front door, my phone rang. It was Meg. I'd arranged for her to call me, just in case I needed a bit more incentive for Kyle to pick up the phone and call his brother—provided he was guilty of something. "Sorry, Kyle. I just have to take this, then I'll be off." I clicked the green button. "Hello, Sergeant. Yes, what can I do for you?"

"You're so naughty, Avery. Honestly. What if the guy is innocent?" I'd told her why I wanted her to call, but I just left out the part about Naomi's ghost hanging around to find out what happened next.

My mouth dropped open in mock shock. "Are you serious?" I flicked my gaze to Kyle. He stared at me, frowning. I looked away quickly, as if I had something to hide. "Is that right? Oh, okay. I'll come down now. I'm just finishing up with a newspaper interview. Okay, bye."

Meg laughed. "Bye, Avery. Come see me on your way back to the office. I want the rundown."

I hung up and looked at Kyle. "The police have some new evidence. They're not sure Naomi's death was random." I slammed my hand over my mouth. "Oops. Please forget I said anything. Oh, God, I'm so sorry. There's no way I should've said anything. The police sometimes give me a heads-up with information, so I can write informative articles. If the police find out the evidence doesn't stack up and that I told you anything, I'm going to be in so much trouble. Besides, I don't want to worry you. I'm sure this is just them throwing ideas around." My backtracking was lame, and if he hadn't done anything wrong, I wasn't just rubbing salt into his wound—I was grinding it in with sandpaper. I was so going to Hell, where I'd spend eternity with my parents and Brad. If it turned out he did nothing after this, I'd call him and tell him it was nothing.

Kyle placed an arm across his middle, rested his other elbow on his hand, and placed his hand over his mouth. He stood there holding himself together or trying to hide. I wasn't sure which. Eventually, he shook his head. "Please, just leave."

"I'm so sorry." I genuinely was, although I got the sense that he wasn't just upset. Something else was going on—his body language hinted he was hiding something. I gave Naomi a nod, but at this distance, Kyle would probably think it was at him. "Bye."

I made my way down to Daisy. Now I just had to wait for Naomi to get back to me. Then I'd know whether I had to apologise to Kyle or write an article about him going to gaol.

CHAPTER 14

I'd almost reached the pub when Naomi popped into the passenger seat. After getting my mini heart attack out of the way, I glanced at her. Her face was pale—and, yes, Naomi was a ghost, but she normally looked like she did when she was alive, and that was nowhere near as white as she was now. "What happened?"

"Maybe you should pull over."

"Oh, it's like that, is it?" What in Hades happened? I pulled onto the shoulder, put my hazard lights on, and turned to Naomi. "Spill."

"As soon as you left, he called his brother." She shut her eyes, then opened them again, the pain in them obvious. Nooooo! "The first thing he said to him was, 'What have you done?' Then he explained about the police. I don't know what his brother said, but Kyle responded with 'Are they coming after me next…, you, Mum, Dad? Who's next, little brother?'" She took a calming breath and wrung her hands in her lap. "Kyle said if Max didn't fix it, he would go to the police himself. Consequences be damned. Then he hung up on him."

I stared out of the windscreen, not seeing anything. What did it all mean? Was he talking about the police coming after them for the murder, or did he mean someone else was involved and was coming after them if Max didn't appease them? I turned to Naomi. "Well, maybe it would be good if Max went to the police. There's obviously something else going on."

"There's something else."

I blinked. "Something else?"

"Kyle ran to the bedroom, threw as much as he could fit into one suitcase, including his passport, and tore out of there in his car. I think he's on the run."

My eyes widened. "Is he running because he's scared of being next on the list or of getting caught by the police? Can you pop into his car and see where he goes?"

"I don't know. I feel like he's scared for his life. He's not a panicker, and he's certainly not someone who makes spur-of-the-moment decisions. He likes to think things through, which is why we made such a great team. I pushed him out of his comfort zone." Her eyes implored me. "Please get to the bottom of this quickly. I don't want him to die."

"But we don't know he's going to die. Let's figure out why he's running before we jump to that particular conclusion." I hated seeing her in a panic, especially since he might be running because he didn't want to go to prison.

She shook her head, tears glazing her eyes. "Okay, but how? If only he could see me. He'd tell me the truth."

"I wish that were possible, Naomi. It would make life a lot easier." If there was a way for me to help others see ghosts, now would be the time to work it out, but I was pretty sure there wasn't.

I considered what she'd told me. Did the new information complicate things or make them easier? Kyle's brother did seem to be involved if I could take the overheard conversation as some kind of admission that Max was tied to everything. Maybe Kyle was being sucked into it after the fact? I let out a frustrated breath. So, if I now assumed the murders were connected for a solid reason rather than just Rusty trying to throw the police off, my big question was: How and why were they connected?

I looked at Naomi. "And you're sure you don't know Mandy?"

She shrugged. "I don't know anyone by that name. Do you have a photo?"

"No. She didn't have social media because she was on the run from an ex. I doubt she would've let anyone take a picture of her and post it anywhere. Hang on." I looked at the back seat. "Charles, could you come here to Daisy's back seat? Charles?" I didn't want two freaked-out ghosts again.

He appeared in the middle of the back seat. "You called?"

"I did. I was wondering if you could take Naomi to the station and see if you can find a picture of Mandy's face. I want to know if they'd ever met, even in passing. The two murders are related somehow, but I have no clue where to start."

"Okay." He looked at Naomi. "Do you want to come now?"

I shook my head. "Not now. She has to check in with her boyfriend and see where he's going. Maybe she could do that, then meet you back here?" I looked at her. "Is that okay?"

She nodded, her expression resigned. "Okay. I'll see him long enough to get some landmarks, then come back here. Bye." She waved, then disappeared.

"So, what did you find out?" Charles popped into the front seat. I was left staring at an empty back seat.

I rolled my eyes and turned to face him. "That's rude."

"What? All I did was change seats. I prefer the front." Spoken like a true child.

"It's like running around when someone's talking to you. You just don't do it."

It was his turn to roll his eyes. "Yes, Mum."

I gave him a look meant to strike fear into his heart, but he just grinned. Argh, I surrendered and gave him an update, including the fact that Kyle was on the run. "So, what do you think?"

He rubbed his chin thoughtfully. "Hmm, I think he's running away because he doesn't want to be killed. I mean, why threaten to call the police on yourself? Sounds like if his brother did do something, he would be reluctant to sacrifice him, but why run? What vibe did you get?" Ha, *vibe*. For someone born so long ago, he was up to date on today's lingo.

"I think he genuinely loves her, and he misses her. He was giving off some signals, though. He wasn't telling me everything. He was hiding something for sure, but was it that he had something to do with her murder? I don't know. I mean, what does he stand to gain from it? There was no inheritance—they were still saving to buy their own place. There doesn't seem to be another woman on the scene. She wasn't stopping him from doing what he wanted. In fact, he said she pushed him to do stuff, so she was an encouraging partner."

Charles folded his arms and tapped the fingers of one hand on his upper arm. "So, it's looking like he's running away because he's scared of being next."

I pushed my guilt aside for thinking he might have killed her—having an open mind and considering all options was essential when trying to solve a crime or get to the bottom of a story. "Looks that way." During the research phase, I often had to change tack. It wasn't like I was psychic. What I thought at the beginning wasn't always what I'd discovered by the end, so I was only too happy to admit I was wrong and go in a new direction. I'd had enough practice. "Which means I really should talk to his brother before he disappears too."

Charles frowned. "Be careful, Avery. I have a bad feeling

about this. The brother knows you're talking to the police. He probably won't want to talk to you anyway. He'll be suspicious."

"You could be right, but he might think he can get information out of me, if that's the case."

He cocked his head to the side and raised an eyebrow. "But it means he could be dangerous. I know I sound like Sergeant Bellamy, but don't go and see him by yourself, please. Take Finn. He'll make sure nothing happens."

I rubbed my forehead. It wasn't the same as letting men take over my life, but it was frustrating that I couldn't just go and do my job by myself. Needing a minder was ridiculous, but I couldn't argue that it was for the best. My hapkido skills could only get me so far. One day, my luck would run out. It still rankled, though. "I suppose I could take Vinegar."

Charles smiled. "Thank you, Avery. I know how independent you are, but if anything happened to you, I'd be sad. You're going into the light for sure, and I'd miss you."

"Thank you, Charles. That's a sweet thing to say. I'd miss you too. Besides, I'm not ready to cross any dimensions just yet. I'm enjoying my life too much to give it up easily. Trust me—I've worked hard to create a life I could enjoy, and I'm not about to lose it." Didn't they say the best revenge was to live a good life? Well, I was revenging it up with the best of them.

"When do you think you'll go and see him?"

"I guess the sooner the better. If I leave it until tomorrow, he might have already done a runner. I'll visit him this afternoon, provided Vinegar can come." If he couldn't, maybe I'd just have to stake the guy's garage out. Which reminded me. When was I going to look for Mandy's son? I hoped against hope that this was what it looked like—connected crimes. Maybe chasing up Kyle's brother would give me a hint as to where Mandy's son was.

"Stay safe, Avery."

I smiled. "I will. I'll update you when I get back."

"Okay. Bye."

"Bye." He disappeared, and I drove to the pub. I'd promised Meg I'd go and see her, and I could do with some food.

I parked out the back, and before I went in, I called Finnegan. "Hey, Vinegar, are you busy in half an hour or so?"

"That depends on what you want."

"I was hoping we could dress like clowns and creep a few people out."

"I'm in! Lucky you asked me today because I was planning on putting my clown suit in for dry cleaning tomorrow."

"I have the best timing." I chuckled. "I actually have a favour to ask. I need to interview someone, or at least see if they're around, and they could be dangerous. I mean, probably not to another guy, but possibly to me… in particular."

"And why would they be dangerous to you 'in particular?'"

"If you say yes, I'll tell you on the way. I wanted to go in thirty minutes. The drive will probably be about thirty minutes. I don't plan on staying too long. If he agrees to talk to me, I probably need about fifteen minutes, and if he's not there, well…."

"Okay. I'm just finishing up something in the office."

"I'm just about to visit Meg. Wanna come by the pub when you're done, and we'll go from there?"

"Sounds good."

"Cool. Thanks. Oh, and please don't tell Bellamy."

He laughed. "It's like that, is it?"

"Meh, don't complain. At least I'm asking you to come with me. Old Avery would've gone by herself. I'm doing my best, but I'm not about to stop investigating stuff because Bellamy gets his knickers in a knot."

"Yeah, or if it's, I don't know, *dangerous*."

I wasn't going to justify that with an answer. "See you soon. Thanks, Vinegar. Bye."

"Bye, Lightning." He sounded resigned, which was good. I

really wasn't about to stop investigating anything, even if things might go badly, and I didn't need the annoyance of people begging me.

I grabbed my bag and went inside. It was a bit before the lunchtime crowd, but there were a few people sitting around, having tea, a beer, or coffee. A couple of people had desserts, and one table had a plate of chips. My mouth watered. Mmm, coffee and a lemon tart would go down super well.

Bailey wasn't at the bar, but Mike the friendly American was. He stopped wiping the bar top. "Hello, Avery. What can I get you?"

"A cappuccino, thanks, and a piece of that lemon tart. Can I have ice cream with it, please?"

"Isn't that too much dairy? Milk and ice cream at the same time?" He looked genuinely worried for my welfare.

I laughed. "Nope. My stomach can handle it."

"Right, well, I just cleaned the bathrooms, so don't go making a mess in there later."

I pulled an ew face. "Seriously? That's gross. I can promise you that unless I find a cockroach in my coffee, there will be no messing up anything with bodily fluids."

"Avery!" Meg pounced from behind and gave me a super hug.

I held her hands. "Meg!"

She released me, and I turned around. "We don't often see you during the day. I'm so happy you could drop by. You know how same, same my life is. I live vicariously through your escapades."

"Well, I needed coffee, and I didn't want to see Joyless. I've had enough of her sour face to last into my next life." It was hard not to give in to the serrated edge of hate that wanted to destroy my self-control and go all hapkido on her. The first rule of the dojang I went to was "never initiate conflict." Technically, she'd started everything, so I was well within my rights to exercise my skills on her. Unfortunately, I didn't think the police would see things quite the same way as my instructor. "Can we please change the subject?"

She laughed. "You brought her up. Come on and sit down. Dad's in the kitchen. He'll be out in a minute, so I have some time to sit and chat before the lunch crowd inundates us." She led me to a four-person table near a window, and we sat. "So, you only briefly explained what you were doing this morning. I want to hear what happened."

I gave her all the details, except for the thing about talking to Naomi's ghost. "He just seemed a bit sus. I really need to talk to his brother."

"So, how did you find out they might have something to do with it? Did Bellamy finally decide to let you into this investigation?"

Yikes. I hated lying to my friends, but I needed to get over it because it had to be this way for the foreseeable future. If only I could let her in, tell her everything. It sure would be nice not to have to check everything I said around her. And sometimes, it would be awesome to get her opinion. I could even facilitate a conversation between her and her dead relatives. "He didn't tell me outright. He said a couple of things, probably not meaning to, but then I did my own research." It was scary how easily falsehoods slid off my tongue.

"Is this brother dangerous?"

"Mmm, maybe. That's why I'm taking Vinegar."

"Ooh, my ears were burning. Are you saying how much you all love me?" Finnegan grinned and sat down. "I know I'm interesting, but it gets tiring being so popular. Even I'm getting sick of talking about myself."

I rolled my eyes. Meg shoved his shoulder. "You're such an idiot. You give my brother a run for his money."

Finnegan looked around. "Where is the old chap, anyway?"

"He's gone on a picnic with Sophia." She looked at me, maybe trying to gauge if I was upset. It stung a tiny bit, but not too badly. It was my choice to back away.

"Don't look at me like that. He deserves to be happy, and she seems really nice. You know I could never date him… if I was, in fact, ever going to date. If anything happened, and we ended up hating each other, things would be mega awkward, and you'd feel like you had to take sides."

"No, I wouldn't. I could be Switzerland." She smiled. "It's okay, though, Avery. I understand." She flicked her gaze to Finnegan and smirked.

"Oh, God no. There's no way I'd ever date him either. Same problem, but different situation. I'm not his type either. Not to mention, he's probably got a hundred diseases of the nether regions."

His mouth dropped open. "Hey, I take exception to that. If it's not on, it's not on. I'm cleaner than a Labrador's food bowl."

I chuckled. "And that's the weirdest comparison ever."

Meg pinched his cheek and moved his head back and forth. She deployed her "talking to a cute animal or baby" voice. "No, it's not. Finny Winny has a soft squishy side, just like a big puppy. Look at that face."

He swatted her hand away and laughed good-naturedly. "If you keep that up, I'll pee on your office rug." I snort-laughed, which made Meg laugh. "Can't take you two anywhere."

Meg's dad arrived with my coffee and tart. "Which one of you delinquents ordered this?"

"Ooh, me. Thanks, Mr Fisher. That looks so good."

He placed everything in front of me. "Please call me Bob. We don't have airs and graces in this place. What you see is what you get."

"Okay. Thanks, Bob." He'd been a bit wary of me when I'd

been introduced to him, but over time, he'd warmed to me because he knew I cared about Meg. At least some of the people in this village trusted me.

"Good choice." Meg stood. "I guess I'd better get back to it. You'll have to fill me in later… again." It was probably a good thing that Finnegan had interrupted our conversation. The more lies you told, the greater the chance of being found out.

"I will. Don't worry."

"And message me when you get back safely. Okay?"

"For sure."

She gave us a wave and headed off to a group of six that had just walked in. She pointed them towards a table in the middle of the room.

I sipped my coffee, then tucked into my lemon tart. "Mmm, this is so good." It had just the right amount of citrusy tang versus sweetness. I was in heaven.

Finnegan stared at it and licked his bottom lip. He turned puppy-dog eyes on me. "Can you save me a bite? Pretty please?"

I frowned. I hated sharing my food because I was greedy, and I wanted all of it. Unfortunately, I was also a people pleaser, plus guilt. "Argh, all right. Just stop drooling. I hate slobbering dogs."

He narrowed his eyes, but a smile broke through. "I knew you'd come through for me. Now we've settled that, give me the deets. What are we hoping to achieve this afternoon, and why do you think he's dangerous?"

I elaborated on what I'd told him on the phone, which hadn't been much. I was careful to supersede my information with the fact that I'd done a lot of research and also spoken to Naomi's mum for the article. *Dig, dig, dig that hole, Avery*. One day someone would find out, but until then, I'd do what I had to. "I waited down the road a bit after talking to Kyle, and after a few minutes, he came tearing out of his apartment building with a suitcase in tow, got into his car, and took off."

His eyes widened. "Did you follow him?"

"Just a little bit, but then I thought better of it because I have Bellamy's voice in my head, not to mention yours, Carina's, Meg's, Bailey's, all telling me to be careful and not go anywhere dangerous by myself. So don't say I never listen. It's cost me this time for sure." I was so good at making things up, I should become a writer. Oh, that's right, I was, just not the kind that was supposed to invent things. Journalists were supposed to report facts only.

"Yeah, okay. I get it. I would've kept following him for sure. If his brother does the same thing, we'll follow him. You've got me now." He grinned and looked at what was left of my tart. "Can I have that last bit?"

"Yeah, yeah. Here." I handed the plate over. He picked up the tarty goodness and slipped it into his mouth. "Mmm, this is really good. Maybe I'll get some when we get back."

I swallowed the last of my coffee and stood. "Let's do this. Your car or mine?"

"I left mine at home today, so yours it is."

We made our way to the car park and got into a clean Daisy. Looked like my days of being vandalised were over. Touch wood. I put Max's address into my phone maps and set it into the holder. Then we were off. We started the trip in silence, the first ten minutes going by when I thought I'd better clarify the usual. "Oh, by the way, all this is for my article. Okay?"

He put his hands in the air in supplication. "Of course. I'm pretty sure all that goes without saying these days. I help you, it's still yours, and vice versa. I might even get your assistance with another story I'm working on. Could you give me a couple of hours to help with research?"

"Of course. I owe you way more than that, timewise." I could get behind this reciprocal thing. He'd helped me a few times now and risked his life. The least I could do was give him a few hours of my time in the future.

"Excellent. We have a deal."

"So, since that's agreed, what's your take on it? I'm pretty sure the two murders are connected. I'm hoping we can find a link by talking to the brother. I mentioned the other woman to Kyle, and he professed not to know her. His body language looked legit on that." When I'd first landed my last journalism job in Sydney, they'd sent me on a two-day course on body language. It had been more than useful. I also loved watching police-interview videos on YouTube. Sometimes the smallest thing could give someone away. It meant you should keep digging. It was also good at helping to figure out when to let something drop so you didn't waste your time chasing up a bum lead.

"So, Mandy was a single woman in hiding?"

"Yes. It appears to be that way." I wasn't giving him too much extra than what I could've feasibly found out from Bellamy.

"I haven't done much reading on the other victim because I knew you were covering the whole thing. What can you tell me about her?"

"Well, she was living with her boyfriend, Kyle, as you know. She worked as a legal secretary, had no kids, wasn't in hiding, had a loving family, no enemies that I can find, except some woman at work, but I don't think she has a strong enough motive. They didn't get along, but she'd never threatened Naomi. Her social media had nothing about Mandy on there. They worked and lived in different places, were born in different cities, went to different schools. There's nothing I can find that links them." *And Naomi told me herself that she didn't know Mandy*. Frustration burbled in my stomach. I was sick of not saying stuff. One day, maybe.... *No, stop that. That's not a road you can go down.* Entertaining that thought was more dangerous than interviewing potential criminals. I mentally slapped myself.

He rubbed his lips. "Hmm, that is tricky. Maybe Max knew Mandy and just didn't tell anyone? What do you know about him?"

"Not too much. His social media is set to private. From what Kyle said, he's a bit of a loser. He's borrowed money from his brother and Naomi a few times and still lives in his parents' converted garage. I don't think he has a stable job, that kind of thing. I can't see Mandy hanging around someone like that. She worked long hours at the salon, wasn't dating anyone that I could find. I mean, she could be a partier and hang out with the guy, but I don't know. It doesn't gel with what I know about her." If only Mandy had more friends I could talk to. Verity didn't know much about her life outside the salon. Mandy kept to herself a fair bit. "Mandy talked to me that morning. She said she didn't know many people here and did I want to hang out sometimes." Leaden sadness settled over me. "She seemed really nice."

Finnegan turned from looking into the side mirror and stared at me, his sad expression matching mine. "I'm sorry, Avery. How are you since all that? I haven't asked much because I figured you would talk about it if you wanted to."

My lips turned up gently. "You know me so well. It's true—I don't want to talk about it. I'd rather block it out." I gave a self-deprecating chuckle. "I do deal with it in my own head, face it, think about it, etcetera, but I don't like talking to people much."

"Okay, but you didn't answer me."

I flicked a glance at him and found his ocean-on-a-sunny-day-blue eyes staring back at me. Pushing away the urge to keep staring into them, I quickly looked back to the road. I could just imagine crashing into something and having to explain why to the insurance, not to mention that Finnegan would know the truth, and that would be the worst thing of all. He'd never let me forget it. "I'm okay. Thanks for asking. You've done your duty as a friend, and now we can get back to our regular programming."

He smiled. "Hint taken. So, you haven't called this guy because you didn't want him running if his brother had said something to him."

"Yep. I figure he might have run anyway since his brother did. But maybe he thinks because his brother is out of the picture, he'll be safe. I don't even know how they're involved in this whole thing." Under Siri's instruction, I put my blinker on and turned the corner.

After a couple of minutes, staring at his side mirror, Finnegan said, "Avery, can you make a left at the next street?"

"Why? Do you know a shortcut? Although, how can you when I didn't tell you the address?"

"I think someone's following us. They're a couple of cars behind. I noticed them about ten minutes ago, but I wasn't sure. Can you?"

"Ah, okay." It was last minute, but I flicked on my indicator a couple of seconds before slowing. I almost didn't make it around and stay on my own side of the road.

Finnegan gripped his door. "Holy moly, Lewis Hamilton. Slow down."

"Seriously? You told me at the last second. What did you expect me to do?"

"Wait until the next left, maybe? Bloody hell. I'm driving back."

I rolled my eyes. "If you want me to wait before carrying out an instruction, you need to be more specific. You should've said, 'take a left when you're ready.'"

"So, if I said to you, 'drink that drink' and pointed to a random bottle, you'd just drink it without checking what it was?"

"No. But we're in a stressful situation. Kind of. I just reacted." Argh, he was so annoying. "So, is the car still following?"

He looked in his mirror. "Yes. It's the one right behind us."

"Maybe it's a fluke?" I looked into my mirror as well. Hmm, that car looked familiar, but I couldn't see the person driving as the car was staying a bit back, and the light was reflecting off their windscreen, making it impossible to see inside properly.

"Okay. See that café up ahead? Get a spot outside, and we'll duck in and see if they wait."

"Ooh, good idea." I knew I should probably be at least a little worried, but Finnegan could be making a mountain out of a molehill. And if someone was following us, maybe it was one of Bellamy's guys keeping an eye on me. If it wasn't, well, it's not like they'd do anything to us in public in the middle of the day. *Yeah, like they wouldn't dare shoot someone in broad daylight with a witness standing right next to them.* Ahem. I ignored the logical part of my brain that was spoiling my day. I wouldn't worry about this unless and until it became a *situation*.

I pulled over and parked. I grabbed my bag, put my phone in it, and got out. Finnegan and I walked calmly to the front door of Caketastic Café. "I like the sound of that. Do you think it's bad if I have two desserts in one afternoon?"

Finnegan grinned and made pig-snorting noises. "Not at all."

I walked up to the counter, not wanting to appear suspicious. "Did the car pull over too?" I hadn't checked because I didn't want the driver to know we knew. If the driver was, in fact, following us.

Finnegan stood behind me. "Face me, Lightning, so you can pretend you're talking to me, and see."

"Good idea." I turned around and looked over his shoulder—there was pretty much no way someone could see us clearly inside from the distance of the road. "Argh, there's a shrub in my way."

"We can just wait until we go back to the car, then." He

looked up at the giant menu behind the counter. I turned around and looked at it too.

"What are you having?"

"I think I'll get a coffee and a piece of carrot cake. What about you?"

"Maybe just a water. As much as I would love another piece of cake, I'm full from earlier."

"Oh, hey, I was only joking with the oinking. Honestly, if you want another piece of cake, have one." Why did he have to be so sweet?

I smiled. "Seriously. It's fine. Now, order. If that person is still there, we know for sure. We've been in here for a while." Finnegan ordered his stuff and my water. "You didn't have to do that. Can I give you the money?"

He chuckled. "No, Lightning. It's two pounds fifty. I don't need it. You can buy me a coffee next time."

"Are you sure?" I hated owing anyone anything. Yes, it was a stupid hang-up, but it lingered from my I-wish-I-could-forget days in Sydney.

He turned, and we stood to the side so the next person could order. When he looked down at me, his gaze locking onto mine, warmth shot through my chest. We were standing close, and it was all I could do not to step into him and close the distance. God, I needed to get a grip. Stupid hormones. He licked his lush bottom lip before answering. "I'm positive." He seemed as if he was going to say something else, but then he shut his mouth and looked towards the front of the shop. Our one-sided moment was over. Which was a relief, really. Any longer, and goodness knows what idiotic thing I'd have done that I couldn't take back.

"Finn Stephen!" The woman behind the counter looked around—it wasn't the one who'd served him. Finnegan was still looking out of the glass. I smirked. "Finn Stephen?!"

I elbowed him. "They're calling your name… or at least a resemblance to it, Finn Stephen." I chuckled.

He gave me a "huh?" look and went to the counter and grabbed his order.

He came back and handed me my water. "Thanks, Vinegar. So, what's the plan?"

"Well, if that car is still there and follows us, I don't know if we should still go see your guy. He could be following you because of Kyle."

"Do you think? But why?" There was no reason anyone should be following me. I was just a journalist doing a job. Unless…. "Mandy's ex got a good look at me when, well, you know." I ignored my increased heart rate.

He swore. "Would you be able to tell if it's him?"

"I think so. He has unforgettable eyes."

He raised a brow. "Unforgettable, hey? In what way?"

Did he think I liked the guy's eyes? "Seriously, Vinegar. I didn't mean I was attracted to his eyes. They were a super-light blue. I don't know that I've ever seen anyone with eyes that colour. They're cold and psychopathicky."

"Psychopathicky?"

"Yes, psychopathicky. But how in Hades am I meant to get a good look at the guy without tipping him off? What if he's got his gun and kills me?" The more we talked about this, the worse the outcome was looking.

Finnegan sipped his coffee. "Okay. Better not to risk it. We'll just get in the car and decide what to do."

"Okay." I unscrewed the lid off my water and drank some. "I'm ready." Finn opened the door, and we strode into the sunlight. At least it wasn't raining. Probably a good thing in case I had to drive fast. I made sure my expression was relaxed as I glanced around, spotting the black car a few spots behind mine. I didn't let my gaze rest on it for more than a couple of seconds because I didn't want to tip the driver off. Unfortunately, I couldn't see the number plate.

When we slid into Daisy, I put on my seat belt and turned to Finn. Hmm, I was thinking of him as Finn rather than Finnegan now, was I? Interesting concept to analyse at a later time. Or not. "Can you try and see the number plate? I'll call it through to Bellamy. Surely he'll help us."

He clicked his seat belt in. "Good idea, but then he'll complain you're putting yourself in danger. Do you really want that?"

"Well, I don't have to tell him what I'm doing, just that someone's been following me."

"He'll put two and two together, Lightning. He's not an idiot." He raised a brow.

"Well, would you rather we didn't know who this person was? And is it a man or woman? I couldn't tell."

"Neither could I. Maybe get onto a four-lane carriageway and try and see."

"Or I could just knock on their window and ask why they're following me?"

Finn scratched the side of his forehead. "What if they shoot you?"

"What if they don't?"

"Well, if it's the murderer, he'll panic, so there's no telling what he'll do. And I hate to say it, but who else would be following you?" Argh, he made a solid point.

"Well, that's a vote for calling Bellamy and telling him. They could get a car to wherever we are and pull that car over."

"That's a good idea. Nice one." He nodded slowly. "I like it."

I chewed my bottom lip. "Ah, I still want to visit Max. We're losing time, but I don't want to head over there and have Bellamy find us there and tell me I can't interview him. He'll want to know what I know, and I have no proof of anything. Besides, if we go there, maybe the person following us will try and stop us. Who knows?"

"So, what, we drive around randomly until the police pull them over?"

I smiled. "Yep. Sounds good to me."

He shrugged. "Fine. You're the boss. Let's get this show on the road, literally."

I started the car, indicated, and pulled out. Finn turned and watched out of the back window. When I was about two hundred feet down the road, the black car waited for another car to pass, then pulled out. "Did you see the number plate?"

"No. That other car is in the way, and before that, a parked car was in the way."

"Bummer." I tapped the steering wheel with my finger. "Hmm, I have a plan, but you have to be ready." I noticed on my maps that there was a dead-end street up ahead on the right. "We're going into a dead-end street. When I turn around and come back, we'll be front on. Can you film the other car? At this point, I don't care if they realise we're onto them. Maybe they'll leave me alone, and we can trace the number plate."

"But the police catching them is a way better plan. I'm calling Bellamy right now. Can you find a cul-de-sac further away?"

"Fine." Maybe he was right. I wanted to force the issue because I was sick of running, but if they caught him, his son wouldn't be in danger any more, assuming Mandy's mum had managed to stay hidden from him.

Finn had his phone on speaker. "Hi, Sergeant. It's Finn."

"Hello, Finn, my boy. How are you?" *Finn, my boy?* Of course he'd be that chummy. They'd known each other for years. It was just a shame I wasn't afforded the same familiarity or access to information.

"I'm in the car with Lightning, and you're on speaker."

"Oh…. Hello, Miss Winters." I smirked. Back to super formal.

"Hello, Sergeant."

"So, why the phone call? Is everything all right?"

"We're being followed by a black sedan, an Audi. I haven't got a lock on the number plate yet, but we're hoping you can send a car out to pull it over. It might be the killer."

"What killer?"

I piped up with "*Mandy's* killer." Yes, I was having a dig at the fact that he hadn't believed me about her hiding her identity. It was hard to resist sometimes.

"Why do you think it's the killer?"

I let Finn answer that one. "Who else would be following Lightning around?"

"Are you investigating anything else at the moment, Miss Winters?"

"No, Sergeant. Just this case."

"Are you sure they're following you, and you're not just being paranoid, Miss Winters?" Oh, for goodness' sake.

"Vinegar was the one who noticed and told me." I explained stopping at the café.

"Okay. I'll send a car out. Where are you?"

Finn told him where we were and in which direction we were headed. He picked my phone out of the holder and studied the screen. "There's a park about seven minutes from your station and about ten minutes from here. We'll head towards that. Let me know when your guy is near."

"What's your number plate, Miss Winters?" I told him. "Okay. Dispatching a car now. Hang tight, and don't engage. If they stop following you, call me back immediately, and don't follow them."

"Okay. Thanks. Bye." Finn hung up his phone, pressed some buttons on my phone to set the new destination, and placed it back in the holder. He looked at me. "If they stop following, what do you want to do?"

I gave him a side-eyed glance. "You mean, do I want to follow them or listen to Bellamy?"

He grinned. "Exactly."

"I'm guessing you want to live on the edge."

"Depends on what you want. Whatever you decide, I'm good with, but I'm up for a bit of adventure this afternoon if you are. That's all I'm saying." How could I resist those twinkling blue eyes. Damn man had me right where he didn't even want me.

"I'm voting we follow." I smiled. I wanted to discover who the creeper was. Information was power, and not knowing was going to prevent me from sleeping. If it was the killer, he could be stalking me to find his best chance of permanently silencing me. Not that I'd seen much, but he might realise I was looking into what happened. Also, if it was the killer, well, this would all be over soon. My heartbeat kicked up a notch at the prospect of more danger, because if the guy was game enough to shoot someone in broad daylight, he was unlikely to go down without a fight. Also, why did everyone say "broad daylight?" Why wasn't just "daylight" enough? Ah, English language, how you bother me sometimes.

Siri told me to turn right at the next street, so I did. We lost the car in between us, and the black car turned the corner. "At least he's not any kind of British Intelligence." Finn laughed.

"Why would they be following me?"

"They wouldn't. I was just saying. It's funny how obvious this guy is."

"Yet, I never noticed him until you said something. Are you insulting me too?" I was feeling kind of down about being so oblivious. From now on, I'd be more observant of my surroundings all the time.

"Don't sweat it. I'm overly paranoid these days. About two

years ago, I had a stalker. It was a guy I'd written an article on who was charged with animal cruelty. He did six months in prison because of me chasing up all the facts and giving them to Bellamy. Also, the article I wrote outed him to his community. He hated me. Anyway, he was following me, and I didn't know until I went out one night to go to a club, and he came at me with a baseball bat. I was with a mate, and we managed to contain him, but he landed one whack to my thigh. Didn't break it, but it was bloody sore for a couple of weeks. So now I watch out, and considering all the crimes you've been getting involved with, I tend to check out our surroundings."

Was he saying he was doing this especially to look out for me, or did he mean he would do it anyway? Hmm, let's go with the latter. He would've done it anyway. "Thanks. I appreciate it. I'll pay more attention from now on."

"Good. We can't have anything happening to you." Was he flirting, or was he being a friend? "We don't want Manesbury getting a bad name, and you've taken workload off Carina and me. It's been a lot better since you settled in." Okay, so not flirting. I knew I should be relieved, but….

I smiled. It wasn't forced… ha! "Excellent. God forbid I'm murdered, and you have to work harder until they find someone else." I glanced at him. He smirked, and I growled.

Finn's phone rang. He didn't put it on speaker this time. "Hi, Alanna. Yep, we're still good for tonight. Meet you there at eight. Yeah, it's got a great vibe. Okay…." He stared out of his window, maybe trying to give himself some privacy, but, well, we were in the same car. "Yep, me too…. Sorry, can't talk. I'm at work with a colleague…. Yep. Bye." Ouch.

Get a grip, Avery. You have a crush on him because he's hot and he's kind, but you don't want to date anyone. Not now, and not for a long time. Stop considering it. You know you need this time. Right. I vowed to myself that I'd stop making cow eyes at him and always remember that we were only ever going to be friends. Besides, I wanted to travel later. I wasn't going to stay in England forever. I took a deep breath and let all the doubt leave me.

Siri directed me for a few more minutes when we spotted a police car coming towards us from the opposite direction. "Is that them?"

Finn stared at the car. "Yep. That's PC Davis driving. Patel's with him." At least I knew both of those officers. It was nice to have backup I could trust.

"So, will I just keep driving or pull over? I assume they'll do a Uey and come back this way.

"A Uey?"

"It's Australian for U-turn."

"Ah, of course." He looked at me like it wasn't obvious and I was a puzzle to be solved. I rolled my eyes. Surely, it wasn't that hard to get U-turn from that.

"So, do I pull over?"

"That would probably make it easier on everyone and stop a potential police chase."

"Okay." It was a little bit later that I found a spot and pulled over. Hopefully whoever was following us wasn't suspicious about what we were doing.

Finn chuckled. "Nice choice of parking. Do you want to go in?"

I looked at him as if he were crazy. "What are you talking about?" He pointed out of his window. I bent so I could see the building sign, which was near the top of the first floor. "The Cheeky Monkey." There was a silhouette of a woman pole dancing. "Is that a strip club?"

He grinned. "Yep."

"Gross." I knew strippers earned their money honestly, but anything that objectified women really got up my nose. Men paying women for showing off their bodies was not advancing the human race towards equality at all. I figured those women mostly did it because they felt they had no other choice, and the money was good, but I didn't have to like it. If only society made it easier for unqualified women to earn decent money at jobs where they got to keep their clothes on.

He exaggerated his sigh. "Okay, then. We don't have to go in. I hate how you spoil all my fun." I glared at him, and he winked. "We do have to get out, though. If we sit here too long, whoever's in that car will get suspicious."

I couldn't argue with that logic. "Okay." I grabbed my bag and took my phone out, in case I decided to film.

As I got out of the car, the police car came our way and pulled up next to where the black vehicle was parked, blocking it in. They put their lights on because they were in the middle of the street. PC Davis got out and looked our way. He nodded at the car as if to ask "is this it?" Finn and I both gave a nod.

I scratched my palm while we waited for the police to do their thing. What if the guy went berserk and started shooting? Ah, stuff it. I started filming. Patel got out and was wearing a vest, thank goodness. Although, they normally wore stab-proof ones. Was this one bulletproof too? I certainly hoped so.

He went to the driver's door, tapped on the window, and made a motion for the person inside to lower it. After a moment, he said something. We were too far away to hear what it was. So frustrating. My muscles tensed in case something happened and we needed to help, or if he started shooting and we needed to duck. Not that I thought it would come to that.

The person in the car passed something out, probably his licence. Patel said something to Davis, who got back in the car and probably put it into the system. When he got out again, he stared at me and shook his head, disappointment and annoyance clear on his face, even from this distance. I turned to Finn and could see my confusion mirrored in his expression. What was going on?

Patel handed the guy back his licence, gave him a nod, and came towards us. In the meantime, Davis slid into the police car and reversed it so my stalker could leave. As he drove past us, I filmed and made sure to get the number plate. I didn't trust this whole situation. How in Hades had they just let him go?

Patel reached us. I couldn't hold it in. "Why did you just let them go?"

He stared at me for a moment. "Miss Winters, we had no cause to arrest him."

"But he's been following us all afternoon. Why? Did you at least ask him that?"

"Yes. He's a private investigator. He wouldn't tell us who paid him to follow you, and since he hasn't broken the law, we didn't have authority to force him to answer."

My mouth dropped open. "You're kidding?"

Finn put his hand on my arm. "It's okay, Lightning. Maybe just stop now before you're the one they haul away in the car." He looked behind us to where Davis had parked.

I took a deep breath. "What colour eyes did he have?"

"Brown."

I folded my arms. "Maybe they're contact lenses."

He gave Finn a look as if to say, "save me from this lunatic." I only just stopped myself from growling. *Keep calm, Avery. Don't show too much emotion because they'll use it against you. They always do.* I blocked out thoughts of the mental hospital I'd been in. They didn't call it that, of course. It was a private psychiatric hospital. Whatever. Tom-a-to, tom-ah-to.

I wasn't giving up that easily. "What was his name? If he's a private investigator with a public business, I have the right to know." This was insane that someone could stalk me and get away with it.

Patel took a card out of his pocket and handed it to me. "Don't bother the man. If I find out that you harassed him, you'll get a warning."

I took a picture of the card and handed it back. It took everything in me not to call bullcrap on everything he just said. How could I end up with a warning for telling someone not to stalk me? Although, it was only a warning. I'd had worse. "This is ludicrous. So, what do I do if he follows me again?"

"Nothing. If he's on public property, there's nothing we can do. This guy is registered as a PI. Our hands are tied."

Anger flared in my chest, and I pressed my lips together. My nostrils flared, and I clenched my fists. It took everything in me not to explode. How was this legal?

Finn recognised the impending danger. Standing behind me, he grabbed my upper arms and steered me towards the car. "Thanks, PC Patel. We appreciate you coming out to help. Have a nice afternoon." He grabbed my keys, opened the passenger door, and gently pushed me in. He went around and got into the driver's side.

Once the doors were shut, I turned to him. "That's absolute bullsh—"

"I know. I know. But that's the law, and there's nothing we can do about it. What we can do is check the guy out and go from there." He gave me a meaningful look.

"Okay, so maybe turn the tables?"

He smiled. "Now you're getting it. If you want to beat deviousness, you have to be even more devious."

"Not that finding out why someone is stalking you is devious."

"True." He adjusted the seat for his long legs, started the car, and put his belt on. "Are you still up for an interview? That guy's gone now, so he won't know we went."

"Yes, please." I took a few deep breaths as he pulled out and did a U-turn. "Thank you for removing me from the situation. I don't know how much longer I could've held it in."

He chuckled. "Yes, I noticed."

At least we were finally on our way to check on Max. If this led to a dead end, I had no idea where to look next. My gut told me time was running out to find Mandy's son and make sure he was safe. *I'm doing my best, Mandy, but why, oh why, did you have to go into the light?* Why couldn't things just be easy?

CHAPTER 15

We made it to Max's without being followed. Finn had decided I wasn't checking if the guy was home by myself. The detached garage that Max lived in had its own entrance, so we at least didn't have to bother his parents. One less barrier to get through.

We stood at the side door. I knocked. Then knocked again. We waited a bit, and I knocked a third time. I hadn't expected him to be home, but disappointment soiled my mouth like a bad oyster. He was the link to everything. I was sure of it. If I could just find the connection, the whole thing would unravel, and we'd find Mandy's son.

I was about to turn and head back to the car when the door opened. A thin, pasty-skinned guy stood there in a ripped T-shirt and blue jeans. His sandy-coloured hair and hazel eyes were so similar to his brother's that I did a double take. He was a bit shorter and much thinner. He had the gaunt, tired appearance of someone who was into drugs or who had been in the recent past, and his skin was spotty. Was Naomi's murder somehow drug related?

He narrowed his eyes. He might have looked half asleep, but he was clearly in his right mind. "You're that reporter. I'm not speaking to you." He pushed past us and looked down the driveway before hurrying back inside. "Leave now, or I'm calling the police. You're trespassing." His pupils widened in what I assumed was fear, and he slammed the door.

My breath sighed out of me. "Damn it." Normally, I would've knocked again, but he'd seemed unbudgeable, and after our conversation with Patel, I didn't want to push things. I might need them on my side before this was over.

"What do you want to do?" Finn was sweet. He wasn't telling me what to do—he was asking what I wanted. Something Brad never did. He chose the wine and food at restaurants. I hated making a fuss, so I just went along with it. It was a total surprise that I could still make my own decisions by the time I reached England. The more time that went by, the more I realised all the insidious ways he controlled my life and kept me small.

"I think we should go. Today's not panning out as I'd hoped."

"Okay."

We headed back to the car, and he handed me the keys. It was a quiet drive to the office as I considered my next move. Today could be summed up in one word—frustrating. After everything that had happened, I was no closer to finding Mandy's son than I was when I was sitting in the salon, cradling her dead body. I'd made her a promise, and I wouldn't stop until I'd delivered.

I parked the car, and just before we got out, Finn looked at me. "What's your plan now?"

"I'm going to put that PI's details into the system, see what comes back. Maybe if I surveil him, I'll figure out who hired him. The only person I could think of would be Max or his brother, but if Kyle's done a runner, why would he want to know where I was? Also, that would be some speedy organisation on his part."

Finn shook his head. "I have no idea. Maybe he wants to know when you get close to figuring things out? Are you sure there's no one else who would put a PI onto you?"

"Joyless? But she couldn't have much money, working in a café. And it's not like she wouldn't follow me everywhere herself, screaming at me the whole time if she thought she'd achieve something. I don't even know if she told her brother to dirty my car. It might've been his idea, a way to please his sister. A PI isn't her style, is it? You know her better than me."

"Yeah, it's not her style. She's not subtle. But then again, if you'd asked me a week ago if she'd insult you on a local Facebook page, I also would've said it's not her style. We guys can be clueless sometimes, you know." He grinned.

"Ahem, yes, you can. *Sometimes* is being generous." I snorted.

"No need to be rude."

I laughed. "On a serious note, thank you so much for today. I was hesitant to ask because I didn't want to be a bother, but also, I'm sick of not being able to just do things by myself because it's too dangerous." I rolled my eyes. "Bellamy thinks I can't take care of myself, and I know my past experiences kind of prove it, but I feel like a big baby. Surely not everyone I interview in relation to a murder is going to hurt me."

"Yes, well, the odds of that are minimal, but I'm glad you asked me. The guy you were going to see today could've been a problem. You did the right thing. And never be afraid to ask me to help. Unless it's impossible, I'll be there for you." He gave me a gentle smile.

"Thanks, and vice versa." It was time to get out of the car before things got awkward. "Okay, time to get to the bottom of who wants to know my movements." I hopped out of the car and shivered. Holy Hades. Had that guy followed me home? He must know where I live—they didn't just follow you every now and then when they were investigating you. They would know everything about me. Ickiness travelled through my body like molasses, thick and sickly.

"Are you okay?" Finn stared at me over the top of Daisy.

"Ah, yeah. I'll be fine." I gave him a fake smile.

He gave me a look like he knew I was lying. "Yeah, okay. If you want to talk, let me know."

"Thanks, but I'll be fine."

Carina was in the office. I stopped without warning when I saw her, and Finn crashed into the back of me. "What are you doing?"

"Ah, sorry. Carina, your hair!"

She looked at me from her desk across the room and grinned. Her blue hair was now a deep, deep magenta. "You like?" She stood and turned three hundred and sixty degrees.

I grinned back. "It looks gorgeous, so vibrant and happy. How is it that you can rock every colour? I bet if I had blue hair, people would think I was trying for an old-lady vibe." I'd never been a trendsetter. Safe was how I described my style.

"Striking," said Finn as he walked around me and to his desk.

"Were you two out together?" Carina's voice was casual, but I knew what she was asking, cheeky minx.

"Vinegar was kind enough to accompany me to an interview. I promised I'd take someone with me if I was going somewhere potentially dangerous."

"And it was a good thing she did." Finn put his laptop on his desk and opened it. He proceeded to tell her about our afternoon.

Carina's gaze snapped to me at the end. "Oh my word! Are you okay, Avery? I would hate to have some creep following me everywhere. And d'e police wouldn't help. Shame on d'em."

I sat and took my stuff out of my bag. "Yeah, tell me about it. I'm going to find out where he lives and turn the tables." I smiled. I wasn't going to cower in my flat, no matter how scared I felt.

"Well, I'm glad you had Finny d'ere to help. If you need anyone, I'm free tomorrow."

How did I luck into such good friends? "Thanks, Carina. If I need someone, I'll definitely let you know. If I can find out where this guy lives, I'll be checking it out tomorrow, and since he's following me, he'll probably talk to me. Maybe I should tell him he can drive me around since he wants to know where I'm going. I'll save money on petrol." I chuckled.

Carina laughed. "Now, d'at's out-of-d'e-box t'inking."

After getting that out of the way, I opened my phone and brought up the photo of the PI's card. Hmm, there was no address on it—just a name, an email, and a mobile phone number. I did a quick internet search of Bob Carnival PI. A short entry with the same details as what was on his card appeared. No reviews, no business address, no website. I knew PIs had to be secretive, but did he really attract clients with no reviews or website? I wouldn't trust someone who didn't give all their info.

The next search I did was for car registration. I found an Audi with his number plate registered in his name. The listed address was in London. I googled it. What? "Vinegar, what would you say if I said that our PI friend has his address for his car registration as a retail shop—Vintage Threads. The upstairs is the shop's office, according to Google."

He came to my desk and looked at my screen. He brought up Google Earth and double-checked. "Well, this is interesting."

Carina had come over too. "And frightening. Is this guy really a PI, or is that card fake? What's his name?"

"Supposedly Bob Carnival." I brought up one of the paid sites we used to research people. "There's one Robert Carnival, but he's seventeen, and he lives in Manchester."

"Poor guy has an old-person's name." Finn snickered.

Carina smacked his arm. "Be nice, child." He rubbed his arm and pulled a mock-pain face.

Finn looked at me. "Can I have a go?"

"Sure." I angled the laptop towards him, and he did all the searches I'd just done. "Right. No new information."

"Yes, so surprising," I deadpanned. Carina snorted.

"Just making sure."

"Mmmhmm. So, now that you've checked my work, what do you suggest, oh wise one?"

"I actually have an idea, but if you're going to be a smart mouth, I don't have to say it. I'm sure you can come up with your own idea since you're so clever." He gave me a so-there look. At least he was having trouble keeping a straight face.

Carina smacked his arm again. "Stop being a pain in the behind. What's your idea?"

"Drive back to Kyle's place, since it's relevant to this investigation. This PI is likely following you because of this case. I doubt the timing is coincidental. This guy is bound to follow you, but maybe he'll change cars since we know the one he already has."

"Not necessarily. The police didn't care, so he knows he can't get in trouble."

"Fair enough, but what I want to do is park mine on the main street near our laneway. When you get going, I'll wait thirty seconds and follow. We'll both be on the lookout for someone following you. In the end, I'll follow them. Just keep driving till we have them on your behind, and then go to a random shop—so it doesn't look sus—then go back to the office. I'll keep following him when he leaves. Chances are, he won't hang around the village all day, but if he does, I'll just watch him."

"But he knows what you look like. What if he recognises you?"

"I could always tag team with Carina." He looked at her.

She grinned. "Ooh, I'd love to be in on d'is."

I nodded. It could work. "That's actually a great idea. I'm in. So, what time are we doing this tomorrow?"

We figured out the logistics, and by the time I went home, I was feeling pretty good about everything. Maybe after tomorrow, I'd be one step closer to finding Mandy's son.

CHAPTER 16

"Avery. Psst, Avery. Wake up." In my dream, Charles stood in front of me talking. "Avery, it's urgent. Wake up!"

Huh? I fought out of sleep and cracked my eyes open. It was dark, but I could still see Charles. "What time is it?"

"How in the hell should I know?"

I grabbed my phone off my bedside table. 1:17 a.m. I sat up and tried to kick my brain into gear. Charles didn't show up when I was asleep unless it was important. "What happened?"

"Naomi came to find me. She said her brother-in-law's been killed."

It took a moment for the words to sink into my sleep-addled brain. "Max has been murdered?"

"Yes. Naomi's outside. She needs to be invited in."

"Of course." I slid out of bed, padded to the kitchen, and turned the light on. Argh, that was painful. I blinked. Squinting, I focussed my thoughts on what Naomi looked like so the universe knew my intention. I wouldn't want any other Naomi Ashfords to float in. "Naomi Ashford, I hereby invite you into my home."

She appeared in front of me. Her face was a picture of stress. "Avery, you have to help. Please. Max has been murdered."

"Okay, let's begin at the beginning. How did you find out?" I had so many questions and no clue what I was going to do. Hopefully I'd have a better idea at the end of this conversation.

"I was with Kyle—he's still in hiding, and thank God he is. Anyway, he was trying to call his brother because they agreed they'd check in at eleven every night. Max didn't answer. Kyle kept trying for an hour, thinking maybe his brother had gone out to a club or something." She put her hand on her stomach. "Anyway, I decided to check on him, but I couldn't get into the garage. Figuring he could be dead, I called out, and he came outside... without opening the door. He could see me too." Her shoulders drooped, some of her energy draining away.

"I'm sorry, Naomi."

She nodded. "Thank you. At least I got to see him again. He apologised to me. He said he felt responsible for my death, but he didn't pull the trigger." She hugged herself.

"So why does he think it's his fault?"

"I don't want this to get out because it would devastate his parents, but I think Kyle must've known, which was why he ran."

"Okay, I won't say anything to his parents. I promise." That was a ridiculous promise because once the police found out, his parents would be next. I wasn't promising not to tell the police, although they might ask how I knew. Maybe it would all just come out without my intervention anyway.

Naomi was so upset that she didn't realise that my promise was useless. "When he left school, he drifted from job to job and got in with the wrong crowd. He started using drugs. Nothing terrible at first—just weed. But then he got into coke, and that's expensive. He tried to quit, but he struggled. Eventually, to pay for it, he became a dealer for someone. I-I didn't think it was relevant before, and it's embarrassing for Kyle and his family, so I didn't say anything."

"That's okay. I understand." This was getting complicated, but how—if at all—did this relate to Mandy? "Did he say who?"

She shook her head. "No. He said the guy he dealt with was lower down the chain, and he called the gang leader Shark." The name suited the predatory head of a drug operation—it was suitably ominous.

I could just see what happened. You didn't have to be Einstein to work this out. "Did he steal from them? How did it get to the point where they started killing his friends?"

"His parents don't know this part. He only spilled when he couldn't pay Kyle back and Kyle was on his case." She shut her eyes for a moment, then opened them. "Max skimmed a bit of the drugs each time, and a couple of the customers complained. Turned out he'd been doing it for a year and had stolen thousands. They beat him up and told him he had two weeks to pay it back. He couldn't of course." She massaged her temples, maybe wondering why he'd been so stupid to take such a risk. I shouldn't forget that he was someone she cared about. "Once that happened, they gave him another two weeks; then they were going to start picking off his friends and family. But this all happened about three months ago, so I didn't really think it would come to that because nothing happened. And Max promised us he had a way to get them the money."

I swallowed. We were dealing with truly evil criminals. Had they killed Naomi? Were they the ones behind the PI following me? My stomach dropped. *Calm down, Avery. You don't know that for sure.* But they knew who I was if their killer was Mandy's boyfriend. Maybe he'd decided to kill two birds with one stone. Oh my God, what a terrible analogy. I needed to stop thinking for five minutes. "Did he tell you the name of the guy he was dealing with?"

"Rusty. That's his nickname, anyway." I sucked in a breath, everything piecing together. She took a few steps to one side of the room, then returned. Her eyes stared into mine. "They killed him, Avery. You have to get there and help."

Now I had a concrete link. He'd killed Mandy because he hated her, and he'd probably killed Naomi because of the drug debt. But had he decided on his own, or had someone ordered him to? And what in Hades was his real name? How was I meant to find this guy? Not to mention, I couldn't take any of this information to Bellamy because I couldn't explain where it came from. "But he's already dead. Besides, what am I supposed to say, turning up at two in the morning? The police are going to think I had something to do with it. How was he killed?"

"They…" She inhaled a shaky breath. "They hung him from the rafters in his garage. He invited me in." She turned to Charles. "Apparently, ghosts can invite other ghosts into their homes. Did you know that?"

"No. I've never had occasion to visit other ghosts in their solid-body homes. Thanks for the information."

She shrugged. "You've helped me so much." Naomi turned back to me. "You have to help, or his parents are going to be broken-hearted."

I didn't get what she was saying. "But he's already dead."

She shook her head. "I know. Sorry. I'm not making sense." She scrubbed a hand down her face. "They hung him to make it look like suicide. They threatened to kill his parents if he didn't write the suicide note and confession to killing me and that other woman." Right, so there was my second confirmation that Rusty was the murderer.

"I'm so sorry, Naomi, but you've done so well. This is the information we needed to link the murders." My legs went to jelly as both fear and relief swarmed my body. We were getting somewhere, but Rusty knew who I was. He could decide to off me at any time.

Tears glistened in her eyes. "His parents are going to be devastated, and so is Kyle. Please don't let them get away with this."

My mouth dropped open. "I… I'm sorry, Naomi. Where is Max? Can I talk to him?" If I could get Rusty's real name, it might be a game changer.

"He… he…" She burst into tears, and I could sense what was coming. When she'd managed to contain her grief to sniffles, she said, "Darkness came. I couldn't see anything but a brownish-grey tunnel. It was as if spiders were crawling all over me, and dread like I'd never experienced overtook me. There was a cacophonous rushing sound and eerie wailing. I collapsed and shut my eyes. Max screamed. Then everything quietened, the ominous feeling subsided, and when I opened my eyes, Max was gone." Her eyes looked haunted, which was saying something since she was the ghost in this scenario. "Kyle's going to be devastated when he finds out Max is dead. He's lost the two people he loves most in the world in a week. What are we going to do?"

This whole thing was an enormous tragedy. And whilst her description of Max going to hell was creepy, it was interesting to get a ghost's side of it. I never heard the wailing when I saw Adriana, the woman who killed her husband, go into the darkness, and I could still see the real world around the tunnel. Add to that finding out Rusty was the key to this, but we didn't know his real name, the amount of information was overwhelming. "I need a moment to think."

I put the electric kettle on to boil and sat at the table. Naomi stood and watched me. Yikes. I couldn't think with her staring like that. I shared a look with Charles. He got my message, thankfully, and led her to the couch, where they sat. He started talking to her, and I tuned out.

So he was dead in his garage, a suicide note proclaiming his false guilt. I rubbed my tired eyes. How was I going to tell the police what I knew? I could try and break in and get rid of the suicide note and leave other evidence pointing to the drug cartel, but what if I was caught? And I doubted I could write a different note in his handwriting. Tampering with evidence would get me thrown in gaol for a while. It was a proper crime. Do not pass Go. Do not collect two hundred pounds.

I scratched my chin, and my kettle clicked off. I poured my tea and sat back at the table. If only I could call Finn and Carina and run this by them. My eyes burned as I blinked back tears. In times like this, I felt so alone. I knew I wasn't a hundred per cent, but in some ways, I was. I sipped my tea and cradled the warm cup in my hands.

Charles got off the couch and sat in the chair opposite me, the table cutting him in half. "It's okay, Avery. We'll work it out. We always do." He gave me a kind smile.

"Thanks, Charles. So, what do we have? Two names—Rusty and the untraceable PI, Bob Carnival. Maybe Rusty paid Bob to follow me around." That was the most likely idea I'd come up with yet. But I still had no idea where Mandy's son was and if he was okay. "We might be able to find out more if we asked around in those druggy circles, but I'm not about to do that. I wouldn't know where to start." Oh, hang on a minute. I had a ghost at my disposal. I sat up straighter. "I have an idea, but it's going to be dangerous… at least for me."

He frowned. "Are you sure you want to do that? Take your time, and think of something else."

"Nope. The longer we leave it, the longer his parents and brother will be tortured, not to mention the likelihood of Mandy's son being taken by her ex. I don't know how it all fits together, but I know it does—Rusty killed them both, but why?" I looked at Naomi, who was still on the couch. "Do you know the places Max used to frequent when he was using or any of his druggie friends, even dead ones?"

She stood and turned. "I know of a couple of places and one of his mates who's alive. Oh, there was one guy who died about a year ago, overdose. Max was really cut up about it. Helped him stay clean for a bit, too, but then, well…." Grief shone in her eyes.

My bag was on the table, and I took out my notepad and pen. "Tell me everything."

Charles took a deep breath. "I hope you know what you're doing, Avery."

"So do I, Charles. So do I."

CHAPTER 17

I wanted to get the ball rolling early to ensure Max's friend Gary was at home, so I left my place at six in the morning. Also, knowing Max was dead in his garage was incentive to do it quickly. The thought of him hanging there for his parents to find…. I didn't know how to fix that. It was horrific, but there was nothing I could do. That suicide note would likely spell the end of the police investigation, except they'd still have to find the driver. It also bothered me that I seemed to be getting further away from finding Mandy's mum and son. I was assuming this direction would lead to finding them, but what if I was wrong? Argh, too many things to stress about.

The guy lived approximately forty minutes away, but in the opposite direction of Max's place. Apparently, Max had lived with this guy for a few months before the thugs caught wind of his stealing. That's when he moved back home because he couldn't afford not to.

For the first twenty minutes of the drive, I kept checking my rear-view mirror. No one had been waiting for me when I'd left home, so I was fairly confident that the PI wasn't aware of my movements so far today. I admit, I probably got a bit slack after that twenty minutes. Charles had come with me because when we finally found people who knew who Rusty was, we were going to talk to any ghosts who were hanging around. There must be some dead addict who could help us or even some other ghost who'd frequented the places Rusty and Max hung out and sold drugs.

About ten minutes from our destination, Charles turned in his seat. "Avery, I think that car's been following us for the last few minutes."

"Maybe they have, but that's not unusual." I ignored the nervous fluttering in my belly because I didn't want to escalate something that would likely turn into nothing. "I think we're up too early for that PI, unless he slept in his car near my place, and if he had, we would've noticed his car before." I glanced in the mirror. "He had a black Audi. That's a red Mazda."

"Pull over and see what happens."

Oh, God, not again. "Seriously?"

"What would Finn say?"

Argh, he knew how to get to me. "Fine." I pulled over to the shoulder without indicating, and the car shot past. We waited there until the car was over the rise and away. "There you go."

"Now keep going, and see if they've stopped."

"But would the guy be that obvious? This is stupid. Why would he bother picking a different car and then let me see him again?"

"I can't answer that. Sorry." *Yes, big help*. I kept that to myself. He was just trying to be a good friend.

As I pulled back out onto the road, the hairs on my arms stood on end. There was a white car coming up behind me, but was that a black car behind it? Argh, now I was getting nervous at any black car. *Chill, Avery*.

We crested the rise, and there was no red car. "Happy? The

red car is gone, and there's no side streets just here. They weren't following us to follow us, if that makes sense."

"Perfect sense." He grinned. "Just being careful. It doesn't hurt. And you haven't told anyone where you're going, have you?"

"No. I didn't want to text anyone and wake them if they forgot to turn their phone or ringer off." Guilt reared its head, but in my defence, Charles felt like company. It was hard to remember he was a ghost sometimes. The obsidian amulet I wore gave him a faint rose glow, as it did for all ghosts, but I was used to it. I just had to be aware that he couldn't physically do anything to help if something untoward happened.

"I think you should pull over again and text Finn." He anticipated my argument because, without waiting for an answer, he said, "Please? I'll never forgive myself if something happens to you, and neither will he."

I huffed. "Fine." This time, I hadn't meant to stop without indicating, but I did. I turned hard towards the side of the road and skidded to a stop, half the car up on the grass. The white car behind me stood on the horn as they passed, and the black car slowed. As it passed, I saw why I'd had chills. "That's the PI. It's the same number plate and a black Audi."

"But we were at least five minutes ahead. How did he know where we were?"

I had a good idea. Anger ignited in my core and shot up my body like a wildfire up a hill. "I bet he's put a tracking device on my car. Piece of trash." I called Finn because he'd be up by now.

"Lightning, what's up?"

"I think that PI put a tracking thing on my car. How would I find it?"

He swore. "Are you sure? Why do you think that?"

"Um…."

"Spill, Lightning. I bet I can guess anyway."

"Fine, so I went out without telling anyone. It's not like I *have* to. I do it as a courtesy to everyone."

"And?"

I explained where I was, what had happened with the cars, and that I'd tracked down one of Max's friends to see if he would talk since Max wouldn't. I left out everything else. "So, what do I do?"

"Come back. I'll find it, and then we can get you a different car, and I'm coming with you."

It rankled because I was only ten minutes from Max's friend's, but if I didn't want the PI—and potentially Rusty—to know where I was and what I was doing, I should just do as Finn said. It was logical, and I was all about logic… well, that was until I discovered I could see ghosts. There wasn't anything logical about that. "Okay. I'll see you at the pub in thirty. Bye."

"Bye." He sounded a little ticked off, the "bye" way more forceful than it needed to be.

If I could've gotten away with following the PI, I would have, but he knew my car, and yellow wasn't a subtle colour. He'd see me in a second. So I turned the car around and headed back. "Good choice, Avery."

"Yeah, yeah." This was one of the most frustrating crimes I'd ever investigated, especially knowing that the killer was getting away with it and a child was in danger. Everything was conspiring against me, and finding a way around it wasn't easy. At least it was a relief to know that Kyle hadn't had anything to do with Naomi's murder. It was one less thing she had to be upset about.

I didn't expect the PI to follow us all the way back now that I was pretty sure he had a tracking device on my car. If I found it, I could go to Bellamy. But how did one prove who put it there? It might be another case of "sorry, we can't help you."

There was one other thing that niggled me—when were they

going to discover Max's body? The urge to call Bellamy was strong, but what excuse could I use? If I lied and said Max called me and they checked my phone, I'd be in big trouble. Maybe I could say I had a dream. Nah, they wouldn't go because of that, and when they eventually discovered I was right, they'd just suspect me of something—whether it was witnessing the crime or being part of it, who knew? By the time I found a spot near work, I was no closer to an answer.

I texted Finn and waited, watching to see if the PI drove past. I didn't want him to see us discovering the bug. If he didn't know I knew, then if I went somewhere in someone else's car, he'd have no idea.

Charles looked at me. "I'm going to go and hang out at the station. I'll see if I can overhear anything that might help. Okay?"

"Thanks, Charles. You've been great company. See you later."

He disappeared as Finn walked up to the car. I got out. "Thanks for coming. So, how are you going to find the device?"

He held up his phone and a mirror-on-a-stick contraption. "These. I got this rig when I had issues. We're going to have to find it by looking."

"What do they look like?"

"Like a small black box, usually. About the size of or a bit smaller than a matchbox."

Yikes. "That's going to be hard to find."

"Not as hard as you'd think." He walked around to the back of my car. "Keep a lookout—we obviously don't want him seeing what we're doing. Let me know if he comes past."

"Will do."

I walked to the end of the laneway and observed the main street through the village. I glanced back. Finn knelt on the ground and looked at the mirror as he ran it under the rim of the car. I folded my arms and turned back to watch the stream of traffic.

At least this gave me five minutes to stop and think about how to get the police to Max's place. Hmm…. Bingo! Three choices came to mind. One of them—knocking on Max's parents' door and telling them he'd agree to talk to me yesterday but isn't answering the door when he said he would—would get us a result today but would be cruel. The second—finding out from Naomi where Kyle was and going to see him, spilling that I can speak to ghosts, and letting Naomi talk to him through me and then telling him what had happened—would take some convincing and a lot of time. The third meant going to see Max's friend and hoping he was home and that he would want to help me. Which choice was best?

"I found it." Finn's voice came from behind me, and I jumped.

I spun around. "For the love of chocolate-chip cookies. Why did you sneak up on me? Are you trying to give me a heart attack?"

Finn's wide eyes made him look startled, and it was kind of funny. He surprised me, and my surprise surprised him. I forced the smile off my face. "Did you find anything?"

"Yep. Come and see."

I followed him back to the car, and he shone his phone torch under the back wheel hub. I crouched and had a look with my phone torch. "That's so small and dark. So hard to see."

"That's the point."

I stood. "Can I borrow your car right now?"

His brows drew down. "Now? Where are you going? I should probably come with you."

I sighed. "I'm going to see Max's friend, the one I was trying to see this morning. I need to ask him some questions." Argh, if he insisted on coming along, that was the only choice I could make. If he'd come with me to see the parents, he'd wonder why I was lying and then be suspicious when we found the body. Going to see Kyle was a definite no-no where Finn was concerned. He'd want to know how I knew where the guy was. I could lie and say he'd called me and told me, but why would the guy do that? More lies I'd find hard to cover up if Finn interrogated him.

"Is it worth the risk? If the PI has any inkling that you were headed there, he might be waiting."

I closed my eyes and rubbed my eyelids. Why couldn't things just be simple? I opened my eyes. "I have to take that chance. Maybe I could wear a wig or a disguise of some sort. Coveralls and a cap? I could pretend to be a handyman."

His gaze raked from my head to my feet and back. "Um, I hate to tell you this, Lightning, but you couldn't pass for a bloke if you tried."

"I so could. Coveralls don't hug the figure. Plus, I could put some padding, like I have a beer belly. I could also flatten my boobs. Carina could help me."

"I'm assuming you have coveralls in your wardrobe." His raised eyebrow clued me in that he was being sarcastic.

"I'm sure the farm shop has them. It's only ten minutes out of town." The other thing I'd need to get was a sports bra that was a size too small. Carina's boobs were smaller than mine. Maybe she had something. If not, I'd have to fork out for that too. The only other way to bind my chest safely would be with a specially made product, which you could only buy online, and I didn't have time. I knew about bindings after doing an article on transgender teens back in Sydney. The things they had to go through to feel right in their own skin were heartbreaking. It was wonderful to see them blossom when they were able to live as their authentic selves. The article I'd done was nominated for an award. I didn't win, but at least Brad's name hadn't been on it, and my boss had been proud of me.

"Okay, then. Let's make this happen."

We made our way to the office. Carina was sitting at her desk eating a KitKat. "Hey, lovelies. Did you get her sorted, Finny?" She kept a straight face, but I stared at her, looking for any sign that she knew she'd just thrown massive innuendo my way. She didn't break. She was good.

"Yes, Miss Magenta. He got Daisy sorted. We found the tracking device, and we're leaving it there."

She shook her head. "D'at's horrible. Is d'at legal as well?"

"No, but proving who put it there might be an issue. At this point, I'm going to pretend it's not there. I can deal with it later." Hmm. I turned to Finn. "Did you take a picture of it? Just in case he removes it at some point?"

"I'm a step ahead of you, Lightning. I filmed it, then spoke over the top of it to say why we checked and the date."

I smiled. "Thanks. Shame we can't get fingerprints off it."

Carina stared at me. "D'at's genius! Who knows? Maybe d'ose fingerprints are in d'e police system."

Finn looked at me as if to ask what we should do. I bit my bottom lip. "I don't know. I guess we could talk to Bellamy and have them see if there are prints. We could leave my car there and go see this other guy in yours."

"That sounds like a plan." Finn went to his desk and packed up his stuff.

I still had to disguise myself. "Carina, I have two questions."

"Shoot."

"Do you have a sports bra, and if so, what size do you wear?"

Finn sat up straight like a meerkat. His eyes widened as he looked at me, then her. "You're going to answer that in front of me?"

She shrugged. "Like I care if you know what bra size I wear."

He looked wounded. I smirked. "Not every woman falls for your charms, Vinegar." I was hoping he took that to mean I was included in that statement. I looked back at Carina. "So? Can you help a lady out?"

She smiled. "I wear a thirty-two B. But I'm smaller d'an you. What do you want wit' it?"

"That should work. I want to squish my boobs. I'm a twelve C. That's a thirty-two in English sizes, I think. That should at least make my boobs less recognisable, and once I add the stomach padding, I'll look more like a man."

"I hope you've practiced how to walk." Carina stood and moved towards me, stomping more than gliding, with a swagger that was distinctly male.

I chuckled. "That's hilarious. Let me try." I hunched my shoulders slightly, bent my knees more than normal, widened my legs, and kind of bounced into each step. "Ha, this is fun. Just strutting my manliness around."

Carina and Finn laughed. Carina slapped my back. "You get a pass from me. Once you have all the gear on, you'll be good. How are you going to cover your head?"

"I have a black cap she can wear." Finn looked at me. "Have you got workman's boots?"

"Funnily enough, I do. They at least look like them. They're a camel colour. They're actually hiking boots, but you can't tell the difference at a glance." We were going to such an extreme. I was going to have to wait for everyone to get their gear, including me. "Let's grab what we need and meet back here in fifteen minutes. Is that doable?" They nodded. "Awesome."

I left my car where it was and walked home with Finn. Carina lived in the opposite direction. We hurried to get what we needed and returned to the office. I put the bra on in the toilets. Now we just had to go and buy some coveralls, and we'd be set. After we did that, we had to pass by the station and see Bellamy.

Finn had parked his car a couple of blocks from the office in a side street so it wasn't obvious when I left that he was leaving at a similar time. I looked out for the Audi or any car that was acting weird, but I didn't notice anyone. Chances were, when the PI realised I was at the police station, he'd bug off. The trick was me getting to Finn's car without being seen. Finn was buying the coveralls for me so that I didn't arouse suspicion by stopping off at the farm-supply shop.

When I reached the station, instead of parking in the street, I drove around the back. It was only for police cars, but once I explained to Bellamy why I was here, surely he'd understand. I didn't want the PI seeing the sergeant poking around the car.

When I went in, PC Adams was in her usual spot at the front desk. She grinned. "Avery! How are you? I hope your car's been staying clean."

"Kind of. Joyless's brother and his mate haven't been around, but I have another car-related problem."

"Oh, what is it?"

"Is Sergeant Bellamy in? My car's been bugged with a tracking device. Vinegar… ah, Finnegan found it for me when I suspected I might be being tracked."

She sucked in a breath. "Oh, Avery, that's awful. Do you know who put it there?"

"Yes. I'm pretty sure, anyway. I'm hoping the sergeant can see if there's any fingerprints on it." I looked at her hopefully. *Please don't tell me he's not here.* I needed to get this sorted ASAP. There were so many unknowns, and my gut told me danger was around the corner. Although, danger had been around the corner and up in my face since I'd gotten here, so I guessed nothing else was new, but still. Until we caught Rusty, I wouldn't feel safe.

"Of course. I'll get him myself. Please wait here." She turned and went further into the station. She probably thought she was more likely to convince him to see me if she did it in person.

Bellamy was a decent guy, and I had to agree that he was probably more moveable in person. All my phone conversations with him lately had resulted in zero help. I managed to do better when he couldn't just hang up on me.

Bellamy came out of the security door as PC Adams returned to her desk. She winked at me, and I mouthed, "Thank you."

The sergeant stopped next to me. "I understand there's a tracking device on your car."

"Yes."

"You bought that car recently, didn't you?"

"Sort of. It was maybe two months ago, give or take." I could see where he was going with this, and I didn't like it. "I doubt it was on my car when I bought it."

"It could've been put there a long time ago. It's probably not even active." He gave me a stern look as if I'd done something wrong.

Argh, I'd had enough. I planted my hands on my hips. "It's pretty suspicious since that PI was nowhere near me this morning, yet when I'm thirty minutes away from the village, he just shows up, following me. What are the odds?"

He harumphed. "Okay, Miss Winters. Let's go and have a look." When we got to my car, I pointed to where it was. He reached under to feel for it.

"Can you not touch it, in case it has fingerprints? Also, I don't want you to take it off. Well, at least if you take it off, don't take it far from here, and then put it back on." He stood and looked at me as if I was a sandwich short of a picnic. "I don't want him to know I've taken it off. Then he'll camp outside my house or just put another one on. Also, I can go places in Finn's car, and the PI won't know."

He folded his arms. "How do you know it's the PI? And before you say anything, my officers told me what happened yesterday. Seems like you're on someone's radar because you don't listen when I tell you to stay out of things."

"I hate to say this, Sergeant, but you're not the boss of me. You can't stop me doing my job." Or fulfilling my promises.

"No, Miss Winters, I can't. And that's more the shame. One day, your luck will run out, and you'll leave many people in this village… unhappy, to say the least." He cleared his throat. "Right. I'm going to have to remove this, or I can't test for prints. You can leave your car here, but you can't camp out all night."

I smiled. "I wasn't going to. Vinegar will be here soon, and we're going to question someone."

"Who? Is it in relation to the murder investigation?"

Would he play ball? "I'll tell you if you answer three questions for me about the murder investigation." I really only wanted to ask one, maybe two questions, but I'd given him a point to negotiate from.

He cocked his head to the side. "I'm not answering three questions, Miss Winters. I'll give you one, and only if it doesn't compromise my investigation."

I lifted my chin. "Two questions and we have a deal."

He pursed his lips, dropped his head back, and stared at the sky. I drove him crazy, but he drove me crazy, so we were even, in my estimation. I started whistling while I waited, knowing it would push anyone off the edge. I made sure it was creepy whistling in the way a rusty, squeaking-swing-in-a-storm-in-a-movie was creepy. His chin snapped back down. "Do you have to, Miss Winters?"

"Sorry. I was bored. If you need more quiet thinking time, I'll go and chat to PC Adams." He always wanted me gone ASAP. Me hanging out here wouldn't give him any joy whatsoever. I smiled.

"Argh. You win, Miss Winters. I have too much to do to argue with you. You get two questions. And be quick about it."

"Thank you, Sergeant." Never let it be said that I was impolite. "I'm assuming you found some of Mandy's old friends. Did any of them know anything about her ex?" I'd been dying to ask him that question. It was just a shame that Mandy hadn't told me his first name. Things might've been a bit easier if she had.

He hesitated. I raised my brows as if to say, "Come on." He looked over my shoulder, then back at me. "None of her school friends knew who he was. There was one friend from her drug-taking days—they were arrested at the same time at a party—and she wouldn't talk. She said she didn't know, but I have a feeling she did."

"So, he's likely a dangerous criminal." I put my hand up. "That was just me musing. It wasn't the second question."

He fought to contain a smile. He managed it, just. "What's your second question?"

"Are you any closer to finding Mandy's mother and son?" That was just for me. I wasn't having any luck, but maybe the police were.

"We're getting closer. We tracked them down to a caravan park near Bath, but by the time we got there, they'd gone." He fiddled with his tie. "I appreciate that you feel you owe Miss Hadler something, but you don't. It's our job to find who did this."

"It's your job, but it's also mine as an investigative reporter." I shouldn't be telling him this, and he might already know, but I was going to spill anyway, now that I had him in front of me. "The other victim, Naomi, her boyfriend had nothing to do with it, and his brother didn't do it either. I've got to speak to someone else, but I have a feeling this has something to do with a drug debt of Max's, Naomi's boyfriend's brother." If he asked how I knew, I'd say I couldn't divulge my source. Thank goodness for that little gem.

"How do you know all this, Miss Winters, or is it a hunch?"

"I have a source, and I've followed a few of my leads."

"Care to pass on those leads?" He tapped his foot, already knowing my answer.

"No."

"Just as I thought. When you're ready to pass on some evidence, come back. Until then, I have a crime to solve before a little boy gets hurt." Ouch. Silly thing was, we both had the same goal. For the hundredth time this week, I lamented that I couldn't divulge where I got my information from. Oh, how I wanted to scream.

"I'm sorry, Sergeant. I'd love to, but I can't."

"Lightning, there you are." Finn walked up to us, a yellow plastic bag in his hand with Farmer's Friend on the front. He handed it to me and then looked at Bellamy. "Hello, Sergeant. Did you check out the tracking device yet?"

Bellamy pressed his lips together and threw an irritated look my way before turning his gaze back on Finn. "No, son, because our Miss Winters wanted to have a chinwag."

I threw an annoyed look back at him. "Seriously, Sergeant? We were discussing the case, and I was trying to help."

Finn looked at me. "Why don't you go into the station and get changed. I'll be out here when you're ready."

"Were you followed?" What if they'd put a tracking device on his car too? I opened my mouth to ask, but Finn was ahead of me yet again.

"No. And I checked my car before I left. It's clear."

Should I be worried he could read my mind? Maybe he was just good at anticipating the next logical step in a conversation. "Right. Good. Thanks." I held up the bag. "I'll be back in two shakes."

I hurried into the station. PC Adams let me in to get changed in the bathroom. I'd already put the small bra on, so it was a matter of donning the navy-blue coveralls over my T-shirt and jeans. Before I did them up properly, I shoved craft padding in there. Carina had come through again. I put my hair in a bun and stuck the cap over the top. Now I just had to keep my head down when I walked into the guy's place. Once I was in the building, it would be fine.

When I went back outside, Bellamy stood next to my car. The tracker sat in his gloved hand. He looked at me and did a double take. "Miss Winters?"

I smiled. "One and the same." I patted my large belly. "Big lunch."

Finn chuckled. "Can you come and fix my plumbing? I haven't had time to call anyone."

I put one hand on my hip. "We can drop by your house on the way home. I'm sure I'll make whatever it is worse, but you're welcome to my substandard service." I smiled pleasantly.

Bellamy looked at me. "I don't like this, Winters." Oh, what happened to the Miss? I must be in trouble… again. "Why can't you leave this one to us? We're close to finding the mother and son, and we have a lead on who did this."

I narrowed my eyes. "Why are you telling me you have a lead on the ex now? You've had plenty of time."

He threw a cautious glance at Finn before looking at me. "I didn't want you asking more questions."

"Why? You refuse to answer them anyway." Oops, bad mouth—it spoke before I gave it permission. Still, the question was legit.

"We received some intel from the Canterbury police about a man Miss Hadler was dating around the time of her son's birth. That doesn't make him the father, but he's our best lead. We have reason to believe he was there for her whole pregnancy."

"Who is he?" And how did the police know? Had they been called in for a domestic dispute or something? Surely if that was the case, Bellamy should have found it on record. Unless no charges were filed. Knowing more than one police station was on this didn't make me feel any better. I had too many unanswered questions.

He shook his head. "Nope. Not going there with you, Winters. Let us conduct our investigation, and you concentrate on staying safe. We'll have this one in the bag soon without your help."

I pressed my lips together. I wasn't quitting until I knew Mr Ice Eyes was locked up. "Sorry, Sergeant. We all have compromises we're unwilling to make." I turned to Finn. "Come on. Let's go." I started off towards the street in my man strut. I felt more powerful with this get-up. Everyone better get out of my way. I was a man with a beer belly ready to conquer the world.

As we drove, I stared in the mirror every five seconds, making sure we weren't being followed. After a while, Finn glanced at me. "You know we don't have to do this. You can just go about your normal day and let the police handle it. If Bellamy says they're close to figuring it out, they're close."

I looked at him. "Like all those other times they didn't need my help?"

He smiled. "You have a point, but trust me when I say they solved lots of crimes before you crossed the ocean. They're good coppers, Lightning. I think the sergeant is genuinely worried about you, and truth be told, so am I." When I didn't answer for a while, he added, "Don't you get tired of putting yourself in danger, of worrying you'll be the next target?"

"Maybe, but my passion for justice never runs out, Vinegar. I'd live my whole life in stress if it meant helping those who need it." It sounded like I was implying that I was such a hero, but that's not what drove me. I hated unfairness. It irked me that bad guys got away with hurting others, and I wanted all of them put away, but that wasn't realistic, so I just put effort in where I could make a difference. With ghosts now asking for my help, that desire had increased tenfold. How could you say no when someone begged you? For whatever reason, I could see these ghosts, and I was pretty sure ignoring them wouldn't only be ethically rubbish; I'd have trouble sleeping at night. My conscience could only take so much. Unfortunately, I couldn't say all that, so I just said, "It's what I do. I'm sorry if it upsets everyone, but I'm not about to stop." Rather than see his reaction, I stared in the side mirror again. A string of cars followed us, but none were black.

"We're almost there. Do you want me to park a bit away from the place?"

"Yes, please." I hadn't told him, but I didn't want him coming in with me. This guy was super low risk. He likely had no clue that anyone had even been killed. Me turning up would be a total surprise.

Finn parked outside a row of 1950s terrace houses. When he was about to open his door, I cleared my throat. "I'm going in by myself."

His head jerked around. His eyes were wide. "No way. I'm coming in with you."

"No. Look, this guy isn't dangerous. He doesn't know anything about what's happened. I need to ask him about his friend and what went down years ago. He's probably less likely to do that with you looking on. I need him to trust me. I'd say that men would look at me and think I'm trustworthy. People confide in me because I appear sweet and harmless."

He frowned. "Not in that get-up you don't."

I cocked my head to the side. "You know I'll explain when I go in. He'll realise that when I take my cap off. I'll take my phone in and have it ready to call you if something happens. Okay? Seriously, Vinegar, this guy isn't dangerous. This is more like a normal interview." He stared at me, his expression determined, unbudgeable. I sighed. "Look, I know you're trying to help, but you know you're all eroding my self-esteem bit by bit. 'Avery can't possibly look after herself. She's hopeless and a walking victim waiting to happen.'" He knew I was right. Although, I was exaggerating things just a little bit. I just wanted him off my case for this one interview. This guy really would likely talk more if it was just me—that, I could tell from years doing this job. I might also have to tell porky pies, and I didn't want Finn questioning me later.

"What if I wait outside?"

I did my best not to roll my eyes. "Seriously, Dad?"

"Look, if anything happens to you, it's my balls everyone will be after. Carina, Meg, Bailey, even Bellamy. As much as Bellamy doesn't seem to be on your side a lot of the time, he is. He just looks at you like someone he has to protect. His daughter's about your age. You remind him of her."

I blinked. "No way. Is that what's been working against me all this time?"

He rubbed the back of his neck. "Um… not the *whole* time. He really didn't trust you at the beginning." He smirked. "Newcomers need to prove themselves in a village."

"Ah, yes, of course. That cliché is alive and well and earning its keep." My head dropped back, and I stared at the ceiling lining. I could stop this argument now with a solution that made everyone happy. I turned to Finn and held out my hand for him to shake. Putting on a deep voice, I said, "Fine. You can wait in some bushes. Don't let anyone see you."

He grinned. "Yes, sir." Why was his hand so warm and soft and large?

"Ah, poop."

"What? You going back on our deal?"

"No, no, but I left my bag in my car back at the station. I don't have my phone or my pad and pen. I guess I'll just have to remember everything he says… providing he says anything worth remembering."

"You'll be fine. I'm not happy about you not having your phone though." He sighed. "Scream if you need me." He got out of the car and shut his door. I hopped out and shut mine. He looked at me over the car roof. "If you're not out in ten minutes, I'm going to come and get you."

"What? That's ridiculous. How many times do I have to tell you that this guy is just a guy? He has no connection to this. This is more a deeper dive into Max's past. If I get lucky, I'll find out who R—" Soggy crackers. That was close.

"What?"

"If I get lucky, I'll find out who some of Max's drug associates are. I have a hunch that they have something to do with all this."

"How did you arrive at that? Also, what drug associates?"

"I don't have time to go through all that now. Come on. This outfit is sweaty as Hades. The sooner I speak to this guy, the sooner I can strip off." I fanned my face with my hand and placed one hand at the top of my chest.

His eyes widened, and he licked his lips. He shook his head as if to clear it. "What? I'm a heterosexual guy, Lightning. You can't say stuff like that and expect me not to react. It doesn't mean anything, so don't worry."

"Of course." I patted my belly. "I know I'm irresistible. I don't hold your reaction against you. If every man who reacted to me that way wanted a date, I'd be booked out till the next century." I batted my lashes and slapped my own bottom. The subject was successfully changed.

As we neared the apartment building, I scoured the street for the black Audi. It was nowhere. Phew. I stopped my swagger two houses away from our target. "The house next door has an accessible garden, and they have shutters covering all their windows. Perfect!" The bungalow next to the two-storey apartment building had a level front yard with a low brick fence. The fence that divided it from Max's friend's place was metal and about waist height. A thick hedge grew from the front brick fence almost to the house along the dividing fence. "You can hide behind the hedge and peek through that gap. You should be invisible."

"Why do I need to hide? You don't have the tracker here. That PI doesn't know you're here."

"What if he figured out where I was headed earlier today and is waiting for me to show up? That was the idea of this, wasn't it?" I gestured to my sexy outfit.

"Well, he'd see you right now."

"Except I don't look like me. But you look like you."

"Oh, yeah. Right. What if he's already seen me?" Finn glanced around.

"He probably hasn't. I can't see his car anywhere. Just hide. I'll be out soon. I don't anticipate this'll take long." I wiped sweat off my forehead. I was going to be a dehydrated husk when I was done.

Finn jumped the fence and made his way to sit behind the hedge. He stared at the house, then me, and shook his head. "If I get arrested for trespassing, you'll owe me big time."

"I'm sure you can sweet talk your way out of anything, Vinegar. Be back soon."

I strutted to the front door of the two-storey 1940s building past knee-length grass and weeds. A couple of beer bottles sat propped on the small porch. Classy. Thankfully, it was my lucky day—the building access door was open. I guessed the guy couldn't afford a block with security access. At least he wasn't in his parents' garage. If Max didn't have the means for a place like this, he really was struggling. Argh, he was dead. He was worse than struggling. Sorrow sighed out of me. Rusty was on limited time, if I had anything to say about it. Mandy's ex was evil.

Flat two was on the ground floor. The number was only screwed on at the bottom and had slid down, so now it was upside down. I knocked. There was a chance Gary wouldn't be home, but there was nothing I could do about that now. I put my ear to the door. There were definite footsteps coming from inside, but no one was answering the door. I wasn't giving up that easily. I banged on the door.

"Hold your horses" came from inside. Finally, the door opened to a faded guy… well, not faded as in ghost faded. He was alive but clearly not living his best life. Everything about him was worn out, even though he looked to be in his mid-thirties. He had thinning hair, a skinny build, and even his T-shirt was worn to the point of holes. Hopefully his patience hadn't got the memo. He stared at me. "What do you want?" His tired voice gave his words zero bite.

I took my cap off. "Hi. I know I'm dressed weird, but I needed a disguise. Are you Gary Pearson?"

He frowned. "Who wants to know?"

"I'm Avery Winters. I work for the *Manesbury Daily*, and I'm doing an article on Naomi Hadley. I understand you're friends with her partner's brother—Max."

He glanced back into the apartment, then back at me. I looked over his shoulder at the open living area. It wasn't as messy as I'd thought it would be. It was relatively tidy, except for a broken coffee cup in pieces on the floor and a dirty bong and car keys on the table in front of a threadbare couch. "Look, I haven't spoken to Max for a couple of weeks. You need to go." He moved from foot to foot. My boot was stopping the door from closing, and I felt the pressure of him pushing on the door. Oh no you don't, buddy. I'd come so close; I couldn't just walk away now.

"Can you tell me about your past? I swear I won't tell the police. I'm just trying to piece a story together. I know he used to deal drugs with a guy called Rusty. Do you know who he is?"

His Adam's apple bobbed. "You'd better leave. *Now*. I have nothing to say. If you want to know anything, ask Max yourself."

It was then I noticed a bump and slight bruise on his cheek. Had he gotten into a fight recently, or had someone anticipated my visit and wanted to ensure he said nothing? I glanced inside again, and he moved to stop me from seeing. "Are you sure I can't come in?"

"No. Leave, please."

"Okay. I'm sorry I bothered you. I guess I'll have to find someone else to talk to. Oh, by the way, there's a car out there with a flat tyre. I hope it's not yours."

He scowled. "I don't have a car."

The sweat on my forehead became less about the heat and more about concern. "Ah, okay. I guess that's it, then. Have a nice day." I stepped back, and the door closed with more force than was polite. I turned quickly and hurried down the stairs. When I reached the next-door house, I jumped over the fence. Finn was already standing, ready to leave. I whisper hissed, "No, get down. Now."

He wasn't computing, so when I reached him, I grabbed his arm and pulled him to sit on the ground. "What the hell, Lightning?"

"Shhhhh!" He was looking at me as if I'd ripped his clothes off or something. The look of confusion and unhappiness radiated from him in waves. I leaned closer so I could keep my voice down. "I think the PI is in there. Gary wouldn't tell me anything, wouldn't even let me in. He looked really nerv—"

"That doesn't mean—"

I put my hand on his mouth. "Just shut up and let me talk. I could see past him to inside. There was a set of keys with a fob on his coffee table, and it had the Audi symbol. I made up a story about a car with a flat tyre out here, and he said he didn't own a car. There was also a smashed cup on the floor." When I'd finished my speed talk, I realised my hand was still on his mouth. His lips were warm under my fingers, and the breath from his nose tickled my hand. My cheeks heated, and I lowered my hand. "Oops. Sorry."

He smirked. "Are you quite finished molesting me?"

"I wasn't molesting you, for crying out loud. Did you hear what I said?" The echo of a door closing made me jump. I crawled past Finn so I could look through the gap between the hedge and the house. My eyes widened. I needed to film this. Oh my God.

I lowered myself and whispered, "Film this. Quickly. Please."

Thankfully, he didn't hesitate. He squished next to me in the gap and put the top of his phone just above fence level. We stayed low and looked at the two men on the phone screen. The taller one was familiar, but I couldn't place where I'd seen him. He had short dark brown hair and broad shoulders. He was dressed in a white shirt and jeans. The other guy was shorter, slim, and had tatts along both arms. He had red hair and a short beard, and I could only see him from the side. One of them had to be the PI. Maybe I recognised something about the taller one because that's who he was. The men were halfway down the path, when the taller one stopped and put his back to us. The redhead turned to face him.

My heart stopped. Adrenaline flooded my body, and I fought the urge to get up and run away as fast as I could. So far away you'd never see me again. I did my best to get my shallow breaths under control. I had to stay quiet. I scrunched further in on myself. Even though there was no way they could see us, my body didn't care.

Their words were too low to reach us until the tall one said, "I don't care, Rusty! Fix this by tomorrow."

Rusty mock saluted. "Yes, boss." My heartrate spiked at near-death level, and if I hadn't been kneeling, my jelly legs would've given way. I'd never forget the voice of the scum who killed Mandy. I took deep, shuddering breaths and tried not to cry.

The taller guy left Rusty standing there and thankfully turned left out of the gate. Finn went to lower the phone, and I shook my head. He gave me a questioning look. I didn't want to be discovered, but I needed to know where Mandy's ex was. Terror clamoured through my body.

Finally, Rusty walked to the gate. He gave one look back at the building, then turned right. I nodded to Finn. He lowered his camera, and I held my breath until Rusty walked past. The urge to vomit was strong, but I held it in. I was a loud vomiter, and if I gave myself away now, I probably wouldn't survive to talk about it.

Finn stared at me. His brows drew down. "Are you okay? You look pale. Are you going to throw up?"

I nodded, then shook my head. Taking my attention away from Finn, I sat up a bit more and peered down the street. Mandy's evil ex got into a red Mercedes. As it passed, I forced myself to stand and look. Hades. I could only get the first two letters of the number plate—LA.

Finn stood and stared after the car. When it was out of sight, he turned to me and grabbed my upper arms. "Talk to me, Lightning. What just happened?"

It took me a moment to find my voice. I stared up into his eyes and tried not to cry. "That was him. That was the guy who murdered Mandy." A flash of the guy pointing the gun at Mandy from the car came into my brain. I'd know those blood-chilling eyes anywhere, not to mention there'd been a russet beard poking out of the balaclava, and that voice.

"Are you sure?"

"I've never been surer about anything in my life."

"Let's get out of here." He must've been worried about me because he grabbed my hand and led me to the car. Once he started driving, he told his phone to call Bellamy on speaker.

"Bellamy here. Unless someone's hurt, I don't have time, son."

"Avery thinks she's just seen the killer."

My heart was still racing. "I have the first two digits of his number plate. He's driving a red—"

"That's impossible, Miss Winters. I shouldn't be telling you this, but we've found the murderer." My stomach dropped. Oh no. I knew what was coming.

"What? Where?" Finn's forehead wrinkled.

"It's Miss Hadler's boyfriend's brother, Max Whitford. He committed suicide and left a note. I'm on scene, and I have to go. Go home, you two. I'll speak to you in the morning." He hung up without saying goodbye.

Finn's voice was gentle, but his words made me feel like vomiting again. "I'm sorry, Lightning. Looks like you were wrong. People often remember things incorrectly when they're a witness to a crime. It's not your fault. Besides, he was wearing a balaclava. You could never be sure with most of the guy's face covered." I stared at him, my face slack. He glanced at me. "I'm sorry, Avery. I know you wanted to solve this one." He turned back to watch the road. "Look at it this way; at least you're safe, and you can write your article now. That PI will be off your case. That has to make you happy. Right?"

There was a word for how I felt, and it wasn't happy. Not even close.

CHAPTER 18

I was ashamed to admit it, but I was too scared to sleep at home. Rusty had been listening in to my conversation with Gary. He'd most probably heard me say I was looking for him. If I hadn't been a target before, I definitely was one now.

After we returned from Gary's, I'd gotten Finn to drive me to get my car. Sergeant Bellamy still had the tracking device, but that suited me fine. The "PI"—if that had been him with Rusty—knew where I lived, and so did, I assumed, Rusty. I also suspected the PI qualification was a cover for whoever ran that drug operation—or at least someone high up—seeing as how that guy with the Audi had ordered Rusty around, and Rusty had called him "boss." Even if they realised I didn't have the device on my car, they knew I was onto Rusty, so being secretive about what I knew didn't matter now, and without the device on my car, I stood a chance at hiding from them.

I'd also convinced Finn to send me that video. After that, I'd gone home and packed an overnight bag, then walked the back way to the pub. It took twice as long because I had to go around a field, but I didn't want any strangers knowing where I was.

The tall guy had told Rusty to "Fix it." Was *it* me?

"Avery. Hey, where have you gone? Earth to Avery." Meg sat on the bed next to me. I was in one of their rooms for rent, and we had our backs against the timber headboard.

I blinked and looked at her. "Sorry. Just going over everything in my head. What were you saying?"

"Why don't you tell Sergeant Bellamy you're sure this redheaded guy is the killer?"

I tried not to sound as despondent as I was. "He won't listen. He never listens. Why do people do that? Make up their mind and close themselves off to everything else?"

"From what you said, he has evidence to prove who killed those women. I hate to say it, but I can't blame him. What have you got to change his mind?"

I sighed. She was right, so I couldn't exactly get cross. I picked at a thread on my dressing gown. "Nothing, except knowing what I saw and heard." And information from a ghost. Had they killed Gary after I'd left? It seemed as if they were the kind of guys to tie up loose ends without a second thought. "It was weird, though. I would've thought the killer would pay the PI to watch me, make sure I didn't stumble onto the truth, but the PI was the one giving orders." What was I missing? "Something else bothers me too. That tall guy was familiar, and I thought at the time maybe it was the PI and I'd recognised him from yesterday, but I never even got a glimpse of him because his side windows were dark, and his windscreen was reflecting everything." Where in Hades did I know him from?

She took my hand. "I'm sorry, sweetie. I have no answers for you. But you can hunker down here for as long as you need. We still have two spare rooms, and it's on the house."

I'd argue with her, but I knew she wanted to help, and I wasn't going to look a gift horse in the mouth. I could afford a few nights here, but after that, it would really put a dent in my savings. "I don't know how this is going to play out. Maybe they'll leave me alone when they think they've gotten away with it."

She bit her lower lip. "I'm sorry to say this, but what if you're wrong? Are you going to dig at this forever? You might be putting yourself in danger for nothing."

I looked at her and shook my head. "If they're not the killers, then I wouldn't be in danger, would I?"

"Oh yeah, I guess not."

"I'm sorry for being snippy, but Bellamy's wrong. Max was set up. I know he was." I stared into her eyes and tried to get her to really look inside me and see I wasn't wrong. The old fear of not being believed clawed up my throat. It was as if I was back at the hospital being fed tablets because what I said couldn't possibly be real. I swallowed the sensation. "I stared into his eyes, Meg. At that exact moment. I will *never* forget that cold stare. Never ever."

She squeezed my hand. "Okay. I believe you. So, what are you going to do now?"

And wasn't that the sixty-four-million-dollar question.

"I have absolutely no idea."

I jolted awake and sat up. "That's where I've seen him before," I said to myself in the dark. The clock radio said it was 1:29 a.m. Every short conversation I'd had with Bellamy over the course of the investigation came back to me. They had him right where they wanted him.

I turned the light on and got out of bed. I needed to tell someone, but who? No one believed me. There was only one person I could think this through with. "Charles. Hello, Charles; it's Avery. Please come to room 205 at Meg's pub."

Charles appeared at the foot of the bed. "Avery! This is where you are. What happened? Ev and I have been worried." Seemed like everyone was worried about me, but no one knew how to actually help. Charles was different, though, and he'd believe me.

"I'm sorry, Charles. I forgot to tell you. I've been so frazzled that I didn't think. I'm sorry. I had to come here because Mandy and Naomi's murderer knows I'm looking for him. I was too scared to go home."

He stared at me. "That's not good."

"No, it's not." I sat on the bed and explained everything that had happened since I'd last seen him, including Bellamy finding Max's body and suicide note. "I don't know what to do, how to prove anything. That guy who I'm thinking is the PI isn't really a PI. I mean, he might have qualifications, but it's a cover. Remember that day we went to find Mandy's mum?" He nodded. "That police car that drove past. That's the guy."

His eyes widened. "He's a policeman?"

"Yes. And he's ordering a murderer around."

He plonked onto the bed, but there was no divot and no sound. It would normally bother me, but I was too wound up to care. If that was the extent of my problems, I'd be sweet.

But it wasn't.

"I bet he'd been there looking for the mother and son too. What does he want with them? How does he fit into all of this?" I knew Ice Eyes was Mandy's ex. Had the policeman dated Naomi at one stage, and she'd broken up with him, so he wanted her dead, and he'd worked with Rusty to achieve it? Or was this guy running the drug ring? Being a high up in the drug ring made the most sense, but I wanted to confirm it. The more concrete information I had, the better. "I need to speak to Naomi."

"Call her."

"Do you think she'll find me here?"

"She'll lock onto your voice. I don't know exactly how it works, but it will."

I yawned, then called her. "Naomi? It's Avery. I need to speak with you urgently. Naomi?"

She faded in near the door. So different to Charles, who generally just appeared all of a sudden. "Avery, what is it?" She noticed Charles. "Hey, Charlie."

"Hey, Nomes." Oh, they had nicknames for each other. Nice to see they were getting along so well.

"Sorry to interrupt, but I need your help, Naomi."

"Of course." She sat next to *Charlie* on the bed.

"Thanks. Okay, so I'm going to show you a video, and I want you to tell me if you know or have ever dated either of these guys." There was a chance she'd recognise the killer, but I didn't want her to be prewarned. I wanted her honest reaction.

I got my phone and played the video for them. Naomi's brow furrowed at the beginning, but when Ice Eyes turned our way, her eyes bugged wide, and she sucked in a breath. "Th—that's him. Those eyes." Her chest rapidly rose and fell with frantic breaths.

Charles stared at the screen, which I'd paused. "That's them? Okay. It's good to know who to look out for. And you're right, that looks like the policeman from Canterbury." His eyes met mine. "And you think they'll keep coming after you?"

"Yes. They know I'm a witness, and they were at Max's mate's today when I showed up asking about them. They probably overheard me saying I thought Rusty did it. Rusty is more likely to come after me because the police guy can deny everything—he'll probably be believed." I turned gentle eyes on Naomi. "Do you recognise the taller guy?"

She shook her head. "I've never seen him before, and to confirm your earlier question—I've never dated either of them."

How did this all go together? I needed to think out loud. "Okay, so Mandy's ex, according to what you said previously, Naomi, is a drug dealer, and he wanted revenge on her, and that police guy might run the drug syndicate or work for whoever runs it, and he ordered your killing to punish Max, and then, when things started to get dicey, he had Max killed."

Naomi nodded slowly. "That sounds like a workable theory."

I stood and got a glass of water from the bathroom, then returned and sat on the bed. "So what does Mandy's ex want with the child? He doesn't seem the paternal type. Surely the child would put a dent in his ability to conduct business. Anyone have any ideas?"

Charles swung his legs back and forth, which made him look so much like a young boy. How had I gotten to this point? Fearing for my life and running it past two ghosts, one who died way before I was even born. The universe was bizarre. My life was bizarre.

Charles's legs stilled. "Don't forget about Mandy wanting you to get that toy."

"Mr Puddles, yes. She said there was evidence inside. Evidence of what, I'm no sure, but it could easily be evidence that could put Rusty and maybe that policeman in gaol." I put my hand on my stomach to settle the churning. If they knew about the evidence, they wouldn't stop till they got it.

Naomi rubbed her arms. "What you're saying is plausible, but we need to find out for sure."

I blew out a big breath. "You're telling me. Bellamy won't listen. Well, at least he hasn't found Mandy's mum yet. If he hasn't found them, neither has that police guy and by default, Rusty." That was something. I had a skerrick more time.

Charles's forehead wrinkled. "No, Avery. Late tonight, they figured out where she was. Bellamy's going to get her in the morning. He called that other station and spoke to a Sergeant Riley. I was there when he did. Bellamy didn't tell them where she was, but he said he'll take him there tomorrow, early. From what he said, it's a four-hour drive."

"Oh God." I jumped up. "Stuff it. I don't care if Bellamy doesn't believe me. I'll make him. There's no other way."

Charles stared at me. "What are you going to do? You can't tell him everything."

"I know. But if I can create reasonable doubt, he has access to more information than I do. If I can just get him to doubt that police guy for five minutes, we can get a head start on reaching the mum."

Charles stood in front of me. "What if you can't convince him?"

I didn't answer because it didn't bear thinking about.

CHAPTER 19

By the time I got dressed, it was close to two in the morning. I called Bellamy's mobile. My stomach clenched, knowing he was going to be livid when I woke him. He'd likely not had much sleep because they would've been dealing with Max's "suicide" and what that meant for the murder investigation.

Bellamy answered on the sixth ring, his voice groggy. "Sergeant Bellamy speaking." He mustn't have looked at who was calling.

"Hi, Sergeant Bellamy. I'm so sorry to bother you at this ungodly hour, but it's important."

"Miss Winters?"

"Yes, Sergeant. I'm sure I'm your least-favourite person right now, but this is super urgent. Can you meet me at the station?"

"Now?"

"Well, in twenty minutes. I have to call an Uber."

"What on earth for?"

"I don't have my car where I am. I have new information about the killer. If you take Sergeant Riley to see Mandy's mum tomorrow, that's a big mistake. As soon as he knows where she is, the killer will know."

His tone was decidedly tetchy. "Are you insinuating he's the killer?" Argh, that was the one piece of the puzzle I hadn't confirmed—was Sergeant Riley the PI, or was it a different officer from his station?

"Yes and no. He didn't pull the trigger. But a policeman from his station is working with Mandy's ex. They could easily get the information from him that you've passed on. I can prove it." Okay, so I couldn't prove Rusty was Mandy's ex, but I could prove they were working together, and I would bet Bellamy had access to staff files. We could match the "boss" guy in my video with the policeman.

"Miss Winters, if this is anoth—"

"It's not. Please, Sergeant, listen to me. If I'm wrong, I'll do whatever penance you want, but if I'm right, you're risking the lives of two people—one of them a child. What's the greater risk—believing me or not believing me?" I hoped he wasn't going to ignore logic.

A huge, tortured sigh came down the line. "If you're wrong about this…."

"I promise, I'm not."

"I'll see you there in half an hour, and this better be good." The line went dead. Relief at getting over hurdle number one flowed through my body. I had about twenty minutes to figure out what I was going to say, but I had a feeling that the footage on my phone would do all the talking. I couldn't *prove* anything, but he wouldn't be able to explain why the guy was pretending to be a PI and following me around.

At least I didn't have to tiptoe down the stairs to avoid Mrs Crabby. The pub was quiet, everyone home in bed for the night. The door to the bar was locked. I made my way past it to the front door and pushed the security button to open it. The Uber

I'd ordered was waiting at the kerb. I fidgeted the whole way to the station.

There was a young male constable manning the front desk. He had short brown hair and a clean-shaven face. It made him appear younger than he probably was because he looked about sixteen. "Can I help you?"

"Yes. Is Sergeant Bellamy here yet? I'm Avery Winters."

"Hello, Miss Winters. I'm PC Falkner. He's just arrived, and he asked me to buzz you through when you got here."

"Thank you, PC Falkner." He seemed pleasant enough.

The door buzzed, and I pushed it. As soon as I walked into the hallway, Sergeant Fox appeared. "What did you do to him? He's pacing like I've never seen. He's even muttering to himself."

Yikes. I just shook my head and shrugged. Talking to an empty hallway wasn't going to look good on the security cameras, so I kept walking.

"Whatever you've done, Miss Winters, please undo it."

I put my head down and whispered, "I'll see what I can do, but no promises."

Bellamy's door was open, and he was standing next to his desk. Even though I'd interrupted his slumber, he'd donned his uniform. He was ever the professional. His under-eye bags made me feel so much guilt, even though I was just trying to help. His voice sounded defeated. "Get in here, Miss Winters, and tell me what I did to deserve being woken after three-hours' sleep."

I hurried in. "I'm so sorry, Sergeant. If it makes you feel any better, I'm tired too."

"It doesn't, but do go on."

"Do you want me to shut the door?" There were two unlucky night-shift constables at their desks in the main area.

"Yes, please." He plonked into his chair. Fox appeared behind it.

I sat in one of the guest chairs and pulled my phone out of

my bag. "Okay, so you know that my car has been tracked, and I think that PI guy did it?"

"Yes, but we have no proof. We found no fingerprints. That tracker could be left over from the previous owner for all we know."

I took a deep breath and resisted the urge to argue. He was right. My assumption was just that—an assumption—based on the fact that he'd followed me everywhere, even when he wasn't waiting outside my place. But anyway, I wasn't here to argue about that right now—we were both tired, and I didn't want this to turn into World War Three. "Fine, whatever. I'll reframe that. You know how that PI was following me, and your officers caught him in the act?"

He nodded. "Yes. I'll allow that." What? Was he a judge now?

"*Thanks*." I wondered if he picked up my sarcasm. "Anyway, I didn't see him at that time. Keep that in mind when I tell you the rest."

"Okay."

"Yesterday afternoon, when I was disguised, Vinegar and I went to interview a man called Gary. He's a friend of Max, the guy you said committed the murder. They used to live together."

Bellamy's forehead wrinkled. "Why did you go and see him? And how did you know they were friends? Your timing is interesting. You were there before I called Finn about the suicide, no?"

I'd been expecting this. "Yes, we were there before you called. I knew Max was linked to one of the victims—Naomi—because I spoke to her boyfriend for my article. I was going to do a piece on her as a celebration of life kind of thing. Kyle, the boyfriend, told me he'd lent his brother money. When I pushed, he admitted his brother was mixed up in drugs." I swallowed. If he ever asked Kyle, he'd deny it, but I could use the excuse he was grieving and probably didn't remember what he'd said. It was the best I could come up with.

"Why would he tell you all that? You were asking about his girlfriend, not his brother." I held in a sigh. Why was he so sharp even when he was half-asleep?

"We got off the track a bit when I mentioned his family must be devastated. He let things slip that he probably hadn't meant to. Like a good little journalist looking into a crime, I might have kept on with that line of questioning until he stopped it." Hmm, my brain was sharper than I'd thought it could be, too, at this time of night.

"Fine." His tone suggested he didn't want to believe me, but he couldn't find the untruth in what I was saying… yet.

"Anyway, I'd tried to talk to Max at his place the day we called you about my car being followed." I rolled my shoulders back to relieve some of the tension. "He refused to talk to me, so then I did some digging and came across an old friend of his on social media." If he asked to see proof, I could tell him the page used to be there and was now gone.

"Right, and what were you trying to achieve by visiting this friend, Gary?"

"I wanted to know if Max had any reason to want Naomi dead—from what Kyle said, he liked Naomi, and they got along well, but I wasn't sure if he was covering for his brother."

He nodded slowly. "Okay, that's a decent line of thinking. Go on." I resisted the urge to say "Phew." At least he was still listening, and he could agree with my reasoning.

"When I tried to go to Gary's the first time, that Audi followed me again, and that's when I came back and Vinegar discovered the tracking device. Yesterday, just before you found Max's body, we went to Gary's. I made Finn hide in the bushes next door."

"What? Why?"

"It's a long story. Anyway, I went in by myself, but Gary wouldn't let me inside his flat. He wouldn't talk about Max either, but I managed to get a glimpse into his apartment. There were pieces of a broken cup on the floor and a set of car keys on the table with an Audi symbol. I made up a story about a car having a flat tyre outside. He said he didn't have a car, and that's when he shut the door in my face."

He leaned forward, placed his forearms on the table, and linked his hands. "And you think those keys belonged to the PI that was following you?" Good that he was getting the gist of it. He would've remembered that Finn said an Audi had followed us.

"Yes. But there's more." I felt like I should be spruiking steak knives right about now. I suppressed a smile. Yes, we were talking about something serious, but I was deliriously tired, and silly things tended to set me off when I was like this. "I figured he could've been in there, listening to our conversation, and I wanted to know what he looked like, so I went to where Finn was—"

"In the bushes next door?" Why did he have to ask that? Was he mocking me?

"Yes. But we weren't actually in the bushes. We were behind them on someone's lawn, looking through a gap in the foliage." Oh my God, why was I explaining it? "Anyway, that's not relevant. It didn't take long before two men came out." Adrenaline flooded my body, and my stomach dropped. I took a couple of deep breaths.

"Are you all right, Miss Winters? Do you want a glass of water?"

"No, no, it's okay. I won't lie; this bit is stressful to tell, even if you don't believe me about who I saw pull the trigger." He opened his mouth to speak, but I held up my hand. "Let me finish; then you can argue all you want." I hurried to continue before he shut me down. "They stopped on the path, and we had a clear view. The guy who I thought was the PI stood with his back to us, but the other guy faced us. He had the exact same ice-blue eyes as the man who shot Mandy. And the other guy called him Rusty. Here, look at the video. I also finally remembered where I'd seen the tall guy before." I got my phone out and brought up the video.

"And where was that, Miss Winters?"

"He was the policeman that drove past when I was outside Mandy's Mum's old place. Remember when they called you from Canterbury station to say I was snooping around? Also, I looked up the PI linked to the car following us and his name, and there is no proper address. The address listed was an office for another company, and the only Robert Carnival I could find was a seventeen-year-old." I hoped he could take the hint that his officers hadn't done the best job in the history of policing. He might have thought it had a low priority, so they didn't want to waste resources, but at the heart of it, no one had taken my concerns seriously.

His brows drew down, and I slid the phone to him. He pressed Play, and I waited, nervously tapping my foot on the floor. If he didn't believe something wasn't right after this, I didn't know what I'd do, short of following him when he went to find Mandy's mum. But I had no doubt that Rusty would beat us all to her once he knew where she was.

Rusty's voice made me shiver this time too. It made me think of Mandy and the terror she must've felt when she looked into his eyes for the last time.

When the video finished, Bellamy stared at me. I'd love to know what was going on in his head.

"I recognised the killer's voice too. You don't ever forget that stuff, Sergeant. What are the odds of finding a random Rusty at the home of a friend of the supposed killer when that was the name of Mandy's ex?"

"I could say there are a lot of people with that nickname, Miss Winters, but I don't like this. Wait a moment." Was he finally taking me seriously? He slid his chair across a bit to access his computer. It was already on. He typed something into it. After a couple of minutes of typing and waiting for things to load, his face hardened. He turned his monitor towards me. "This looks like him. Is this the man you saw, Miss Winters?"

I put my hand over my mouth and nodded. "Yes, Sergeant. That's him." No wonder Mandy had run. Her boyfriend was in bed with a police sergeant. He could cover everything up. She must've been living in terror most of the time. That's why she'd told me not to tell the police about the evidence. Maybe Riley didn't know, and he just wanted to pass on the information about Mandy's son to Rusty because he knew he wanted the boy? And I imagined as much as he was Rusty's "boss," he would want to keep him happy, so he didn't dob him in.

Bellamy turned the monitor towards him again. His expression oscillated between seriousness and anger. "I have a phone call to make. Just a moment." He picked up his desk phone and dialled. "Hello, yes, it's Sergeant Bellamy from Cramptonbury police. I need urgent information on a police sergeant. I need to know if he's involved in any undercover operations." He listened for a moment. "Yes. You can find our number on our website. Yes. Bye." He looked at me. "They're ringing me back to confirm who I am. You can't be too careful, and this is extremely sensitive information."

"I get that." Police could easily be killed if they were undercover and the crims found out. I wasn't going to say it, but there was no way he was undercover. He'd gone way past the point of the gathering-information stage. He would have enough to send Rusty to gaol for the rest of his life. If he knew that much about his murdering spree, he probably knew all about how the drug operation worked. My money was on him being a higher-up or boss. He was in a position to facilitate so much. And all the while, time was ticking away. I looked at my phone. "What time are you meant to be leaving to go and get Mandy's mum?"

His desk phone rang. "Sergeant Bellamy speaking." He nodded, not that the person on the other end could see him. "Okay, thanks for that. Bye." When his gaze met mine, his disappointment was palpable. "He's not undercover." He stood, went to his door, and opened it. "Williams and Campbell, I want you to go pick up Gary Pearson. I want him in for questioning about the Hadley murder." He turned to me. "What's the address?" I looked it up on my phone and told him. He relayed that to the officers. They jumped up and left.

Fox looked at me from his spot behind Bellamy's chair. "Good work, Miss Winters. Sorry for giving you a hard time when you arrived."

I gave him a subtle smile just before Bellamy turned and went back to his chair.

I waited for Bellamy to sit before I asked, "What do we do now, Sergeant?"

He put his thumb and pinkie on the outside of his eyes and massaged. "I'm thinking. Whatever I decide to do, I'd like you to stay here, where you'll be safe."

My eyes popped wide. "I'm sorry, Sergeant, but I don't think so. I'm coming with you when you go to get Jan and Mandy's son. Shouldn't we go right now? As soon as Rusty knows where they are, he'll be going for them." I hugged my middle. This was cutting it too fine. We were so close. If anything happened to Jan or Adrian now, I was going to lose my bananas.

"We? No, Miss Winters. It's too dangerous. And as for us having to rush off, I'm about to take care of that." He grabbed his mobile phone from his top pocket, brought up a phone number, and pressed Call. Whoever he was calling took a few rings to answer. "Hello, Sergeant Bruce, it's Sergeant Bellamy. Sorry to wake you." It was the night for waking people up. He outlined the situation, then said, "Can you bring them in and keep them safe at your station."

I couldn't keep quiet. "Make sure they have Mr Puddles with them."

Bellamy frowned at me, his eyes shooting daggers.

"Mr Puddles is a toy duck. Mandy told me her son will be devastated without it." I wasn't ready to say it held evidence. I'd promised Mandy, and until I knew who I could trust, I wasn't telling anyone, not even Bellamy. I didn't think he'd accidentally spill the beans, but what if someone's phone was bugged?

"Did you hear that?" He listened. "I personally don't care about the duck. Just get them to your station and keep them safe. I'm heading down soon. It's going to take a while.... Okay, thanks, Sergeant. Bye." He looked at me. "That interruption was unnecessary."

I couldn't give an excuse, so I said nothing. "Now what?"

"This situation is... tricky. The only evidence I have against Sergeant Riley is your video, and he could explain it away. He didn't say anything about any murder. He could be talking about fixing a broken pipe for all we really know." I opened my mouth to speak, and he put his hand up. "I'm not saying that's what's going on here, but I have to tread very carefully. We're dealing with another police officer, and if I get this wrong, it will be my career down the toilet. And if I were under suspicion of something, I would like the investigating officers to make very bloody sure before they made public accusations or arrested me. Understood?"

"Yes, Sergeant." I was so sure I was right, though, that I'd bet his career and my life on it. Selfish, I knew, but that's how positive I was about Riley's involvement in this. "What about Rusty?"

"He was wearing a balaclava when he committed the crimes, and with Max's confession, again, we only have your word for it. We don't even have Rusty's real name, for crying out loud. We haven't even found the car they used. The evidence we have isn't worth more than a pack of chewing gum. I'm going to tell the coroner to have a closer look at Max's body for signs of a struggle. But at this stage, I won't put out a BOLO for Sergeant Riley or Rusty. I want to interview this Gary fellow, and depending on how that goes, I have an idea of what we can do. But as of this minute, everything so far is circumstantial and relies on one witness."

He didn't need to tell me who that witness was.

I was in more danger than I thought.

"So we have to wait till Gary gets here?" *Please don't be dead.* Although, if they murdered him, my video would put them at the crime scene. They wouldn't be that stupid, would they?

"Yes. Why don't you grab a cup of tea or coffee. The kitchen is at the other end of the office."

"In a sec. First, I want to know what your plan is if Gary confirms our suspicions."

He leaned back in his chair and folded his arms. I pressed my lips together under his observation. I wanted him to know I was going to be as stubborn as a determined mule on this. I wasn't budging. When he opened his mouth, I knew I'd broken his resolve. He usually wasn't this easy to break, but he'd only had three hours of sleep, and the stress of investigating another officer wouldn't be helping his energy levels. "I'd like more proof, and we don't have much time."

"I'd agree with you in terms of making sure Mandy's mum and son are safe, but if they're with the police down there, isn't that safe?" I sat bolt upright. "Don't you trust the sergeant you just called?"

Guilt crossed his face, and he looked into his lap for a

moment before looking at me again. "It's not that I don't trust him—we go way back. He's one of the most upstanding people you could meet."

I narrowed my eyes. "So, what is it, then?"

"If everything you've said is true, and your suspicions are correct, the only loose thread is you. They murdered two women and potentially killed Max to frame him for the crime, and they heard you say you were after Rusty at Gary's. If we can't wrap this up tomorrow… or today, rather, I'll be advising that you go into witness protection, which will likely involve you leaving the country. I'm sorry to say this, but even if we manage to get a conviction, they could order a hit on you from prison. I've seen it before." Way to make me feel better. But he wasn't trying to. He was trying to get me to go home to Australia. The problem was, it wasn't home any more.

My mouth dropped open in shock. Nausea forced me to close it again and swallow. This couldn't be real. I shook my head over and over. "No. This can't be happening. You're basically saying unless they both somehow die, I'm in danger indefinitely?"

"Yes. That's worst-case scenario, but do you want to risk it?"

"I think I'll get that coffee now." I stood and walked to the other end of the office. There were two doors on the left. One was open and was obviously the kitchen, with a sink, a drainer tray with clean dishes, an el-cheapo coffee machine, and an electric kettle. There was a small round dining table with two chairs. I plonked in one of the chairs and stared at nothing.

Was my new life about to implode? How was this fair? I was in the wrong place at the wrong time, and now my life was in danger. I'd seen how cold Rusty had been when he'd laughed at Mandy and pulled the trigger. I'd been crazy lucky that he hadn't decided to shoot me, too, but now? Now he knew he'd made the wrong decision back then. Because of me, hopefully, he was soon going to be arrested. Would he make it his life's mission to ensure sure I met an early death?

I placed my elbows on the table and put my head in my hands. Was this it for my time in England? How could I walk away from Meg, Carina, Finn, and Bailey? I'd never had such incredible friends who actually cared about me and got the quirky weirdo that was me. They'd accepted me from the beginning. And how could I face my parents again? They'd be ready with the "I told you sos" and the putdowns. Maybe I could move to Perth, which was a four-hour flight across Australia from Sydney. But I didn't want to live in Perth. I wanted to live here. I had to deal with a few unusual people and Joyless, but I loved my job so much.

I shut my eyes against the burn of tears, but they leaked out anyway. *This can't be happening. This can't be happening.*

A voice I wasn't used to being so gentle said, "It's going to be okay, Avery. Look at me."

I wiped my eyes and opened them. Sergeant Fox sat in the other chair. At least he wasn't cut off in the middle—someone had left the chair out a bit. I didn't bother hiding I was talking because anyone would think I was just talking to myself after hearing that shocking news. I still kept my voice low, though. No sense in attracting attention. "How is it going to be okay?"

"I have connections in the ghost world, other police and prison officers who died but didn't leave. They're like me—they frequent their previous jobs and their homes. They like to keep an eye on things… not that they can do anything, but they like to know." I wasn't sure where he was going with this.

"And?"

He smiled. "And… we all keep in touch. Sergeant Bellamy will arrest those monsters, and wherever they go, I'll put the word out. If they so much as try to sneeze in your direction, I'll know about it. I can tell you, and we'll shut it down. I promise to keep you safe, Avery."

Was that really possible? Would Bellamy listen if I told him they were arranging to have me whacked? "What if no one listens to me when I tell them?"

He gave a nod slightly to one side. "That's a possibility. Maybe you'll have to expose your secret to Bellamy."

I put my hand on my stomach. There was only one secret he could be talking about. "No offence, but that sounds like a terrible idea."

"I think you'll find that Sergeant Bellamy has a more open mind than you give him credit for. Trust me on this, Avery. I wouldn't steer you wrong. I'd hate to see anything happen to you. You deserve to have a long and happy life, not to mention, Charles would never speak to me again if I failed you. Besides, you've given me a new lease on the afterlife." He laughed at his own joke. "I can actually get involved now. You help me make things happen. You have no idea how frustrating it is to be able to help and no one can hear you."

I chuckled. "I think I have an idea how that feels. Bellamy might be able to hear me, but he doesn't often listen. I also can't pass on all the intel I have because I have no way to explain it or back it up."

"Ah, so maybe you do know how I feel." His smile fell. "I know how you feel too. Don't let them win, Avery. You've made a good life for yourself here. I don't mean to overstep, and I promised Charles I wouldn't say anything, but I know about your family and your ex-boyfriend. I know how much it means to you to make your own life here. I know you don't want to go back there, and I know how much your friends here mean to you."

"Um, would I be able to see you and Charles if I went back?" That's something I hadn't even thought about. Could ghosts go anywhere on the planet?

"I think so, but I've never tried to appear outside England. Technically, it should be possible." Footsteps came towards the door. I shot Fox a "conversation's over" glance. He responded with a meaningful look. "You can handle this, Avery. I've got your back. Never forget that. Whatever decision you make, make sure it's what you really want. I won't force you to decide one way or the other." He stayed where he was as Bellamy came in.

"Just checking to see if you're okay. You've been a while."

"I needed time to think, Sergeant. Thanks for caring." I gave him a sad smile.

He cleared his throat and gave a nod. I grinned. He was so awkward. Typical man, not wanting to talk about feelings. "I won't ask you to give me an answer on what we talked about right now, but I think you should make a decision by tomorrow."

I stood so that I could more or less look him in the eye. I was still shorter than him, but it was better than sitting. "I've already made my decision, Sergeant."

"Oh, good. I'll start the process. I'll have to contact the authorities in Aust—"

I shook my head and held my hand up. "I've decided to stay. I'm not giving up the life I want for anything. The only way I'll move home is if those two pieces of garbage don't end up in prison. Once they're there, I'll be fine. Besides, Riley will be put in protective custody, since he's a cop. I would imagine it's hard to arrange a hit from there, especially since most other criminals would hate his guts."

"Let it be known that I'm strongly advising you against this, Miss Winters."

"I know, Sergeant, but when I left Australia, I promised I wouldn't let anyone dictate what I did and how I lived my life. I'm not about to give up on that promise to myself so soon. I'm never living that way again, Sergeant. And if death is the price I pay for my freedom, so be it." I smiled. "But I have a feeling it's not going to come to that." I gave a quick side-eye to Sergeant Fox, and he gave a nod. "So, Sergeant Bellamy, how long till Gary gets here?"

He shook his head and gave me a stern look, but at least he'd dropped the send-Avery-back-to-Australia conversation for now. "My officers should be with him in about twenty minutes. The return trip is about forty-five minutes if they drive at the speed limit. I've asked them to get here as soon as possible."

"I know you're going to hate this, but I have a plan for after you've spoken to Gary, providing he tells you something that backs me up."

"You're right, Miss Winters. I am going to hate it. I don't want to know." He turned to leave.

"That's too bad, Sergeant, because I'm going to tell you anyway." Fox was right—I did deserve a happy life, and the only place I could be happy was here. Bellamy would just have to get used to it. Now, to make sure Rusty and Riley were off the streets.

I hurried after Bellamy. The poor dear—I wasn't taking no for an answer.

CHAPTER 20

I'd had to make Bellamy two promises in order to get him to agree to my plan. One, if they didn't manage to arrest both men, I'd go back to Australia. Two, if they did arrest the men and I did stay in Manesbury, I had to never stick my nose into another investigation. He wouldn't compromise on that. I agreed.

I lied.

He'd never trust me again when he realised my deception, but by then, it would be too late. It was a price I was willing to pay.

It got me the privilege of lying in the back of a police van so anyone sitting in the cab couldn't see me. Riley had turned up at the station at their pre-appointed time, and Bellamy made sure PC Patel wasn't around since he'd pulled him over the other day.

Bellamy was driving with Riley sitting up front with him. Bellamy agreed to have me there because, as dangerous as he knew it was for me, he also knew I could identify both men, and he wanted me to do that in front of other officers so there were plenty of reliable witnesses. He also conceded that neither man would kill me in front of the police. After that, I told him that I wanted to give Jan a personal message from Mandy. I pretended she'd wanted me to tell her mum how much she loved her and to make sure her mum looked after Adrian.

In any case, I'd managed to convince Bellamy, and by the time we reached Northampton, I'd have the bruises to show for it. Man, who knew there was a way other than waiting on hold to a government department to make three hours and forty-five minutes seem like an eternity.

Part of the plan was to let Riley in on the mum's location five minutes before Bellamy left. We wanted to give Rusty just enough time to beat us there and incriminate himself before we arrived. Bellamy had officers waiting in the house while Jan and Adrian were at the police station. Thankfully, Gary had spilled everything he knew about Rusty and Riley. It wasn't as much as I'd hoped, but he could testify to buying drugs off Rusty and that Riley had roughed him up. He also said that Rusty had threatened that if he spoke up, the same fate Max had would be awaiting him. It might be enough to send the men to gaol for a little while, or maybe not, depending on what they could prove. In any case, it was enough that Bellamy wanted Riley out of the force and in prison. Bellamy also planned to deep dive into Sergeant Riley's affairs. Maybe what we knew was just the tip of the iceberg.

But it would all be for naught if I was wrong and Rusty didn't show up. The other reason Bellamy thought my plan was good was that it would flush Rusty out where they were ready to grab him. As for Sergeant Riley, Bellamy had due cause to ask for a departmental investigation into him, but it would mean I'd be shipped back to Australia. Might as well kill me now.

I shouldn't complain too much because I had company in the back of the van. Naomi and Charles sat on either side of me on the van floor. Charles had shown up at the station wanting to know what was happening, and when I told him, he called Naomi, knowing she'd want to see those scum taken down. Who knew watching criminals get nabbed was cause for a group outing. "How much longer, Avery?" Naomi asked.

I looked at my phone and brought up Google Maps, then put in the address. Oh Hades, we were almost there. I showed it to Naomi. She bit her bottom lip and stared at me, a mix of fear and excitement in her eyes. I mouthed, "I know." She was dead, but as I'd discovered by spending time with lots of ghosts, your old fears didn't just vanish. Whatever I was feeling, she was experiencing it tenfold.

If they'd taken the bait, she was about to come face-to-face with the man who'd murdered her for no good reason at all. To take a life because someone owed you money? Unfathomable. We were dealing with cold-blooded psychopaths.

The van slowed. A minute later, it stopped.

Was it hot in here? I fanned my face and shared an apprehensive look with Naomi. The doors up front shut, and I jumped at the sound. *Deep breaths. It's okay, Avery.* I whispered to Naomi, "It's okay. They can't hurt you now."

She nodded. "I know, but it's still scary. I don't know why. I guess I'm angry too. I want to hurt them, but I don't want to kill them. I'd love to see them rot in gaol for the rest of their lives. Scum."

I smiled gently. "That's the spirit."

Charles chuckled. "That was punny, Avery. Nice one." Naomi smiled. Nothing like a bit of ghost humour to release the tension.

Bellamy had made Riley think that this was a small operation. Just them and one other police unit to make sure Jan and her grandson got into the car safely so they could be taken back to Cramptonbury station. We figured Rusty would strike at the house. Trying to stop a police car on the road was probably harder, unless he'd brought help. Still, he'd be making it way harder for himself than sneaking into the house, killing Jan, and snatching the boy.

Bellamy was going to approach the house with Sergeant Riley while another officer opened the back of the van. I was under instruction to stay at the van and watch. After it all went down, I was going to check the house for Mr Puddles, just in case they'd left him behind. I hadn't told Bellamy that, but by then, it would be safe.

The van door rattled, sending adrenaline shooting through my already-shaky body. If this wasn't over soon, I was going to be as shattered as that coffee cup at Gary's yesterday. God, was it only yesterday I'd spoken to him? At least I was getting my money's worth in England. Every twenty-four hours felt like a lifetime.

The door opened, and a policewoman stood there. "Avery Winters?"

I gave her a tentative smile. "Yes."

"I'm PC Zhang. I'm under instructions to stay with you at the van, but we can watch from the front."

"Okay. Thanks." It struck me that Charles and Naomi could've slipped out of the van at any time, but they'd waited for me. How sweet.

I hopped out, shook my legs, and massaged my sore bottom. At least on the return trip, I wouldn't be the one in the back.

As I walked around to the front of the van, I could see Jan's small house about a hundred and fifty feet away. It was surrounded by other unremarkable 1950s bungalows. Her home had a side driveway, a low brick front fence, and a silver Kia in the driveway. I had the address, but the fact that Bellamy was standing in front of it with another officer was a second giveaway. Bellamy appeared to be giving the guy a serve. His arms were folded, his body language stiff, and his mouth opened wider than normal every time he spoke.

Another two officers stood nearby, a handcuffed man between them. He was short, maybe my height, and had short, dark curly hair. Had Rusty sent someone else in his stead? I swallowed. This wasn't going to plan, well, not to my plan, maybe to Rusty's.

I tried not to panic. My heart beat double time. I glanced around. Where was Riley? Had he gone into the house? "I don't like this," Charles said from next to me.

"Neither do I."

PC Zhang looked at me. "What was that?"

"Oh, ah, nothing. Just talking to myself."

She gave me a weird look, then turned back to watch the discussion at the front of the home. We were a fair distance from the action, and at least PC Zhang was here to protect me. But I still didn't feel safe, especially since Rusty wasn't here. What would I do if this all went pear-shaped? Knowing I'd have to go home made me want to cry. I swallowed the urge because it wasn't over yet. The problem was, if they didn't show their hand right now, Bellamy would have to go the investigate-Riley route, which would mean waiting for a result for who knew how many months. There was no way my job would still be here for me to return to later, and what if Riley got wind of the investigation and did a runner? What if Rusty had already fled? Had they figured out our ruse? But how?

Naomi turned to me. "I'm going to go listen to what's going on. I'll be back."

"I'll come with you." Charles was good. Naomi must be scared, and he was going to keep her company. Besides, I had PC Zhang here. They weren't leaving me alone. I gave them a slight nod. It would be good to know what Bellamy was ranting about.

I went back to glancing around. Something wasn't right… well, obviously. Who was the guy in handcuffs, and where were Rusty and Riley? My stomach gurgled. I'd been too nervous to eat before we left, not to mention it had been way too early for food. We were on the road by six. I also had to take into account that there would be no toilet stops for almost four hours. Even though my stomach complained now, I still wasn't hungry. If I ate anything, it would probably come straight back up. I fought the urge to jump back into the van where I was hidden and safe.

Naomi and Charles were standing next to Bellamy. Maybe they'd have news that Rusty had already been taken back to the police station. God, I hoped so.

My eyes jerked wide. Was that a footstep behind us? I turned.

Rusty stood there, a baton in his hand, his arm held out wide, ready to strike. Before I could scream, he struck PC Zhang in the side of the head. She went down like a bag of cement. Oh my God, was she dead?

Instead of running, my lizard brain told me to stop Rusty from getting away, which was stupid because he wanted to kill me. Why did my fight or flight reflex have to be fight?

He pulled out a gun. *Good one, lizard brain. Now we're totally stuffed.*

Rusty grinned, his ice-blue eyes shining with happiness. "It's about time, Avery. No loose ends will be left, hey, boss?"

Sergeant Riley rounded the back of the van. "No, Rusty, no loose ends."

My heart was beating so fast, it was going to explode. This couldn't be it. I couldn't be about to die. It was time to scream. Which I did, so loud, I made my own ears ring.

Riley leapt to Rusty's side, slid one arm around the upper arm of Rusty's gun hand, and grabbed the gun with his other hand. Without hesitation, he shot him in the heart.

What. Just. Happened?

Finally, my scream came, which was good because the gun had a silencer, and none of the police had noticed.

Sergeant Riley checked for a pulse, but if the blood pumping from Rusty's chest was anything to go by, he was already gone. Oh, look, his ghost appeared. He stared down at his body and then at Sergeant Riley. "You double-crossing sack of shit." Hatred shone from his evil eyes. He turned them my way. "He'll come for you later."

Riley stood. "Are you okay, Miss Winters?" That's right; he didn't know I'd seen him at Gary's. Maybe he didn't know I knew who he was. Did that give me some time?

I leaned my jelly body against the van. "Um, yes, no. I need a minute."

"I understand."

Bellamy ran towards us, two officers on his heels.

Rusty scowled. "PO Box 129 Canterbury, Dunstans Street. You'll find some interesting things there." He smirked, but then the rushing noise began. A dirty-grey hole opened behind him. His mouth dropped open. "That's not… not Hell, is it?"

I smiled and nodded. "Mandy would be so pleased. I'm sure she sends her regards from heaven. That's where she went, you know."

Rusty gave me a look that could strip paint, and Riley stared at me as if I was nuts. Who cared? Maybe he'd doubly leave me alone if he thought I was crazy.

Naomi and Charles had stopped halfway between the house and the van. I would imagine the sight of a portal to hell was terrifying for them, especially after what Naomi described earlier. If I were a ghost, I'd want to stay far from one. Naomi's voice still reached us, "Rot in hell, scumbag!" Rusty stared at her, eyes wide. It gave me joy that she'd got her jab in before he disappeared.

Bellamy reached us just as Rusty was sucked into the void, screaming. It couldn't have happened to a nicer person. Riley was crouched and checking PC Zhang's pulse. I guessed he had to pretend he was one of the good guys.

Sergeant Bellamy stared at Rusty's body, then me, then Riley and Zhang. He normally had a serious poker face, but even I could see there were a million questions waiting to rush out. But if Riley didn't know we knew about his involvement in the whole thing, that's what mattered. When Bellamy looked at me again, I gave him the subtlest of headshakes. I hoped he understood that we'd speak about this later.

Unfortunately, Riley was still free, and there wasn't anything we could do about it right this second. Riley looked up at one of the constables who'd arrived with Bellamy. "She's alive." The constable nodded, spoke into his body two-way, and requested an ambulance.

Bellamy finally said something. "Miss Winters, are you okay?"

"I seem to be… at least physically."

He looked at me as if to say, "you got lucky this time." For once, I agreed with him.

"Sergeant, I just need to go into the house and take some pics for my article. Thanks for letting me tag along to get the story. The *Manesbury Daily* is excited to get this scoop. I wasn't expecting it to be quite so… dramatic." I looked at Riley. "You'll be a hero once this story gets out." I needed an Emmy for this performance.

"Just doing my job, Miss Winters." Yeah, right. "Getting rid of loose ends" was more like it.

There were six police crowded around, plus Bellamy and Riley, and poor Zhang on the ground. The guy they'd arrested had been loaded into another police car and taken away. Where did he fit in? Was he someone who knew nothing about what was really going on? Some shmuck acquaintance of Rusty's who'd agreed to do this for money? Or did he know more about Riley? *Argh, don't worry about that now. Just go get that duck.*

Bellamy looked at me. "I don't trust you to not get into trouble. I'm coming with you."

"But it's just there. Rusty's dead. I'll be fine."

"Nevertheless. I made a bad call bringing you here. This almost ended terribly, Miss Winters." It was then slow Avery realised he wanted to talk to her. Duh.

"Okay, Sergeant. I guess you're right."

He looked at me in shock but said nothing. Ha, I could still surprise him by agreeing.

We headed off to the house, and chatter started up in the group we'd just left. Charles and Naomi followed me and Bellamy to the house.

When we got inside, Bellamy wasted no time. "What the hell just happened, Winters?" Ha, we were back to last name only.

I told him everything, including both "loose ends" comments. But I couldn't work the post office box thing into the conversation. If he said it as he was dying, that would mean Riley would be likely to knock me off ASAP. Maybe I could just tell him and say he wouldn't believe me? Hmm, I wasn't ready to take that step yet. I'd see what Mr Puddles had to say first.

"Right. Well, you're lucky he didn't let Rusty kill you before taking control and killing him."

"I screamed. He wouldn't have had time to make it look good. Officers would've seen him just standing there as I was shot."

"That's a good point." He shook his head. "You're going to be the death of yourself and me one of these days."

"What can I say? It's a skill. I hope you don't mind, but I need to look for Mr Puddles."

"What is it with that stupid toy?"

"I can't tell you right now, Sergeant. Trust me. Please?"

He rolled his eyes. "Hurry up."

I scoured the two-bedroom home to no avail. Sergeant Bellamy even helped. "Well, the boy must have it with him,

Winters. Maybe we should've checked with Northampton station first and saved ourselves some time?"

"I guess so." Okay, so I was stupid, but in my defence, I'd just been through a crazy, stressful situation. "Can we go there now?"

"Yes, Miss Winters, we can." Phew, we were back to cordiality.

We arrived as a large group at Northampton station, but Bellamy insisted on seeing Jan and her grandson alone in an interview room. He agreed with me that keeping them away from Riley was a good idea at this stage. On the other hand, I had to wait in the waiting room. At least Riley had gone into the main station to give his statement to their sergeant, and I didn't have to endure his creepy presence.

I took out my phone and pretended to be on it. "How are you feeling, Naomi?"

She smiled. "Emotionally spent but happy Rusty's dead. It gave me such satisfaction, watching him go to Hell. I thought he'd suffer in gaol, but I'm sure Hell is much worse."

"Ah, yeah, much." I chuckled.

"I'm worried about that Sergeant Riley, though. He got away with everything, and he'll sow more tragedy as time goes on. He might even decide to come after you."

"I know, but I'm working on it. I'm waiting to see what's in that toy. Once I know that, I can decide what to do."

I was stuck waiting for over an hour. A kind constable gave me a coffee and chocolate croissant from their kitchen stash. Apparently, they took turns bringing in breakfast each day. I wasn't complaining.

Finally, Bellamy called me into an interview room. When I entered, he said, "Avery Winters, meet Jan Hadley and Adrian."

My tears took me by surprise. "Hi." I smiled sadly.

Jan stood, hurried to me, and gave me a huge hug. I reciprocated. She whispered, probably so her grandson didn't hear, "Thank you for being with my daughter at the end. I'm so glad she wasn't alone."

"Me too, Jan. She was a beautiful human. We're all going to miss her. Her last thoughts were of you and Adrian."

She let me go and nodded, her eyes full of glistening grief. She looked at her grandson and back at me. "Thank you for helping the police too. Sergeant Bellamy told me how much you've done to make sure we're safe. You have no idea how grateful I am."

"I'd do it again too."

Sergeant Bellamy gestured. "If you'd like to sit, I have something to show you both." We sat at the interview table. "While we've been talking, we've recovered a small storage stick from Mr Puddles. The videos have been transferred to my phone. There's about ten minutes, but I'm only going to show you a couple of minutes." He looked at me. "There's nothing on here about anyone other than Rusty, I'm afraid." My stomach shot to the floor. I was going to have to tell him. There was no other way.

Bellamy gave us each one earbud and me the phone to hold so that Mandy's son couldn't see or hear anything. It was Rusty doing a drug deal. Another section was him grabbing Mandy, shaking and threatening her. There was probably more graphic stuff, but he wasn't about to show that to her mother. When we'd seen what he wanted, he took the phone off me. "We had enough here to put him away for a long time. Your daughter was a very brave woman, Ms Hadley. You should be proud of her."

"I am, Sergeant. Thank you for everything."

"Sergeant Bellamy, can I speak to you in private, please." It was now or never. I didn't want to live in fear, and as per my agreement with Bellamy, I'd be on a plane home soon. To be fair to him, he wasn't wrong about me still being in danger. Riley might decide at any time that I was a liability.

Nausea clawed up my throat as we went to another interview room. Bellamy shut the door. "What is it, Miss Winters?"

"I was hoping it would be in the video, but it wasn't. I might have proof about Riley's wrongdoings."

"*Might* have proof?"

"When Rusty was shot, he was obviously shocked that Riley would do that, but he looked at me and said, PO Box 129 Canterbury."

He gave me a shrewd look. "Then why aren't you cowering in your boots? If you heard, then Riley did, and he'd be after you ASAP."

Oh, God, was I really going to do this? I supposed I had nothing to lose since I was going to be shipped off if Riley wasn't nailed for something and put in gaol. I gulped. "You're not going to believe me, but set aside your sceptical side for just a moment."

He looked at me, confusion on his face. "Oookay. I guess I can do that."

"I see ghosts." My breath came faster. If his reaction was anything like my parents' and Brad's, I was in for a rough time.

His eyes narrowed, but all he said was, "Do go on."

I licked my lips and leaned from foot to foot. "Rusty told me to look at that PO Box. It was his last act of defiance against his 'boss.' Riley didn't kill him to save me. He killed him to shut him up, and Rusty knew it. I guarantee that if you go to that PO Box, you'll find something worthwhile."

He put his hands on his hips and stared at the ground for a moment. Finally, he looked at me again and nodded slowly. "Okay, Miss Winters. The worst that can happen is we find nothing. I'll get a warrant."

I blinked. "What?"

He smiled. "At this stage, I'm willing to listen to anything. You were right about the toy. You seem to be right about a lot of things, but all I get from you is it's from an 'unnamed source.' Give me a moment." He made a phone call to Cramptonbury station and gave them instructions. When he was done, he looked at me. "Now, we wait."

So, I wasn't the only one with surprises. "Please don't tell anyone I said I can see ghosts, Sergeant. I know it sounds loopy. I got enough grief from everyone back home. I don't need it here, too, and, well, you know how much Vinegar hates anything woo woo. He'd cut ties with me in an instant."

"I do know. And even though I'm not 100 per cent on board with that stuff, I've worked a couple of cases with a psychic. Her information helped solve the case when we were at a dead end. If this information is false, however, I'll be putting this down to you being in shock. Agreed?"

I chuckled, whether in relief or at his joke, who knew? I was in such a flurry of emotion after everything that had happened, that I didn't know if I was awake or dreaming. "Agreed, Sergeant."

"Besides, if you're wrong, you'll be going home anyway, as per our agreement." His smile fell. "I'm sorry, Avery, but it's just too dangerous for you here otherwise."

Wow, he'd used my first name. Things were worse than bad. I sighed. "I know, Sergeant. I know."

"Come on. Let's head back. We'll bring Jan and her grandson to make sure they're safe."

"Okay, Sergeant."

The longest twenty-four hours of my life just got a lot longer.

CHAPTER 21

By the time we reached Cramptonbury station, there were answers waiting. Bellamy let me sit in his office for the debrief. We both stared as PC Patel placed three evidence bags on the table. "We found twenty thousand pounds in the locker, this bag of MDMA—a sizable commercial quantity—and this firearm. The serial number has been removed, but we'll send it to ballistics and see if we can link it to any unsolved shootings."

"And that PO Box was registered to that PI name Riley gave you."

He smiled. "Yes, Sergeant." Bellamy had shown Patel Riley's picture, and he confirmed it was the PI.

"Excellent work, Patel."

"Thank you, Sergeant. Oh, and as per your new instructions, we canvassed the street where Max was found dead. Two homes had video recordings, and we spotted a car arriving at Max's house around the time of his death. Two men got out, went into the garage, and returned about fifteen minutes later."

Bellamy looked at me. "So, he could easily have been coerced into confessing to a crime he didn't commit, and then they killed him."

"That sounds about right, Sergeant." I gave him a small smile.

"Well, we'll look into this more closely, but at this stage, there's more than reasonable doubt that Max killed those women. Max is looking more innocent with each new piece of information we have. You were adamant about the killer's blue eyes, and Rusty had those plus motive for killing Miss Hadler. Miss Hadler's mother also confirmed that Rusty was Adrian's father and that he and Mandy were on and off for a while before Mandy ran away to escape him. He threatened to kill her more than once." So depressing. It was more than sad that she felt no one could help, and that she had to go it alone to get away from him. In the end, he found her anyway. "Rusty's prints are in the system for car theft when he was sixteen. Riley probably left them there as insurance, in case he ever needed a scapegoat. Rusty's real name is Brian Foley. Comes from a broken home, father was in and out of gaol for Brian's entire childhood. He died of a heart attack seven years ago. Not that Max was an angel, but his parents should at least know their son wasn't a killer."

"What about the getaway driver?" I hadn't forgotten about that.

"We're questioning the other man we caught at Jan's house today. We have reason to believe he might be the one, so it's all working out roses."

"What's the plan for Riley?" It was beyond fantastic that they had everything they needed to put him away, but there was that little matter of actually arresting him. I couldn't relax until I knew he was locked up.

Bellamy smiled and looked at his watch. His gaze met mine. "Just a moment, Miss Winters." He picked up his phone. "It's time…. Yes, I know. This whole situation is… unfortunate." He listened for a bit. "Yes, thank you, Chief Inspector. Please let me know when it's done. Bye."

We waited tensely for the call. When it came, Sergeant Bellamy answered it on the first ring. "Yes." He nodded. "Thank you. Okay. Bye." Sergeant Bellamy looked at me and smiled. "It's done, Miss Winters. You are hereby cleared to stay here."

I grinned through my happy tears. "Thank you, Sergeant."

And with that, my very long day was almost over. I just had one more thing to do before I could go home.

Kyle was hiding out two hours from home. Thank God he hadn't fled the country or decided to go five hours away. As it was, as soon as I parked the car, I yawned. Boy, did I need to sleep.

The sun was setting as I unclicked my seat belt. Naomi was next to me in the car. "Thank you for doing this tonight, Avery. I appreciate it."

"Don't worry. I didn't want to leave this undone. Once I've spoken to Kyle, I can go home and sleep for two days." I laughed because I wasn't exaggerating. "Okay, let's do this." I got out and went to room five. It was on the ground floor at the front. Kyle's car was parked outside the door. I put my ear to the door. A TV was on inside. I knocked. Nothing. I looked at Naomi. "Is he in there?" His car was there, so he should be inside.

"He was last time I checked. Hang on." She faded away, then reappeared about ten seconds later. "Yep. He's there. He's wearing the bunny slippers I gave him for our second dating anniversary."

I grinned. "I guess that will help me get in."

"Thanks again, Avery. I know you're scared to do this, but he won't tell anyone if you ask him not to. He's a good guy."

"But will he believe me?"

"I think so. Come on. I really want to speak to him." She grinned and clapped. I couldn't blame her for being excited.

I knocked again. When he didn't answer, I said, "Kyle, it's Avery Winters. I know you're in there and you have bunny slippers on, the ones Naomi gave you for your second anniversary. I came to tell you that the killer is dead. It's safe to come out. If you don't believe me, call Sergeant Bellamy at Cramptonbury police station."

Thankfully, that got his attention. The door lock clicked, and he opened it. His three-day growth had turned into the start of a beard, and dark circles rimmed the skin under his eyes. He poked his head out and glanced around. When he didn't see any threat, he looked at me. "What did you say about the bunny slippers?"

"Can I come in and talk? I don't want to do that out here. I've had a long day. Like, really long, and I'm likely to collapse right here if I don't sit down."

"Fine." He moved out of the way. I didn't waste time and headed inside, sitting on one of two plastic chairs at a small dining table. "Is the killer really dead?"

"Did you see the news about Rusty, or Brian, rather?"

He nodded. "Was that him? I wasn't sure because they didn't say too much."

"Yep. Accused of killing two women is what they said, but they didn't give names because Sergeant Bellamy wanted to tidy things up before releasing more information to the media." He'd also wanted to give me time to get my story out. I'd typed it up in the hours we had to wait for Riley to be arrested. As soon as that call came through, I'd sent my article to Julian. I'd save writing Riley's article for after he was convicted, which would probably take months. The court system was backed up, but because he was a police officer, I imagined they wanted to try and hurry it through so it was out of the news.

Kyle plonked onto the other chair. His breath came out in a

whoosh. “So, my brother was innocent?” He must’ve spoken to his parents after they found Max’s body.

“Yes. He was forced to write that note.”

“How do you know so much? Are you an undercover officer?”

I smiled. “No. It’s something much worse and harder to believe.”

His forehead wrinkled. “What do you mean?”

“Don’t throw me out. Give me time to convince you, okay?” I rubbed my hands down my jean-clad thighs. Sweaty palms were the worst.

His expression turned wary. “What do you mean?”

“Just get to it, Avery. I’m dying here.” Naomi was hopping from foot to foot.

I looked at her. “You’re already dead.”

“Yeah, yeah, very funny. Just hurry up.”

“Fine.”

“Who are you talking to?” He was now openly staring at me as if I’d gone mad, and really, I couldn’t blame him one bit.

“Naomi. She’s the one who told me you were wearing those slippers.” He sucked in a breath. While he was shocked, I thought I’d better continue before he kicked me out. “I met her ghost after she was killed. I didn’t actually know her in real life. Sorry for lying to you, but you wouldn’t have believed me.”

“You’re right. What kind of depraved person are you, telling me you’re talking to her ghost?”

“She wanted to talk to you. She misses you like crazy.”

He narrowed his eyes. “Okay, if she’s here, answer this: What happened to me last New Year’s Eve?”

I looked at Naomi. “Oh, that was funny.” She started laughing. “He got so drunk that when it struck midnight, his friend, as a joke, pushed me out of the way and snogged him. He didn’t even realise until he heard me laughing.”

"Oh wow." I turned to him and repeated what she'd said. "How did you not feel the dude's whiskers?"

"I had a beard at the time. I couldn't tell." He looked at me thoughtfully. "Ask her what underwear she wore on our last anniversary." Tears pooled in his eyes, which set me off too. He was in so much pain. Was I helping or making it worse?

"I wore my red, lacy, crotchless set."

"Oh, wow, too much information." I turned my gaze to Kyle and told him.

He smiled. "She did. And what a night I had. Tell her I'll never forget."

"I don't need to. She can hear you."

Naomi had her own tears now as he turned to where I'd been looking. "Is she on the bed?"

"Yes, she's sitting there looking at you and tearing up. Why don't you talk to her, and I'll sit next to her and repeat everything she says."

He looked at me with so much pain and grief that my breath caught. "Thank you, Avery. I believe she's here. I didn't want to sound crazy to anyone, so I haven't said anything, but since she died, I can still feel her. I know she's with me most of the time." He shook his head as if it were impossible.

"You're right. She has been with you a lot. She's heartbroken that she can't be with you."

"So, can we start now?" His eyes held such hope.

I stood and moved to sit next to a joyful Naomi on the bed. I smiled. "We sure can."

If you enjoyed *A Deadly Drive-by*, you might want to grab book 6, *A Caffeine Hit*. It will be out in March 2023. Watch out for it on preorder online. And if you're looking for more cosy mysteries and haven't tried my Paranormal Investigation Bureau series yet, why not grab *Witchnapped in Westerham*. It has over 3000 positive Goodreads ratings and reviews.

All it takes is one morning for Sydney Photographer Lily Bianchi's life to go off the rails and over a cliff.

A well-dressed English woman turns up at her door, swearing she's a witch. If that's not crazy enough, she explains Lily's brother, James, has been kidnapped and the Paranormal Investigation Bureau needs Lily's help finding him. And the craziest part? The Englishwoman tells Lily she's a witch too.

Before she can say, "Where's my coffee?" she's on a plane bound for Westerham, England. Unfortunately, England's not as welcoming as she hoped--she's barely arrived before she gets set up, arrested, and almost shot.

Things can only get better from here, right? Yeah, right…

ALSO BY DIONNE LISTER

Paranormal Investigation Bureau

Witchnapped in Westerham #1

Witch Swindled in Westerham #2

Witch Undercover in Westerham #3

Witchslapped in Westerham #4

Witch Silenced in Westerham #5

Killer Witch in Westerham #6

Witch Haunted in Westerham #7

Witch Oracle in Westerham #8

Witchbotched in Westerham #9

Witch Cursed in Westerham #10

Witch Heist in Westerham #11

Witch Burglar in Westerham #12

Vampire Witch in Westerham #13

Witch War in Westerham #14

Westerham Witches and a Venetian Vendetta #15

Witch Nemesis in Westerham #16

Witch Catastrophe in Westerham #17

Witch Karma in Westerham Book #18

Witch Showdown in Westerham Book #19

Westerham Witches and an Aussie Misadventure (Coming March 2023)

Haunting Avery Winters

(Ghost Cosy Mystery)

A Killer Welcome #1

A Regrettable Roast #2

A Fallow Grave #3

A Frozen Stiff #4

A Deadly Drive-by #5

A Caffeine Hit #6 (Coming May 2023)

The Circle of Talia

(YA Epic Fantasy)

Shadows of the Realm

A Time of Darkness

Realm of Blood and Fire

The Rose of Nerine

(Epic Fantasy)

Tempering the Rose

Forging the Rose

ABOUT THE AUTHOR

USA Today bestselling author, Dionne Lister is a Sydneysider with a degree in creative writing, a love of storytelling, and two Siamese cats. Daydreaming has always been her passion, so writing was a natural progression from staring out the window in primary school, and being an author was a dream she held since childhood.

Unfortunately, writing was only a hobby while Dionne worked as a property valuer in Sydney, until her mid-thirties when she returned to study and completed her creative writing degree. Since then, she has indulged her passion for writing while raising two children with her husband. Her books have attracted praise from Apple iBooks and have reached #1 on Amazon and iBooks charts worldwide, frequently occupying top 100 lists in fantasy and mystery.

Printed in Great Britain
by Amazon

36066453R00144